P9-CRR-585

*"I'll be close by,"* he said, letting go of her hand and pointing. *"Because we're neighbors."*

She stared.

The house on the hill was his.

The house that was so incredibly beautiful. She'd spent more than one night watching the wooden and stone lines of it sleep in the moonlight when she hadn't been able to find any such rest.

*"You* lived behind my father."

"Yes."

She didn't know what to do with her hands. One was still tingling. The other felt cold.

She forced them to remain at her sides, fighting the burgeoning need to ring them together. "Who built the house?"

"I did."

"You?"

"I'm capable, too," he drawled, his voice impossibly dry.

She ignored the small jab, not doubting his capabilities for a second. The man undoubtedly exceeded "capable" on every front.

Dear Reader,

Well, we're getting into the holiday season full tilt, and what better way to begin the celebrations than with some heartwarming reading? Let's get started with Gina Wilkins's *The Borrowed Ring,* next up in her FAMILY FOUND series. A woman trying to track down her family's most mysterious and intriguing foster son finds him and a whole lot more—such as a job posing as his wife! *A Montana Homecoming,* by popular author Allison Leigh, brings home a woman who's spent her life running from her own secrets. But they're about to be revealed, courtesy of her childhood crush, now the local sheriff.

This month, our class reunion series, MOST LIKELY TO…, brings us Jen Safrey's *Secrets of a Good Girl,* in which we learn that the girl most likely to…*do everything* disappeared right after college. Perhaps her secret crush, a former professor, can have some luck tracking her down overseas? We're delighted to have bestselling Blaze author Kristin Hardy visit Special Edition in the first of her HOLIDAY HEARTS books. *Where There's Smoke* introduces us to the first of the devastating Trask brothers. The featured brother this month is a handsome firefighter in Boston. And speaking of delighted—we are absolutely thrilled to welcome RITA® Award nominee and Red Dress Ink and Intimate Moments star Karen Templeton to Special Edition. Although this is her first Special Edition contribution, it feels as if she's coming home. Especially with *Marriage, Interrupted,* in which a pregnant widow meets up once again with the man who got away—her first husband—at her second husband's funeral. We know you're going to enjoy this amazing story as much as we did. And we are so happy to welcome brand-new Golden Heart winner Gail Barrett to Special Edition. *Where He Belongs,* the story of the bad boy who's come back to town to the girl he's never been able to forget, is Gail's first published book.

So enjoy—and remember, next month we continue our celebration….

Gail Chasan
Senior Editor

Please address questions and book requests to:
Silhouette Reader Service
U.S.: 3010 Walden Ave., P.O. Box 1325, Buffalo, NY 14269
Canadian: P.O. Box 609, Fort Erie, Ont. L2A 5X3

# A MONTANA HOMECOMING

## ALLISON LEIGH

# SPECIAL EDITION®

Published by Silhouette Books

**America's Publisher of Contemporary Romance**

If you purchased this book without a cover you should be aware
that this book is stolen property. It was reported as "unsold and
destroyed" to the publisher, and neither the author nor the
publisher has received any payment for this "stripped book."

For my girls, Amanda and Anna Claire.
I'm so very proud of you both.
Love, Mom.

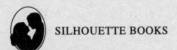 **SILHOUETTE BOOKS**

ISBN 0-373-24718-4

A MONTANA HOMECOMING

Copyright © 2005 by Allison Lee Davidson

All rights reserved. Except for use in any review, the reproduction
or utilization of this work in whole or in part in any form by any
electronic, mechanical or other means, now known or hereafter
invented, including xerography, photocopying and recording, or in
any information storage or retrieval system, is forbidden without
the written permission of the editorial office, Silhouette Books,
233 Broadway, New York, NY 10279 U.S.A.

All characters in this book have no existence outside the imagination of
the author and have no relation whatsoever to anyone bearing the same
name or names. They are not even distantly inspired by any individual
known or unknown to the author, and all incidents are pure invention.

This edition published by arrangement with Harlequin Books S.A.

® and TM are trademarks of Harlequin Books S.A., used under license.
Trademarks indicated with ® are registered in the United States Patent
and Trademark Office, the Canadian Trade Marks Office and in other
countries.

Visit Silhouette Books at www.eHarlequin.com

**Printed in U.S.A.**

**Books by Allison Leigh**

Silhouette Special Edition

*Stay...* #1170
*The Rancher and the
    Redhead* #1212
*A Wedding for Maggie* #1241
*A Child for Christmas* #1290
*Millionaire's Instant Baby* #1312
*Married to a Stranger* #1336
*Mother in a Moment* #1367
*Her Unforgettable Fiancé* #1381
*The Princess and the Duke* #1465
*Montana Lawman* #1497
*Hard Choices* #1561
*Secretly Married* #1591

*Home on the Ranch* #1633
*The Truth about the Tycoon* #1651
*All He Ever Wanted* #1664
*The Tycoon's Marriage Bid* #1707
*A Montana Homecoming* #1718

*Men of the Double-C Ranch

---

## ALLISON LEIGH

started early by writing a Halloween play that her grade-school class performed. Since then, though her tastes have changed, her love for reading has not. And her·writing appetite simply grows more voracious by the day.

She has been a finalist in the RITA® Award and the Holt Medallion contests. But the true highlights of her day as a writer are when she receives word from a reader that they laughed, cried or lost a night of sleep while reading one of her books.

Born in Southern California, Allison has lived in several different cities in four different states. She has been, at one time or another, a cosmetologist, a computer programmer and a secretary. She has recently begun writing full-time after spending nearly a decade as an administrative assistant for a busy neighborhood church, and currently makes her home in Arizona with her family. She loves to hear from her readers, who can write to her at P.O. Box 40772, Mesa, AZ 85274-0772.

Dear Gram,

Coming home to Lucius after twelve years hasn't been easy. I'd forgotten what it's like to live in a small town. Everyone wants to know if I'm here to stay, if I'm going to sell Daddy's house, if I'll take a job at the local school. And then there's Shane Golightly. He's the town sheriff now, and he lives next door. He's really been looking out for me—even though sometimes I feel like he's just being overprotective, it's been nice to have him around. I can't even seem to get a good night's sleep anymore unless he's nearby. I think I might be falling for him again but I'm so afraid—afraid of getting hurt, afraid of hurting him, but mostly just afraid of facing the past I left behind. I wish you were here, Gram. I miss you.

Love,

Laurel

## Prologue

"**W**hat do you mean *you're leaving?*" Laurel sat up, clutching her cotton dress to her chest. Her bare back felt itchy from straw that only a half hour earlier had felt like the sweetest of mattresses. And there was a horrible hole yawning open inside her.

Shane didn't look at her. He yanked his T-shirt over his head. His thick hair looked more brown than blond in the dwindling light of the ancient barn and was messy, as much from her fingers as from the shirt. "I have classes." His deep voice was clipped.

"Starting tomorrow?" She couldn't hide her disbelief. She knew good and well that Shane's graduate school classes weren't beginning for another few weeks. She knew, because he'd told her so himself.

His gaze finally slanted toward her, and he crouched next to her, leaned toward her—making her heart stop with hope that he really *couldn't* be serious about leaving her, not like this, not *now,* after they'd—

He plucked his sock from the straw beside her, and his hand brushed her bare thigh as he pulled back, straightening. He didn't even bother to sit on one of the hay bales. Simply balanced easily on one foot and drew on the sock, then did the same for the other, then shoved his feet into his scuffed athletic shoes.

Her eyes burned. "Did I do something wrong?"

He made a low sound. Shoved his hands through his hair. "Laurel—"

Laurel. Not *songbird,* which he'd been calling her for weeks now.

It had been her first time. But not his. "I didn't cry because it hurt, Shane, I—"

"God, Laurel." He kicked the bales of hay so hard that suddenly the top one tumbled off the stack and landed with a thud. A cloud of dust and bits billowed out, making her wince and squint against the shower of debris.

He swore again, which made Laurel's eyes burn even more, because Shane just didn't swear.

"I should never have touched you. I'm twenty-three. You're barely eighteen."

"But I *am* eighteen." Her voice was thick with tears, which wasn't at all the way she wanted to sound. She scrambled to her feet, awkwardly pulling her dress over her shoulders and fumbling with the buttons that ran all the way down the front. But her fingers couldn't seem to match up any of the buttons with the proper holes and she finally just clutched it together at her waist. "And we love each other." Didn't they?

He looked pained, his gaze fastened on her white knuckles. He took a step toward her. Then another.

She nearly stopped breathing.

He put his hands over hers and slowly unclenched her fingers from the pale-yellow fabric.

Then he just stood there, staring down at the hands he held. Her dress, soft from too many summers and too many washings, parted a little.

He swallowed. She saw it work down his strong, tanned throat. Then he squeezed her hands just a little and released them. And reached for the top of her dress.

Her knees—not particularly steady after what they'd just done, anyway—felt like her mama's strawberry jam left out on a sunny counter.

His fingers were so long. A little bony, and a lot callused. He might be a preacher's son, but he'd spent the summer working for old Hal Calhoun right here on his farm.

"Shane." His name was barely a whisper on her tongue. She loved his name. She loved him. He was tall and good and golden and so incredibly gentle.

"I shouldn't have touched you," he said again. And as deliberately as he'd unbuttoned each and every one of those tiny white buttons, he began doing them up again. "I'm sorry, but it was a mistake. It's my fault. So go ahead and hate me all you want."

By the time he reached the hem, just below her knees, the tears were crawling openly down her cheeks. The bleeding from her heart, broken wide, wasn't visible at all.

He rose.

She was glad that he didn't bother hunting around for her bra or panties. She could see them from the corner of her eye, tossed carelessly aside near her sandals.

"I'll drive you home."

She didn't want to go anywhere. She wanted to stay there in Calhoun's barn with Shane. She wanted him to put his arms around her again, to press his lips to hers, to breathe softly against her ear and make her feel as if everything in life was good and fine.

They'd barely had a summer together, but it had been the best summer of her life.

"I'd rather walk," she said quietly.

"Laurel, I'm not leaving you here—"

"Yes, you are," she interrupted, feeling a curl of anger nip at the yawning pain inside her. "That's *exactly* what you're doing."

He shoved his hands in his front pockets. She could see the shape of them, fisted against the worn-white denim. "I never made it a secret that I was going back to school." He looked away for a moment, and she saw the muscle in his jaw flexing. "You're starting college classes soon, too, dammit."

"Preachers shouldn't swear," she murmured.

He snorted and looked back at her, then pointedly looked at the bed of straw, then her underwear. "I have no business becoming a preacher, either."

Despite her cracking heart, she reached out to him. "Don't say that, Shane." He had plans. Wonderful, admirable plans. He wanted to be like his father, to help people however best he could. On someone else, those plans would just be dreams. But Shane would make it happen. He was just that way.

His lips twisted. "Get the rest of your things. You can't walk home. It's nearly dark." He ignored her outstretched hand and walked to the barn door, sliding it open enough to walk out. A moment later she heard the rumble of his old truck engine cranking to life.

Dashing her hands over her cheeks, she snatched up her panties and yanked them on, balled up her bra into her pocket and shoved her feet into her sandals.

She didn't look at him as she joined him in the cab of his truck. But she had to close her eyes against a fresh rush of tears when he silently reached over and pulled a long piece of straw from her hair.

Then he put the truck into gear and drove her home.

## Chapter One

$W$ho was inside the old Runyan house?

The car—dark blue and dimmed by a thick layer of dust—was still parked in the cracked, uneven driveway when Shane drove past. It hadn't been there when he'd gone to the station in the morning. But it had been there when he'd driven out to his brother's place that afternoon. And it was still there this evening on his way home for the day.

He could have kept on driving. Instead he pulled in to the rutted driveway and parked behind the small blue sedan.

A light shone from the front picture window of the house. Old Roger Runyan had been dead five days now, but the house he'd lived in for as long as Shane could remember looked more welcoming in that moment than it had in years.

Question was, who was inside the house, turning on lamps as if they belonged there? Roger had no kin except Laurel, and she hadn't been in Lucius for twelve years.

Twelve years. He sighed and climbed out of his SUV.

There were three steps leading up to the front door. Wooden and nearly rotting through. It would be a merciful day when Shane finally got the deed to this place and tore it down. Just the thought of it was almost enough to put a smile on his face.

He planted his boot on the top of the porch and climbed up, bypassing the steps altogether, and tilted back his hat a few inches to peer through the metal-framed screen door as he rapped his knuckles on it.

He already knew from dealing with Roger's death that the furnishings inside the house hadn't changed over the years. Considering the old man had rid himself of his wife, Violet, twelve years ago, Shane had been surprised Roger hadn't done a thing to eradicate her little touches from his home. But they'd still been there. Fussy little glass lamps with beads hanging from the fading shades, bowls of dusty plastic grapes and apples, vases of unnaturally bright flowers that never needed a drop of water.

Just another thing Shane would never understand about the man.

He figured the person inside the house was the real estate agent. Only, he didn't recognize the car, and Shane knew all the cars around his town.

All part of the job.

He knocked again. "Hello?"

"Coming."

The voice was female.

Throaty.

Young.

He straightened and absorbed the shock of it.

He was pretty sure he recognized the voice, and it was definitely *not* anyone from down at Lucius Realty.

The woman neared the door, her form blurred by rusting metal mesh. The porch light flicked on. The door screeched as it began to swing open. "I'm sorry. I was in the back and didn't hear…" The woman's voice trailed off as Shane stepped away from the screen door enough for her to open it.

She looked up at him. Her eyes widened a little. The color in her cheeks rose, then fell.

Recognition, all right. "Hello, Laurel."

Her lips—damn, but they looked as soft as ever—rounded into a little *O*. She wore a tidy white blouse tucked into a slender beige skirt. Little gold hoops hung in her ears, visible because her hair was pulled back from her face in a snug knot. She looked about as finished and polished as she'd looked ravaged and pained the last time he'd seen her.

Except for her eyes.

Her eyes looked positively shell-shocked.

And he felt like the proverbial bull in a china shop.

Then her lashes swept down for a moment, and when she looked up at him again, the shock was gone. Everything was gone. There was nothing but politeness, and for an awful moment Shane thought maybe the stories had it wrong and that Laurel Runyan had never climbed out of the pit of despair she'd been tossed into that long-ago summer when her family had disintegrated before her eyes.

"Hello, Shane. What are you doing here?" The greeting was considerably less welcoming than the light shining from the front window had been.

But at least she remembered him. That was good. He'd rather have her still hate him than be feeling the emotional numbness that had gripped her for months after that summer.

"Saw the light," he said, looking past her into the house. But he couldn't see hide nor hair of another person. Had she come alone to Lucius? Had she married? Did she have a little tribe of kids now? He wished he could blame the questions on simple curiosity. But nothing about Laurel had ever been simple. "Wanted to check it out."

Her eyebrows drew together a little, and the corners of her lips lifted a little. "Check it out. For what? New church members?" Her hands lifted to her sides for a moment.

A moment long enough for him to see there was no ring. A faint tan line where one had been, though.

Recently.

"Sorry," she went on, oblivious to his cataloging. "I gave up going to church years ago."

He had, too. For a while.

"Thought maybe you were one of the agents from Lucius Realty," he admitted.

"Well, as you can see, I'm not." Her voice was still pleasant. But the edge of curiosity was still there, not quite hidden. "I…didn't think you were still in Lucius," she said. "I saw the sign outside your dad's church. He's still pastor there. And there was a name I didn't recognize listed as the associate pastor. Um, Morrison or something."

"Morrissey."

She nodded and leaned slightly against the opened screen door. Her position was clear. She had no intention of inviting him in.

But she was still curious.

Hell. So was he. If he'd had any way of reaching her, any way of knowing where she was, he would have notified her himself about her dad.

"I'm sorry about your father." He should have said that right off. No wonder he hadn't ended up in the ministry. Unlike his father, Beau, Shane's people skills were miserable. He took care of his townspeople's safety. He left it to people like his father to take care of their sensibilities.

Her head tilted a little to one side, and a few strands of silky hair drifted from the knot to lie against her slender throat. Her hair was darker than he remembered. Almost the color of walnuts. Back then, it had been streaked with blond from the summer sun, a shifting mass of burnished gold that had felt like silk against his rough fingers.

"Condolences?" she asked. "I know what you thought of him. What everyone in this town thought of him."

"He was still your father." He wasn't sorry about Roger. But he was sorry if the loss hurt Laurel. He was always sorry when something—or someone—hurt Laurel.

Her lips pursed a little and her lashes swept down, hiding her expressive brown eyes again. "Yes," she murmured after a moment. "He was. Thank you."

"If you need any help with the arrangements, just ask."

She lifted her hand and tucked the stray strands of hair behind her ear. She pushed the screen door the rest of the way open. It was so worn, it merely settled open with a sigh and she stepped out onto the porch. Even with her high-heeled shoes—pretty for her ankles, but still a conservative tan color—she didn't reach past his shoulder.

How could he have forgotten how small she was compared to him?

"I'm not sure my father would have wanted a religious service," she admitted. "His lawyer, Mr. Newsome—I can hardly believe my dad *had* a lawyer—said he didn't have a will when he notified me about his death. He didn't say if Dad had specified any instructions at all. Only that he'd asked Mr. Newsome to contact me." Her voice faltered a little. "I, um, I haven't had a chance to go through any of Dad's records here yet." The prospect clearly held little appeal for her.

He couldn't blame her. Even under the best of circumstances, such a task would be difficult. "The lawyer might not have known, but your father went to Sunday service every week. Talk to Beau. He'll be able to help you figure it all out."

"He went to *church?*"

"Regular as rain," he assured. But he couldn't fault her for her skepticism. Unlike Roger, who had never gone to church until after his wife died, Laurel had once been a regular presence at Lucius Community Church. Her grandmother had taken her every Sunday, and then when Lucille died, Laurel had continued going on her own.

Until the summer she turned eighteen.

Twelve years ago.

A lot had changed that summer for the Runyan family. And for Shane.

"So," Laurel finally said, as if she were anxious to move on from the notion of her father having discovered religion. "Your name wasn't alongside your father's on the sign at the church. So I guess your ministry took you elsewhere, after all."

"I didn't go into the ministry. Don't know why I ever thought I could."

Her eyes widened again at that, and for a long moment she stared at him. "You'd planned it all your life."

"Planning doesn't mean the same thing as having a calling."

She finally unfolded her arms and propped one hand on the doorjamb near her shoulder, which let the lamplight behind her shine through the fine weave of her lightweight blouse. He could clearly see the outline of her bra beneath it.

"But you're here. In Lucius. So what *do* you do?" she asked.

*Look at you and still want.* He wasn't quick enough to cut off the realization. "I'm the sheriff," he said.

She closed her hand over the screen door latch, that brief moment of softening, of near welcome in her demeanor drying up as surely as the grass in the yard behind him had.

"Sheriff. I see. No *wonder* you wanted to check things out at the Runyan place. But as you know, my father's dead. There's no one here anymore for the law to come after."

Without another glance at him, she stepped back into the house and firmly pulled the screen door shut.

Then she turned away, closing the wooden door with a thud. He heard the lock sliding into place as she disappeared into the house where, twelve years ago, her father, Roger Runyan, had gotten away with killing his wife.

Laurel was shaking.

The moment the door slammed shut behind her, she reached out for the arm of the couch and shuffled around to sit before her legs simply quit functioning.

Shane Golightly.

She closed her eyes, her hand pressed against the base of her throat.

She'd known that returning to Lucius—to this house—would stir up memories. She could handle memories.

Most of them.

But why, oh why, hadn't she prepared herself for *this?* Why had she let herself believe that he would've followed through, chapter and verse, with his long-ago plans?

Because the Shane she'd known had never deviated from his chosen course. Not ever.

Except for *her.* She'd definitely been off the path for Shane.

"Foolish Laurel," she whispered aloud, and nearly

jumped out of her skin at the imperious sound that drowned out her hoarse whisper.

A fist pounding on the front door.

"Laurel, open the damn door."

Her heartbeat skipped right back into triple time. She stared at the door, half expecting it to open even though she'd flipped the flimsy lock.

"Laurel." He'd moved to the grimy picture window next to the door and was looking in at her through the limp curtains. As if he had every expectation of her jumping right to her feet. "I'm not leaving," he said, and he didn't even have to raise his voice to be heard through the thin pane.

Voices had always been easily heard through the walls of the Runyan place. Particularly the raised voices.

She didn't want to open the door. She didn't want to see Shane. She didn't want a lot of things, and for that reason alone, she forced her muscles into motion and rose from the couch. He moved away from the window and was standing in front of the screen again when she unlocked and pulled open the door. She leaned her shoulder against the edge of it and was glad he couldn't see the death grip she had on the inside knob.

Weren't sheriffs supposed to wear khaki-colored uniforms and badges in full view to warn all innocent bystanders of their position? Shane was wearing a charcoal-gray shirt, open at the throat, and blue jeans that fit entirely too well.

"I'm busy, Sheriff."

"I could see that through the window." His voice—droll though it was—was deeper. Everything about him seemed deeper. His gray eyes. His golden hair. His...intensity.

"Where are you staying?" he asked.

It was the last question she expected. Not that she'd expected *any* questions from him, since she had been naive enough to believe he'd be far, far from Lucius. That had been his plan that one summer. To finish seminary and take his ministry wherever he could help people the most.

"I'm staying here," she told him.

His mouth tightened. Then, in a clearly conscious effort, his entire expression gentled. "Do you think that's wise?" His voice was even more gentle. More careful.

Her spine stiffened. "You needn't speak to me like I'm deranged, Sheriff."

"I wasn't." Again in a gentle, careful tone.

She understood where it came from, and why, but she still hated it. Hated that it was coming from *him,* most of all. "Yes, you were. Are." She also hated the fact that she was the one sounding defensive. She swallowed and scrambled for her wits. Her composure. She was a composed woman. Had always been a composed woman.

Except for the brief time when she was more than a girl but not yet a woman and had spent more hours than she could remember in a room where there were no sharp corners.

"This is…was…my father's home. I'm staying here. Unless there's some law against it?"

He didn't look pleased. "By yourself?"

"Yes," she managed calmly.

Something in his eyes made him look even less pleased. Anyone else and she might have blamed it on the dwindling light, or on the bare bulb that would have sufficed as a porch light if it had been a higher wattage.

"Here." He abruptly pulled out his wallet and slid a card from it. "Call me if you need anything." He extended the business card.

She plucked the card from his fingers, careful not to

touch him. "I won't need anything," she assured him stiffly. "But, thank you."

"I'll come by and check on you in the morning."

"I don't need to be checked on."

"You're not—"

"Capable enough to stay alone in the house where I grew up?" She crossed her arms. "I'm not crazy, *Sheriff.*" Not anymore.

"Nobody said you were, *Laurel.*" His deep voice was smooth, so incredibly smooth, that they might just as well have been exchanging pleasantries on the steps of his daddy's church. "But this place is—"

"What?"

"Falling apart," he said simply.

Truthfully.

The defensive balloon that had puffed up deflated, leaving her feeling off-kilter. "I'll be all right."

"The furnace stopped working last year. Roger never had it fixed."

"It's the middle of June. I won't need the furnace yet."

He barely waited a beat. "Yet?"

She unfolded her arms. Folded them again. She'd been debating the idea of staying since before she'd driven back into the town limits. It wasn't as if she had anywhere else to go. Not since two weeks ago when she'd called off her own wedding at the very last minute. Finding out that Shane was still in Lucius didn't change a thing where her plans, her nonplans, were concerned.

Did it?

"It won't be cold for months. I'll have plenty of time to fix the furnace," she said more confidently than she felt.

She had time, yes. Money? That might be another matter. A matter she intended to keep to herself.

"You can't be planning to stay."

He actually sounded horrified, and it surprised her enough that she managed not to get defensive over the flat statement. "Why not?"

He jammed his hat on his head. "This house isn't fit for anyone to live in it."

"How do you know?" She highly doubted he'd spent Sunday afternoons visiting with her father.

"Because I make it my business to know what's going on in my town."

"Including the habitability of my father's house."

"Yes."

"How sheriffy of you."

"You've earned yourself a smart mouth somewhere along the way."

She managed an even smile. But the truth was, she *didn't* have a smart mouth. The only thing she'd done in her entire adult life that wasn't agreeable and sensible was walking out on her wedding to a perfectly decent man. "Maybe I've picked a few things up from the third-graders I teach. You went from the Lord to the law," she observed. "Time brings all sorts of changes to a person."

"Time doesn't change everything," he said flatly.

She didn't know what on earth to make of that, not when they were both living evidence to the contrary. So she just stood there. And the silence between them lengthened.

Thickened.

She cast about in her mind fruitlessly for something—anything—to break the silence, only to gasp right out loud when a metallic chirp sounded.

Shane made a muffled sound and pulled a minute cell phone off his belt. "Sorry," he murmured and flipped it open. "Golightly." His voice was brusque.

She, for one, was perfectly happy for the intrusion as she drew in a long, careful breath. His call, though, was brief, and when he snapped the phone shut, he was very much in lawman mode.

"I'll check on you later." He settled his hat and turned on his heel, clearly expecting no arguments from her this time as he stepped off the porch past the rotting steps.

She didn't have the nerve to argue, anyway. Not when he looked so grimly official. Instead she stood there in the doorway, hugging her arms to her waist, and watched while his long legs strode across the tired yard toward the tan SUV parked behind the little car she'd rented at the airport in Billings.

He wasted little time backing out and driving up the road toward town, but she still had plenty of time to study the word that was emblazoned in dark-green printing on the side of his SUV: Sheriff.

Shane was the sheriff.

And it was a sheriff who'd arrested her father one hot summer night for something he hadn't done. Something she'd never, ever believed he'd done.

The brake lights of Shane's truck—the *sheriff's* truck—disappeared and Laurel finally drew in a full, cleansing breath.

It didn't quite stop the trembling inside her, but it helped.

She let her gaze drift up and down the road. One way, the way Shane had driven, lay the town proper. The other way, beyond a sharp curve that skirted the stand of tall, centuries-old trees, lay nothing but miles and miles of…nothing.

She'd come back to bury her father.

But once she'd done that, once she'd dealt with his belongings, with the house, there was nothing else for her here. As much "nothing" as what lay beyond the curving highway.

Unfortunately, Laurel knew as she finally turned and went back inside the house, there was nothing for her to return to in Colorado, either. No job. No home. No fiancé.

Maybe she *was* just as crazy as Shane probably thought.

## Chapter Two

"I heard you were here, but I had to see it with my own eyes." The voice was deep and smooth as molasses and definitely amused.

Laurel set the heavy bag of weed killer in the cart next to the bucket and cleansers she'd already put there and turned toward the voice, a smile already forming. "Reverend Golightly. I was going to call you later today." She dashed her hand quickly down her thigh, then extended it. "It's so good to see you." The pleasure in her voice was real. In fact, it was the first real pleasure she'd felt in weeks, and definitely since she'd arrived in Lucius the previous day.

He cocked an eyebrow and his light-blue eyes crinkled at the corners. "Oh, Laurel, honey, we can do better than that." He swept her up in a great hug, lifting her right to the tips of her toes there in the aisle of Lucius Hardware. "You're the spitting image of your grandmother, do you know that?"

She laughed and very nearly cried as she hugged him back. "I'll take that as a compliment."

"It was meant as one. In her day, Lucille was the prettiest woman in five counties. Until my Holly came to town, that is." He grinned and settled her on her feet, keeping hold of her hands and holding them wide as he stepped back to look at her. "I'm as sorry as ditch water that it took something like this to bring you home, Laurel."

The knot in her throat grew. "Me, too." She swallowed harder and peered up into his face. "You haven't changed a bit, Reverend Golightly. How is your family?"

His eyes crinkled again. "Beau. And they're all fine. Stu's fit as a fiddle," he told her. "Still single and he's got a small spread outside of town a bit—Hal Calhoun's place if you remember it—plus he runs the garage down on Main Street. Evie's running Tiff's. She has three kids. They're all getting on their feet a little since she and her husband divorced."

Laurel would be better off if she *couldn't* remember Calhoun's place. Or his barn.

"Your wife doesn't run Tiff's anymore?" For all of Laurel's childhood, her mother had been employed as a maid at the bed-and-breakfast operated by Beau's second wife, Holly.

"She passed away some time ago," Beau said quietly.

Laurel pressed her hand to her chest, dismayed. "Oh, I'm so sorry. I had no idea." Her conversation—if one could call it that—with Shane hadn't gotten to such matters. And she hadn't talked with anyone else in town since she'd arrived.

"No reason you would, child," he assured gently. "But she'd be pleased as punch to see you back in Lucius. Hadley took over running Tiff's after we lost her mother, but she got married not long ago to Dane Rutherford, and now Evie's trying her organized little hand at it."

Laurel paused at the name. "Dane Rutherford?"

Beau grinned, his eyes brightening again with amusement. "*The* Dane Rutherford. Didn't they have newspapers where you lived? Sure did make the news around these parts."

"I'll bet," Laurel murmured. The Rutherford name was as familiar as Rockefeller and Kennedy. She shook her head, amazed. Hadley was a few years younger than Laurel and had always had her nose in a book. How on earth had she met someone like Dane Rutherford? "Well... wow."

"He puts his pants on one leg at a time, too," Beau assured mildly. "So far he seems good enough for my Hadley. And then there's Shane, of course. He's the sheriff, if you can believe it."

Her face felt a little hot. They stepped aside to let a woman bearing a flat of daisies pass. "I know. He told me my father started going to church."

"You've talked to Shane?" Beau was obviously surprised.

"He stopped by the house yesterday." And surprised *her* greatly by not coming by that morning as threatened.

"He didn't mention that when I saw him this morning at the hospital."

Her nerves jangled. "Hospital?"

"Nasty three-car accident on the south side of town. Aside from handling the reports and such, he's friends with one of the women who got hit. He's probably still there."

Even as relief that Shane was at the hospital in his official capacity doused her nerves, an odd sense she couldn't quite identify took its place. "I hope she's all right." Shane obviously hadn't been as unsettled by their encounter as she had been, or he'd have mentioned it to his father.

"Fortunately, no one was seriously injured," Beau said, mercifully oblivious to Laurel's undeniable sense of… what? Pique? Disappointment? Relief? "Now, what about you? Your father said once that you'd become a teacher."

Laurel nodded. In a way she was as surprised that her father had told anyone anything about her as she was that he'd evidently found religion. "Elementary education. I, um, I've been at a school in Denver—Clover Elementary—teaching third grade."

"Surprised you're not teaching music."

She shook her head. She hadn't sung in public since the day her mother died.

Fortunately, Beau let that topic lie as he surveyed the items in her cart. "Looks like you're planning on exercising your elbows a bit."

"I'm staying at Dad's place. It needs some work." He probably knew that.

"Well, if you decide you prefer staying elsewhere, you just give Evie a call. I know she can come up with a room for you at Tiff's that would be comfortable."

Whether or not she could, Laurel wouldn't be able to afford it. Not even if Tiff's room rates hadn't budged a dime in the past decade. "I'll keep that in mind."

Beau's smile was ever kind, as if he'd divined her thoughts perfectly. "It's good to have you back, Laurel. Everything is going to be fine." He hugged her shoulder. "Now. We'll need to talk about the service for your father sooner or later, but I can see you're plenty busy and I'm on my way over to the hospital for my afternoon visitations. You just let me know when you're ready to talk about it, and I'm at your disposal. In the meantime, though, you can still call me if you need anything at all."

Why it was so much easier to take that advice from Beau

than it was from his son, Laurel didn't know. But where she'd bristled at Shane's command, she was touched now by Beau's concern, and she gave him a hug back. "I will. Thank you."

He gave her a little wink and headed down the wide aisle.

Laurel finished loading up her cart. She appreciated Beau's matter-of-factness about her father's service. Her father had died nearly a week ago. The attorney who'd contacted her had informed her that the funeral home would simply wait for instructions from her. The only rush for a funeral and burial would be whatever rush Laurel felt.

And she didn't really know *what* she felt.

So she concentrated on the immediate reality.

Her father's house was a pigsty. And she needed to clean away the mess left by years of neglect before she could begin to figure out what repairs the structure needed. Then maybe she'd consult a real estate agent.

She made her purchases and headed back to her father's home. On Main Street she passed the busy-looking garage and auto-body shop that undoubtedly was the one Beau had mentioned Stu ran.

The sheriff's office was a little ways up the road. She didn't allow herself much more than a glance that told her the brick-fronted building hadn't changed during her absence.

She passed the Luscious Lucius, which used to serve up the best breakfasts she'd ever had, and which—judging by the cars parked in front of it—was still doing a fine business for lunch.

A little further, beyond the businesses, she passed Tiff's. The enormous Victorian house looked just as distinctive as it always had, its sharp angles softened by curlicues and lace. The colors hadn't changed, either, over the years; still an eye-popping combination of pink and green.

It seemed hard to believe that Beau's wife was gone

now. That Evie was running it. Laurel's memories of Evie were of a light-hearted blond beauty more interested in winning the county science fair than helping with her stepmother's business.

At her father's house she parked in the cracked driveway bordered by overgrown weeds, yellow grass and bare dirt. There was no point in trying to enter the small, detached garage that sat next to the square house. It was filled to the rafters with about a million years of old newspapers and other junk. Her father's rusting pickup truck was parked in the center of it all, and since there was nothing under the hood but cobwebs and yawning space, the pickup wasn't going anywhere.

She unloaded her trunk, dumping everything on the porch next to the front door and nearly tripped over the cat that appeared out of nowhere. The animal yowled and streaked around the side of the house.

Probably belonged to the owner of the lovely rambling house built high on the hill behind her father's. The house certainly hadn't been there when Laurel was growing up, and as far as Laurel could determine, it was the only thing new in this area.

She eyed the worn, tired house where she'd grown up. A person would have to be desperate to buy it in its current state when there was an entirely new and modern development on the other side of Lucius.

A person might have to be desperate to *stay* in it.

She pushed aside the thought. She wasn't desperate. She was just…at loose ends.

After unloading the trunk, Laurel went inside the house, stepping over the porch steps. She'd already made the mistake of stepping too firmly on one. It had creaked ominously. The treads would definitely have to be replaced before some unwary soul went right through them.

How had her father lived here this way? As if he'd just given up on having any sort of decent home a long time ago?

She grabbed the box of trash bags she'd purchased and went inside. She'd start upstairs and work her way down.

It was a nice, sensible plan, and just *having* a plan made her feel better.

She went up the narrow staircase and paused at the first closed door. Her parents' bedroom. She hadn't gone in there yet. She started to reach for the iron knob. But her stomach clenched, and she curled her fingers into a fist, lowering her hand.

Later. She could clean out that room later.

She went into the only other bedroom. Her own. The narrow bed still had the afghan her grandmother had given her for her eighth birthday, folded neatly at the foot. The ancient student desk where she'd done her homework still stood beneath the single window that overlooked the front yard.

Nothing had changed since she'd been a girl. Yet everything here—as in the rest of the house—was covered with the thick layer of years of neglect.

She pulled out an enormous trash bag, flipping the plastic open. She dropped into the bag the glass jars that she'd painted one summer and filled with dried wildflowers. She yanked out the slender center drawer of the desk and tipped it into the bag, a childhood of bits raining out. She shoved the drawer back in place and slid out the second, tipping it, too. Magazines. More pieces of nothing. Then several canvas-covered books fell out from the bottom of the drawer.

She caught at them, her haste fleeing as quickly as it had struck.

Her journals. She set them on top of the desk, her fingers lingering on the top one. The canvas was dull, but the delicate lines of the flower printed in the center of the cover was still clear. Sighing a little, she looked from the diary out the window in front of her, then back to the bedroom behind her.

So long ago, she thought, since she'd been in this house. Her childhood bedroom. And she wasn't certain if she was grateful for the intervening years or not.

She looked at the journals again. Flipped the top one open randomly. The pages were stiff from age, but they parted easily midway through the book. She looked at the handwriting. Her handwriting. All loops and curls.

The handwriting of a girl.


Dear Gram,

Did you ever have one of those times when you were doing something you almost are always doing—like taking out the trash or washing the car on a Saturday morning—and then all of a sudden, time kind of stands still?

That's what happened to me this morning. I was washing daddy's truck, on account of he'd left it all muddy and Mom was totally mad about it and they were fighting. (They do that a lot, Gram, but I guess you can see that from up there in heaven.)

So there I was, standing in the truck bed hosing it down when Shane Golightly drove down the street in his dad's pickup truck. He stopped in front of the house and said something. Gosh, Gram, I don't even remember what it was he did say. Isn't that silly? He was wearing a plain white T-shirt and his arm was hanging out the open window and he stopped and said something—maybe it was about Mom's job at Tiff's. See? I can't remember even when I'm trying.

I haven't seen Shane since he went off to go to college several years ago. And I hadn't heard he was back, which was interesting, 'cause Jenny Travis usually calls me the very second she hears something major like that.

Anyway, there he was. And, oh Gram. He lifted his hand to wave and the sun was shining on him and everything else sort of disappeared.

Except for him.

The water, the mud, the yelling inside the house behind me, it was all gone.

Shane Golightly, Gram. I've known him—and Stu and Evie and Hadley, too, of course—all my life, seems like. He was always nice enough to me, probably because I was a little kid to him. But that moment—and I swear on a stack of Bibles that I'm not exaggerating like Mom's always saying—that moment was…special, that's all. Special!!

I just knew, Gram, that I'd remember that very moment, that I'd remember *Shane* in that very moment. The way he looked and the way the muddy water ran cold on my feet and the sun burned hot on my shoulders, and the grass smelled sweet, like it had just been mown.

I knew it.

I knew that I'd remember that moment all the rest of my life.

Laurel carefully closed the journal on those girlishly written thoughts, but doing so didn't close her mind to the memories.

She wished she could say the memories at the end of the summer were as clear as those from the beginning, when the sight of Shane Golightly had struck with such singular clarity. If only the entire summer were so clear.

So much of her life would have been different.

She sighed again and stacked the diaries in the bottom drawer, which she slid back into place in the desk.

She was sweating by the time she finished with the bedroom and the single bathroom, a state that wasn't helped by the sight of the sheriff's vehicle parked at the curb, or the presence of Shane studying the pile of supplies she'd purchased from the hardware store.

"What are you doing here?"

"What are *you* doing?"

She gestured at the trio of weighty bags full of trash she'd pulled from the house. "What does the evidence tell you?"

He didn't look amused. "You shouldn't be staying here."

She crossed her arms, staring down at him where he stood below the porch. "Because I have to take out some trash?"

He picked up one of the bags and tossed it at the steps. The wood cracked sharply and splintered beneath the bag.

"Well." Laurel eyed the half-buried bag. "You can pull that out."

"You're missing the point." With no seeming effort, he hefted the bag free of the jagged wood without managing to tear the plastic. "That could be you falling through the steps."

"Instead, it was an innocent garbage bag. I'm staying, so if that's your only reason for coming out here, you can go." The sooner the better.

He just gave her a look and held out his hand for the remaining bags. She tightened her hold on them. "I can manage."

"Hand me the bags, Laurel."

She made a face and dragged the bags over to him. His hands brushed hers as he took hold and lifted them off the porch, carrying all three around to the trash bins next to the garage.

It was a fine time to realize that Shane Golightly's touch still had the ability to make her mind go completely blank.

He was back in seconds, and the hope that he would simply leave died rapidly when he stepped up onto the porch and lowered himself onto the faded wicker love seat near the door.

She leaned against the wall. "What do you want, Sheriff?"

He doffed his hat, balancing it on his knee. His hair was darker than it used to be. Particularly near the nape of his neck where it was cut severely short.

The last time she'd seen Shane so closely, his shoulders hadn't been quite so wide, his chest not quite so deep, his forearms, where his white shirtsleeves were rolled up, not quite so sinewy. And his deep-gold hair had been long enough at the nape for her fingers to tangle in it.

She swallowed and looked away. Her gaze fell on his SUV. *Sheriff*.

She swallowed again. "I saw your father earlier. I was sorry to hear about your mother." Holly Golightly had been his stepmother, actually, but Laurel knew he'd considered her his only mother, since his natural mother had walked out on her family when he'd been very young.

"Cancer. It was fast," he supplied. "And a long time ago."

"Does that make it hurt less? Time?"

His wide shoulders rose and fell. "Yeah. But it doesn't stop us all from missing her. I moved back to Lucius when she got really bad, and decided not to leave again once she was gone." The toe of his boot jiggled. "This place isn't safe for you."

She exhaled, impatience swirling through her. "I'm a big girl. I think I can avoid the bad steps until they're fixed."

"Who is going to fix them?"

"I will."

His eyebrows rose. "Really."

"Yes, *really.*"

"Gonna buy the lumber. Get the tools. Rebuild the supports that are rotting underneath."

"If I have to." She propped her hands on her hips. "Women are perfectly capable of—"

"Whoa, whoa, whoa." He stood. "I'm not getting into that argument with you. I know plenty of women who can frame a house better than men. My point is that you're a—"

"A *what?*" She angled her head.

"A third-grade teacher," he finished mildly, and smoothly circled her wrists, turning her palms upward. "Without a single callus on these pretty hands of yours to indicate you're accustomed to this sort of work."

She curled her fingers into fists. He wasn't being chauvinistic. His attitude was strictly based on what he knew—or thought he knew—of her.

"I'm perfectly *capable* of learning." And hadn't she learned her lesson where Shane Golightly was concerned?

His thumbs worked across the knobs of her knuckles. Soothing. "Of course you're capable of learning anything. That's not the point."

The point. Remember the *point.* "This house is the only thing left of my father. Maybe I don't want to abandon it the way he abandoned me." She pulled her hands away. "Now, if you'll excuse me, I have a lot of things to take care of this afternoon, not least of which is planning a funeral." She reached for the screen door, turning away from him.

"Laurel."

Why did hearing her name on his lips make her heart still skip? She didn't want to hesitate, but she did. "What?" When he didn't respond, she finally looked back at him.

His eyes were unreadable. His expression no more helpful. Did she even *know* this man anymore?

"Be careful," he finally said.

She nodded once. "I plan to be." Then she went inside.

## Chapter Three

The funeral service for Laurel's father was on Friday morning, just three days after she arrived in Lucius.

Beau Golightly handled most of the details. When they'd met to discuss the service, he'd told her that Roger had left a plan a few years earlier. What hymns he wanted sung. What scripture readings.

The fact that Roger had left *any* sort of instructions had stunned Laurel.

He'd even prepaid for an arrangement of flowers, had prearranged his burial, had done nearly everything.

The only thing Laurel had done was purchase him a new suit, and she'd had to depend upon the funeral home director to advise her on the size.

She could have avoided that particular embarrassment if she'd only had the nerve to enter her parents' bedroom.

But she hadn't.

Picking out the navy-blue suit, white shirt and burgundy striped tie at the new department store on the far end of town was the most familial task she'd performed for her father in twelve years. And he had to be deceased for her to even be allowed the task.

She'd gone back to his house and had a glass of wine, after she'd delivered her purchases to the funeral home, and had felt guilty that she'd been unable to shed any tears.

She should be able to cry for her father, shouldn't she?

Even now, sitting in the front row of the Lucius Community Church while a woman Laurel had never before met played "Amazing Grace" on the organ and Beau Golightly stood at the pulpit with his Bible in hand, and the unprepossessing casket rested ten feet away from her, Laurel wasn't able to summon any tears.

Maybe there was still something wrong with her, after all.

There were no other mourners. She hadn't expected there would be. Roger had worked for the town of Lucius all of his adult life. Even after the charges in her mother's death had been dismissed against him, he'd kept his job with the town. He'd certainly never considered leaving Lucius to join her in Colorado, even though she'd asked him.

There was a small arrangement of summer flowers that had been sent by his department.

But there were no people who'd interrupted their day to attend his final service. Even the funeral home director, who was there to take care of transporting the casket, had chosen not to come in for the service but was waiting outside.

Nobody had loved Roger Runyan. Most people hadn't even liked him. Even before that awful summer, he'd been sullen, standoffish and made it plain that he liked others as little as they liked him.

He may have begun attending church after Laurel left

Lucius, but it seemed that nothing else about him had changed.

The organ notes slowly faded, and Beau gave her one of his unbearably kind looks. He opened his Bible and began to read.

Laurel closed her eyes and prayed for forgiveness. She'd loved her father, even if he hadn't loved her.

So what was wrong with her that she couldn't cry for him, now?

For a moment—a weak moment—she almost wished she'd asked Martin to come. Despite the way she'd left him only a few weeks earlier, he would have been here for her.

Which would have been as wrong as going through with the wedding.

A rustle sounded behind her and she glanced over her shoulder, starting as two people slid into the pew.

Evie and Stu Golightly.

She would have recognized them anywhere.

Evie, with her short, fluffy blond hair and blue eyes, and Stu, with his brown hair and eyes. He was Shane's twin, but the resemblance between them was limited to their size and facial structure.

Evie sat forward, closing her hand over Laurel's shoulder. "I had to find a sitter for my kids," she whispered, "or we'd have been here on time." She squeezed her hand a little, then sat back and pulled a hymnal from the rack on the back of Laurel's pew and dropped it on her brother's lap.

"I didn't expect anyone," Laurel whispered, feeling numb. This had to be Beau's doing.

Evie's smile was sympathetic and very much like her father's. "Maybe not, but here we are."

Beau continued reading, his voice beautiful and soothing and after a moment Laurel gathered herself enough to turn back around in her seat. Then the organist played again. The small congregation rose and sang the two hymns that Roger had requested. And that was it.

The end.

There was to be no graveside service, in accordance with Roger's wishes, and Laurel rose as Beau stepped down from the pulpit and approached her. "Thank you." She held out her hands to him.

He took them and gave her a hug. "Your father would be very proud of you, Laurel."

Behind them, the funeral director and his associates were efficiently removing the casket. Laurel watched them for a moment. There was an awful, hollow feeling inside her, and it surpassed the emotional black hole that had prompted her to call off her wedding. "Proud? I can't imagine why."

"Remember? He told me you were a teacher. That you have a master's degree in education from the University of Colorado, even. He was proud," Beau assured. "Now, there's a table waiting for us over at the Luscious. Evie, Stu, you'll join us."

Neither seemed inclined to argue. Evie tucked her arm through Laurel's as they headed out of the church. Within minutes their small caravan arrived at the café and, just as Beau promised, there was a table waiting.

The waitress had barely delivered their water glasses and menus when Evie sat forward. "You know, Laurel, the school here has been short staffed for over a year."

"Geez, Evie," Stu groused a little. He didn't bother with a menu. "Give her a chance to settle in first." He focused on Laurel. "How long do you have that rental car for?"

"Er, through the weekend."

"Well, you let me know if you're gonna be in the market for buying something more long term. I'll make sure you get a good deal."

Her mouth dried a little. She had a car back in Colorado. It was still parked at the apartment complex, where the rest of her worldly goods were stored in a locked garage. None of it would be moved to Martin's as they planned to do once they returned from their honeymoon. "Thank you," she said. She didn't know how to tell them that the permanency of her stay in Lucius was still undetermined.

"Stu knows what's under the hood of all the used cars around here," Evie said. "It's one of his few skills."

Stu shot her a look. "I'll remember that when you need your engine rebuilt."

Evie grinned.

The tears that had been painfully absent earlier now seemed to clog Laurel's throat. She looked down at the menu, blinking hard. Why was it that she could cry just because this family behaved so normally? Because they just let her be, didn't seem to expect her to break down and didn't seem shocked that she hadn't.

Around her, the café was alive with conversations, the clatter of dishes, the aroma of coffee and grilling hamburgers. And after a minute she could actually absorb the words that she was staring at.

The menu, aside from a few modern additions like grilled-chicken wraps and low-carb hamburger buns, held few changes. "Is the fried chicken here still good?"

"Better 'n ever," Beau assured. "Oh, good. There's Shane. I was hoping he'd be able to join us."

Laurel's water glass tipped precariously when she knocked into it with her menu, but Stu stretched out a long arm, capably catching it before it spilled.

"Sorry I couldn't make the service," Shane murmured

as he took the seat beside her. Beneath the square table, his thigh brushed against hers as he returned the few hails sent his way from other diners. "Stuck in court."

"I, um, I didn't expect anyone at all," she admitted, carefully shifting away. She felt a little steadier if she focused on the other members of Shane's family. "It was just…so…nice of you to be there."

Evie smiled. "If we're nice enough, maybe you'll decide to stay in Lucius and look into a teaching position. Julie goes into third grade in the fall and I really, *really* don't want her to have to have Mrs. Cuthwater as a teacher."

"Mrs. Cuthwater still teaches?" Laurel remembered the woman. Any child who passed third grade was left with the desperate fear of not sitting up straight enough or of slanting their cursive writing the wrong way.

"She substitutes," Shane supplied. "Out of necessity."

"See?" Evie leaned forward, her blue eyes merry. "Think of my sweet, innocent baby, Laurel."

"I could be worse than Mrs. Cuthwater," Laurel warned.

Evie, Stu and Beau all chuckled at the prospect, and Laurel felt her tension begin to leave again. The waitress came by and they ordered.

"I probably should thank you," she told Shane after the waitress departed. "For the plywood. I assume that was you." Before evening had fallen on that day, an enormous sheet of wood had been laid across the steps, creating a rough but sturdy ramp. It had been a nice gesture, though it had rankled her that he'd done it without consulting her.

"What plywood?" Beau asked.

Shane plucked the lemon out of his iced tea and dropped it into hers, as if it were perfectly natural for him to do so. As if he remembered, from those few weeks they'd once spent together, just how dearly she loved lemon in her tea. "To cover the steps at the house before she breaks a leg going through them." His voice was flat.

Laurel's cheeks went even hotter at the tsks that statement elicited. Nobody questioned, of course, *which* house, as if Roger Runyan's house was the only one in all of Lucius that could be in such disrepair.

"It's not that bad," she defended.

"Maybe you should stay at Evie's," Stu suggested, and Evie immediately nodded.

"I have an empty room right now. The tower room, in fact. Nicest one at Tiff's."

Laurel remembered it, having helped her mother occasionally. "I'm fine where I am. Really." Even if the entire Golightly clan did believe she'd be better off staying in a cardboard box than in her own father's house.

"She thinks she's gonna fix things up there by herself," Shane said.

"'She's' sitting right here," Laurel interjected, "and can speak for herself. The house needs repairs if I'm going to sell it."

"If?" Shane's voice was incredibly mild.

"Mrs. Cuthwater needs a reprieve," she reminded, and saw the triumphant look passing between Evie and Stu.

"Without a reason to get up in the morning, Mrs. Cuthwater might as well lie down next to Mr. Cuthwater in Lucius Cemetery."

"Shane," Beau cautioned.

"She shouldn't be staying in that house, much less wasting time and energy fixing it up, and we all know it."

Laurel angled herself away from Shane. "You've made your opinion more than clear about that house. I don't really need to hear it again."

"Evidently, you do. Because you're still there. You don't have to fix it up to sell it."

Her eyebrows shot up. "Who on earth would buy it in its current condition?"

Evie made a faint sound.

"All rightee, here we go." The waitress arrived, bearing plates of food. She brushed her hands together when she finished unloading. "I'll be back to top off your drinks. Anything else I can get for you?"

Laurel's appetite for her fried chicken was definitely waning, but mindful of the concerned look in Beau's eyes and not wanting to add to it, she picked up a drumstick.

"Probably should have a contractor look at your dad's place," Stu said. "Jack Finn's the best around. He wouldn't have to do the work, necessarily, but he could steer you in the right direction."

Stu either possessed a remarkable ability to remain oblivious to the irritation rolling off Shane in waves or he simply didn't care. Either way, Laurel wanted to lean over and kiss him. "Finn? He's Freddie Finn's dad, isn't he?" She was surprised at the ease she had recalling old names, old faces.

Stu buried his attention in his burger as he nodded. "Call Jack. You won't regret it."

Laurel glanced at Evie. She would have to think about calling the contractor. It certainly made the most sense to get advice from a professional. But the cost was a consideration she couldn't ignore, no matter how wise it would be. "Is Freddie still in Lucius? She was in your grade, wasn't she?"

"Yes. And she's still here."

Stu made an unintelligible noise.

Evie rolled her eyes. "Ignore him. He's just irritated because he signed a lease for her to rent the barn he converted a while back. And she's holding him to it, even though they can't agree on the color of rice."

Laurel buried her nose in her glass of tea. Stu's barn was probably old Calhoun's barn, unless he'd built another one.

She didn't dare glance at Shane.

Evie, fortunately was chattering on. "Freddie runs a tow service with Gordon, but if you ask me, she's the brains behind keeping the business going since her brother hardly has the sense God gave a goose." Evie flicked a look at her father. "Sorry, Dad. But it's true."

"Gordon's a hard worker," Beau said, looking slightly amused. "There's a lot to be said for that. But I agree with Stu about calling Jack Finn, Laurel."

Shane breathed an oath that only Laurel heard. "Laurel shouldn't be *in* that house at all, and we all know it."

Silence settled over the foursome, and Laurel wished she were anywhere but there.

"So, Dad, have you heard from Nancy?" Evie finally broke the silence, her voice deliberately cheerful.

"Nancy Thayer," Beau supplied to Laurel. "She directed our junior choir. Kids in fifth grade through eight. She eloped last week. And no. I haven't," he told Evie.

"Far be it from me to stand in the way of true love," Evie's voice was a little tart at that, "but she couldn't have timed it worse." Her blue gaze shifted to Laurel. "The junior choir still spends every year raising enough money to travel to Spokane to participate in the choir festival there. Now they won't be able to go."

"Never put my truck through so many car washes." Stu dumped more ketchup on his French fries.

"Or bought so many homemade brownies," Beau added. "Think you financed two kids' expenses on that alone."

Stu just grinned.

Laurel didn't quite see the problem. "If they have the money, why can't they go?"

"Without a director, they won't be able to sing." Evie shook her head. "Rules."

"You can't hire someone else? Or maybe have a parent fill in temporarily?"

Evie's eyebrows rose pointedly. "The only other parent aside from me who's even willing to try that is Tony Shoemaker, Shane's senior deputy. And he can't carry a tune in a bucket."

"Neither can you, Tater," Shane drawled.

"A person doesn't have to sing themselves in order to direct a youth choir. Surely you can find someone." She flushed when she realized Beau was studying her.

"The festival is next weekend," he said.

"What about you or your associate pastor?"

"Jon is on study leave for a month, and I can't leave for three days without someone to fill the pulpit on Sunday. Believe me. If I could figure out a way of not disappointing Alan and the others, I would."

Alan, Laurel knew, was Evie's eldest son. "There's not *anyone?*" Her stomach felt in a knot. She wasn't so oblivious that she didn't know where this was headed. The hopeful look in Evie's eyes was enough to tell her that.

"Not so far." Beau dropped his napkin on his empty plate. "Some things just can't be helped. They'll have a chance to go next year."

Laurel swallowed. "Maybe I could, um, fill in as director. Just to get them through the festival."

"No." Shane's voice was flat.

Laurel bristled, her nervousness shriveling into irritation. "Why not?"

"Joey Halloran is in that group. He's hell on wheels. He got caught shoplifting last week at the thrift store."

"All the more reason for him to keep involved with more appropriate pursuits. But I suppose being the *sheriff*, you think anyone who even slightly breaks the law ought to be punished, rather than resolve the issue at the root of the problem?"

He looked equally irritated. "I didn't say that."

She turned in her chair and looked at Beau. "It's been a long time since I've sung—" a severe understatement "—but I can probably keep a group of kids on key."

Shane shoved back his chair. He was surrounded by people bent on ignoring reality. Laurel didn't need to be filling in for that twit who'd eloped, any more than she needed to be fixing broken steps. "I've gotta get back to the office." He tossed some cash on the table and ignored the disapproval in Beau's eyes as he turned to the door.

The wounded look in Laurel's eyes, though, followed him all the way back to his office.

When he got there he stopped at Carla's desk and picked up the stack of pink messages awaiting him.

"How was court?" she asked.

"Too long." He knew she wanted a blow-by-blow account because she always did. And, as always, she'd have to get her gossip from somewhere else. He flipped through the paper messages as he headed back to his office, only to stop. "What's this number?" One of these days, he needed to get the county to spring for a voice-mail system. Carla's writing had never won any awards for legibility.

Carla craned her neck, peering at the message. "Um, a five."

He nodded and started for his office again. Behind him the door jangled.

"I'd like to make a complaint."

He stopped cold. Slowly turned.

Laurel stood in the doorway. Her hair was still pinned back the way it had been in the café, but her cheeks were flushed, her golden eyes snapping.

"Excuse me?"

"I have a complaint." Her voice was as crisp as her eyes.

Carla was watching them avidly. She liked hearing gossip almost as much as she liked sharing it.

"We'll talk in my office."

"I don't want to talk in your office."

"Laurel—"

"Good heavens. You're little Laurel Runyan. I should have recognized you the second you walked in." Carla was around her desk in a flash. "Carla Chapman. I used to sit in a quilting circle with your grandmother. She was the oldest, I was the youngest. Neither one of us could abide any of the other women. She used to bring you with her, though. You'd sit in a corner in the quilting room with your own squares and a big ol' darning needle and yarn. I've heard you're a teacher. That's a fine thing. Lucille would be proud. And my condolences on your daddy passing," she added belatedly.

Laurel looked a little dazed. "I remember the quilting circle."

Carla looked pleased and only slightly abashed when she caught the look Shane was giving her. She cocked her eyebrow and returned to her desk.

Shane grabbed Laurel's arm, ignoring the start she gave, and led her back to his office. He let go of her as soon as they entered his cubicle and flipped through the messages again without bothering to look at them. Mostly he wanted to rid his hand of the feel of her supple arm.

"Okay, what's the complaint?" He sat down behind his desk.

She, however, didn't sit. She crossed her arms, looking at him with a schoolmarm look that probably did wonders for straightening up mischievous third-grade boys.

For a thirty-five-year-old man, it did *not* have the desired effect.

"Just because you loathed my father, and dumped me the second you'd finished with me, does *not* give you the right to harass me about what I choose to do or not do with his house, or to dictate what I do with my time while I'm here!"

"I didn't dump you." He kept his voice low. His conscience, however, was screaming at him with the ferocity of a freight train.

Her eyes went even chillier. "There may be some things I don't remember, Sheriff, but I remember *that* quite well."

He wished she'd sit. Or pace. Do anything but stand there the way she was, looking as cold and brittle as a narrow icicle. An icicle that could snap in two as easily as a whisper.

"I didn't know how much you remembered." He'd been an ass. An ass who'd been old enough to know better than to get involved with her. Eighteen or not, she'd still been too young and innocent.

Neither fact had stopped him back then.

He hoped to hell he'd learned something in the years since.

Her expression remained glacial. "Not remembering what I saw the night my mother died does not mean I cannot remember the exact details of how you dumped me an hour before it happened." Her chin lifted a little. "Therapy," she clipped, "does wonders for enabling a person to state...unpleasant...*facts*. And the unpleasant fact is that you don't want me in Lucius at all. You probably figured that with my father's death, your town was finally free of Runyans."

He leaned back in his chair. The springs squeaked slightly. "That therapy may have done you a world of good, but you are way off the mark when it comes to reading me."

"Really. You can't wait for me to sell my father's house. To dump it, really. You nearly came unglued when Evie was talking about someone—me—replacing Mrs. Cuthwater. And then this festival business? What's the matter? Are you afraid a Runyan will bring rack and ruin to the innocent children of Lucius?"

"No. I'm afraid Lucius will bring rack and ruin to *you*." He exhaled roughly, wanting to rip out his tongue. Where the hell was his control?

Her lips parted, and all the color drained from her cheeks.

He went around to her, taking her arms. "Sit."

She shook off his hold. "I don't need to sit."

An icicle. Too easily snapped in two. "Laurel, please. I didn't intend to upset you."

"Of course not. Heaven forbid you upset the crazy lady. She might just lose her mind again."

"I never said you were crazy." Maybe *he* was. Maybe that was why he sometimes still—all these years later—woke up sweating in the middle of the night with the vision of her inside that room at Fernwood, rocking herself to sleep, her eyes roiling pools of despair.

"You didn't have to say it," she whispered. "When everything you do makes it obvious you think it."

Then she turned on her heel and walked out of his office.

## Chapter Four

The next day, Laurel took the bus back to Lucius from Billings after returning the rental car there. Keeping it longer was simply an excuse she couldn't afford. But standing in the depot, she very nearly changed her mind about climbing on the bus.

Wouldn't returning to Colorado be preferable to returning to Lucius?

She could find another teaching position. She did have good credentials, after all. She'd left her last school on good terms. Had even helped find her replacement. She'd been planning on marrying. Martin had wanted to travel. See the world. He was forty-five and more than financially able to take an early retirement. Giving up her job had been perfectly understandable, considering the circumstances.

There was no earthly reason why she *had* to return to Lucius. The junior choir would survive without her intervention. Mrs. Cuthwater could keep on substituting for third grade. Laurel could contact that attorney—Mr. Newsome—and put him in charge of disposing of her father's house and personal effects.

She didn't have to go back.

The worst memories of her life lived in Lucius.

But so did the very best memories.

When she went up the ramp of plywood that covered the perilous porch steps at her father's house, she couldn't pretend that she hadn't chosen to return willingly.

None of it had anything to do with Shane, of course. Heavenly days, no. Where would be the sense in that?

Whether or not he admitted it, at worst the man thought she had a screw loose. At best he thought she needed coddling to make sure her screws *didn't* come loose.

So she unlocked the flimsy lock and went inside, leaving the door open for the fresh summer air. Even after only a half a day of being closed up, the house felt stuffy and close.

In her marathon cleaning sessions before the funeral, she'd managed to rid the house of its suffocating layer of dust, but instead of making the house look better, she'd only managed to make its rundown condition more evident. Yes, the windows were clean and shining again, but the cracks only glistened more. Yes, the cobwebs were gone, but the walls and ceilings now screamed for fresh plaster and paint.

She dropped her suitcase on the couch. She knew she needed to get to work on the place. She'd done enough vacillating. Whether she fixed the house up to remain in it or fixed it up to sell it, either way the work needed to be done.

While in Billings, she'd called Martin and asked him to sell her car. It wasn't worth much, but it had been reliable enough for her needs. Going all the way to Denver to retrieve it though seemed more effort and expense than it was worth. His son from his first marriage—a high school senior—had been begging for a car for a year. Now he'd have one. She'd hung up feeling better and worse. Better that she'd made a productive decision. Worse because Martin was simply too good. He hadn't deserved her treatment, and she still felt badly about it.

But not badly enough to go through with a marriage that had put her in the worst panic attack she'd had since she'd been a patient at Fernwood

She'd left Denver. She had no intention of going back. She'd had friends, but no one—other than Martin—who'd been truly close. Aside from him, she'd spent nearly all of her time teaching. Teaching during the regular year. Teaching during the summers.

And dwelling on it all accomplished nothing.

Martin was sending her money for her car, and she'd find something economical in Lucius. On Monday she would open a bank account in town, have her funds transferred from Colorado. She'd have enough to tide her through the summer, hopefully enough to accomplish the most necessary repairs on the house, if she was careful. And then…and then, she would see.

Concrete plans. Achievable goals. Such behavior had gotten her through a lot of years. She could do this.

She *would* do this.

"Laurel?"

She started, pressing her hand to her heart when it jolted. She turned to the doorway. She hadn't seen Shane since she'd gone to his office. "What do you want, Sheriff?"

She didn't need to see his expression clearly through the screen to know he was irritated. The way he yanked open the door and stepped inside told her that quite well enough.

He swept off his dark-brown cowboy hat and tapped it against the side of his leg. "What are you doing here?"

"Where else would I be?"

"You left town this morning."

"How'd you know that?"

"The grapevine is as active now as it was when you were a girl. More so, I 'spose, considering half the town has cell phones now. You drove out of town and word spread."

"And I wasn't allowed back?"

"Don't be ridiculous."

She felt herself flush when she realized she was staring at his legs, strong and long and clad in fading blue jeans that fit extremely well. He looked delectable and she looked…as if she'd just spent a few hours on a bus. "I had to return the rental car in Billings."

"How'd you get back to Lucius?"

"The bus." Looking at his dark-blue pullover didn't help her any, either, because the fabric did little to disguise the massively wide chest beneath.

She settled for focusing on the faint dent in his stubbornly square chin.

He tossed his hat and it landed unerringly on the corner of the coffee table, right next to a footed glass bowl of ugly plastic purple grapes. "For crissakes, Laurel. You could have called someone."

She sank her teeth into her tongue for a moment. "Is it the bus you object to, or the fact that I didn't *remain* out of town?"

"I never wanted you to leave town in the first place."

"No, leaving was what *you* liked to do." Her words seemed to hang in the air, giving her mortification plenty of time to set in good and deep.

If she'd wanted to prove that the brief past they'd shared

was completely irrelevant to her now, she was doing a miserable job of it.

"Leaving is what I had to do," he said finally. "If I'd have stayed, I wouldn't have been able to keep my hands to myself again. Not after we'd—"

"Stop." Heat filled her face. She had only herself to blame for opening up the matter, but she really didn't want to go into *those* details. "It was a long time ago. No need to rehash it."

"Maybe not for you. I always meant to tell you that I was—"

"Please, this isn't—"

"Sorry."

"—necessary."

He frowned at her, looking very much as if he had plenty more to say. After a moment, though, he just raked one long-fingered hand through his hair, ruffling the deep gold into soft spikes. "So you really do mean to stay while you work on this house."

She could feel her scalp tightening. "Yes."

"Despite what happened here."

There was no possibility of pretending she didn't know what he referred to.

"Was Holly in the hospital when she died?" she asked. His eyes narrowed. "No."

"Hospice care?"

"She was at home." His voice was clipped.

"With your father."

"Yes."

"Did he leave his house after? Sell it?"

A muscle flexed in his jaw. "No."

"And you still visit your dad there. At the house where you and your brother and sisters grew up."

"Apples and oranges, Laurel. My father didn't—" His teeth snapped together. "God. What is it about you that pushes me right off the edge of reason?"

She crossed her arms, stung. "Why don't you just finish it, Sheriff? Your father didn't *kill* your mother. And you believe—just like your predecessor, Sheriff Wicks—that my father killed mine. Well, he didn't. Her death was an accident." She dropped her arms and stepped closer to him, forcing the words past her tight throat. "I may have been stuck in a straitjacket five-hundred miles away, but even I knew the charges against my father were dropped. Sheriff Wicks obviously changed his mind. So why can't you?"

"You were never in a straitjacket."

"How do you know?"

"Because I visited you there."

Shock reared her back. "I…what?"

He stepped past her, pacing the close confines between the faded couch and the equally faded rocking chair. He rounded the back of the couch. Stopped. Closed his palms over the back of it. "Guess I don't have to ask if you remember *that*."

She stared at him. His fingertips were white where they sunk into the faded floral upholstery.

"You…saw me there. At Fernwood."

"Three times a week for three months."

She couldn't breathe. Her lips parted, but she simply could not draw a breath. She sat down on the rocker and pressed her forehead to her hands.

Everything she'd thought about him for all these years tilted.

She finally dragged oxygen into her lungs. "I didn't know."

"There was a sunroom there. Plenty of windows. A lot of fake palm trees planted in pots."

She didn't even have to close her eyes to recall the room. To this day she preferred any tree other than a palm. "It overlooked a parking lot. The nurses tried to brighten it up with the plants."

"Right."

She remembered the room, remembered so much of Fernwood.

But not his visits.

Which meant he'd been there only at the first. She knew, because she'd been told, that she'd been moved to Fernwood within a month of her mother's death. But the time between that and the wintry morning when she'd sat looking out at the falling snow and her mind had just…clicked on again…had been nearly six months.

"Your father told you I was at Fernwood, I suppose." She wasn't sure how she felt about that. She knew Beau had been instrumental in getting her placed at Fernwood, a private mental health facility outside of Denver, where she received more care than she would have through the system in Lucius.

"Holly told me. She came to visit me at seminary. Came to give me a piece of her mind, actually, for going for weeks on end without calling home. That's when I learned what your father had done. What had happened…to you. After I'd dropped you off that evening, I picked up my suitcase from the house and kept driving. I didn't know about any of it until Holly came to see me in California."

She pressed her fingertips into her eye sockets. "My father didn't *do* anything."

"Then you remember that? You remember what happened that day, but not the hours you and I spent sitting in that bloody sunroom at Fernwood."

"I remember enough!" She dropped her hands, staring

at him. Wondering why the pain of it was as sharp as it was, when time was supposed to dull this sort of thing. "You slept with me in Calhoun's barn, and then you dumped me, and after you drove me back to my house—insisted on it, in fact—I arrived in just enough time to see my mother accidentally fall down the stairs. I don't *care* what everyone said. My father did not push her."

"Because you remember it."

Her eyes burned. The truth was that she didn't remember anything beyond the sight of Shane driving away in that old pickup truck while she stood on the porch, silently crying. "My father wouldn't have hurt my mother."

"Did you ever talk to him after you left Lucius?"

The question came like a slap. "Yes." Often, once she left Fernwood. Then over the years dwindling down to just once a year. On his birthday. Calling him more often might have been the right thing to do, but she hadn't been able to bear the constant disappointment.

"And? What'd he say?"

"What does it matter to you? It wasn't a confession, I promise you that." She knew her father would never have made such a confession. Not to her. Not to anyone.

He had been a miserable man, but he hadn't been an abusive one. No matter what the rumors around Lucius had said.

She ought to know.

She'd lived under his roof.

He'd often raised his voice, but he'd never once raised his hand.

That had been her mother's particular domain.

"Laurel." Shane's voice went soft. Careful. Gentle. "I'm just trying to—"

Coddling.

She hated it.

"He told me not to come home to Lucius," she said baldly. "So I didn't. He never came to visit me. His actions were perfectly clear. He *didn't* want to be around me. But now he's gone and what he wanted doesn't matter anymore. I'm here whether *you* like it or not."

"I don't want you to get hurt again."

"There's nothing in this house that can hurt me."

"Hurt doesn't have to be physical."

She knew that as well as anyone.

And she was still grappling with the revelation that he'd visited her at Fernwood. "I'll be fine."

Something came and went in his eyes. "I guess I'll be close enough by to make sure of it."

"What's that supposed to mean?"

He merely straightened and rounded the couch, stopping in front of her. "Come with me."

Wariness edged in again. "Where?"

He held out his hand. "You'll see."

She swallowed. Eyed his palm. She could see the row of calluses, the signs of a man perfectly accustomed to physical labor, despite his position as sheriff. His fingers were long. Square-tipped. His wrist corded.

She swallowed and gingerly placed her hand in his.

And even though she'd braced herself, the contact felt electric.

If he noticed, he hid it a lot better than she did.

She rose.

He led her out the front door. The plywood vibrated under their feet as they went down it. There was no sign of Shane's SUV. Instead, there was a small blue sedan parked at the curb.

It didn't look at all like a car he'd ordinarily drive.

But then, what did she know?

She absently noticed that a breeze had cropped up. It felt welcoming, given the heat of the afternoon. Given the heat charging up her arm to her elbow to her shoulder and beyond…

He walked the length of the house, then around the southern side. Fifty yards behind the house, the land rose sharply. Growing up, she'd done a lot of sledding in the wintertime on that hill.

"I'll be close by," he said, letting go of her hand and pointing. "Because we're neighbors."

She stared.

The house on the hill was his.

The house that was so incredibly beautiful. She'd spent more than one night watching the wooden and stone structure sleep in the moonlight when she hadn't been able to find any such rest. She'd admired the gleaming windows, the stone chimneys, the inviting porch. The house had been built while she'd been gone from Lucius, yet it didn't reek of newness at all. It possessed only a timeless beauty.

"*You* lived behind my father."

"Yes."

She didn't know what to do with her hands. One was still tingling. The other felt cold.

She forced them to remain at her sides, fighting the burgeoning need to wring them together. Her appreciation for the house now seemed like another betrayal of her father. "Who built the house?"

"I did."

"You?"

"I'm capable, too," he drawled, his voice impossibly dry.

She ignored the small jab, not doubting his capabilities for a second. The man undoubtedly exceeded *capable* on every front.

Even if he *was* the sheriff.

The *sheriff*.

Who'd lived within eyeshot of her father.

She finally identified the feeling that was hollowing her out.

Disappointment.

"Were you so set on keeping an eye on my father that you chose to live behind him?"

Not even strictly behind him. Above him. Like some almighty watchdog waiting for the moment to attack.

Had her father been bothered by the sheriff's proximity? Had he felt as if the law were breathing down his neck, just waiting for the moment to strike again?

Or had he been as unconcerned about that as he'd been unconcerned about his daughter?

Shane's dark brows had jerked together over his sharp nose. His lips were thinned.

He was displeased, definitely. But he didn't deny the truth in her sharp question. "I chose to build there because of the view," he said.

The view of what? Her father's rooftop?

The hollowness inside her widened. What had he expected her father to do? Once her mother was gone, when Laurel was gone, when the charges against him were dropped, he'd lived alone. He'd still worked as a maintenance engineer for the town of Lucius, but he'd still... been...alone.

Her father's attorney had been very clear on that point.

She'd had no reason to doubt him.

And it made her ache inside to think of her dad being

watched by the sheriff, as if his life was continually on display, under a microscope, awaiting a misstep.

*If only he'd let me come home.* The futile whisper screamed through her. Some portion of her mind realized she'd said it aloud even before Shane spoke.

"You could have come home if you'd wanted," he countered.

"There was nothing here for me." Her father had been adamant. *Don't come back.*

Shane's lips tightened even more, as if he'd taken her remark personally.

Which was simply ridiculous.

"You had friends," he finally said.

She rubbed her palms together. The tingling stubbornly remained. "Jenny Travis moved away to college that year." That year. As if there were only one year that was important.

"I wasn't talking about Jenny."

She knew that. "You left, too."

A muscle ticked in his jaw, but he couldn't change history. He *had* left. And he hadn't returned permanently until his stepmother was stricken with cancer. He'd already admitted that to her.

"I really don't want to rehash the past," she said suddenly. She didn't. She just wished she could get the past out of her mind for two minutes. But every time she looked at Shane, all she could remember were those summer days, when everything had been fresh and beautiful and full of promise. When she'd awakened each morning with anticipation and enthusiasm and hope.

Until it had all ended on one terrible, terrible Sunday.

"Suits me. The present is interesting enough. What are you doing about a car?"

It was such an abrupt switch, she was momentarily unnerved. "I, um, I thought I'd talk to Stu about it."

He pulled something from his pocket. "You can use this in the meantime." He held out his hand.

"That's a key."

His lips twitched. "So it is."

"I don't need any favors."

"Consider it a neighborly gesture," his voice went silky.

At least she retained enough good sense to recognize that the silkiness was *not* an auspicious sign. "It's not necessary. I'll have funds for a used car in a few days."

"It's Beau's spare car and it's parked out front. He'd have brought it by himself, but he's tied up with some stuff today."

Her breath escaped. He'd won handily. He knew she had a particularly soft spot for his father. That she could deny him almost nothing.

She carefully plucked the key from his palm, only he closed his fingers around hers before she could draw away.

She went still, her gaze snapping to his.

"You call me if you need something."

They were both older. The years had brought plenty of changes. He even had laugh lines arrowing out from the corners of his eyes.

But those eyes were still the same silvery gray that haunted her memories.

His thumb rubbed across her knuckles. "I mean it, Laurel. Promise me."

She moistened her lips.

He'd visited her at Fernwood.

She slipped her hand free of his, holding on to the key.

"I promise." Her voice was little more than a whisper.

But he heard.

The lines beside his eyes crinkled.

And she forgot all about the hollowness that she'd felt earlier.

Evidently, some things never did change.

Shane Golightly's effect on her was one of them.

## Chapter Five

Laurel didn't go to church the next morning, despite nearly every member of the Golightly family offering to give her a ride, even though they knew full well she'd accepted the loan of Beau's spare car.

Fortunately, neither Stu nor Evie had challenged her decision. They both thought she was still recovering from the funeral service, and she left them to their assumption.

She felt slightly guilty at that.

Her parents, her gram, hadn't raised her to lie.

But the truth was, she was simply too tired.

She hadn't slept more than thirty minutes at a stretch all night long.

It was no better than before the funeral service, and if she didn't start sleeping better soon, she wasn't going to be in any shape whatsoever to wield a hammer or a paintbrush, much less accompany a choir she'd yet to meet to an out-of-state festival at the week's end.

She'd tried sleeping in her old bedroom.

She'd tried sleeping on the couch.

She'd tried the basement, the dilapidated wicker love seat on the porch and had even eyed the bathtub as a possibility.

She'd ended up with a blanket and pillow on the dining room floor where she could see out the picture window to the cool rise of sun above a stone and wood house high on a hill.

And when she figured the Golightlys would be collectively occupied with Sunday services, she bathed and dressed in a lightweight sundress and drove Beau's spare car through town.

Lucius had never been short of churches. When she was a girl, they'd all been located on church row. Poplar Avenue was the official name, but she'd never known anyone to actually use it.

Until her grandmother died, Laurel had gone with her every single Sunday to Lucius Community. And after Gram died, Laurel walked to church. If the weather was particularly bad, her friend Jenny could be counted on to get her parents to drive out and pick up Laurel.

Laurel's parents, however, never sat in one of those pews.

But that wasn't strictly true, for her father had begun attending Beau's church *after* his family was no longer around.

While the sight of church row with its congestion of vehicles was a familiar sight as she drove beyond the older part of Lucius, she encountered plenty of the unfamiliar. There was a shopping center with an enormous discount store. There was a small hospital with an adjacent medical complex. There were apartment buildings and houses that looked so new she wondered if the exterior paint was even dry.

The cemetery—not at all new—was amidst all the recent

buildings springing up around it, but even it showed signs
of progress in the profusion of bushes and trees and pictur-
esque bits of stone walls that hadn't been there before.

She turned her borrowed little sedan through the opened
iron gates and depended on memory to guide her around
the winding, narrow road. So many landmarks looked different. Small trees had become towering hardwoods.

Her grandmother's grave was still recognizable, though.
The family headstone had been put in place when her
grandfather died long before Laurel was born. She wasn't
sure how old she was when she could first remember visiting the grave with Gram. Three? Four?

It was one of her earliest memories.

Holding Gram's hand. Dusting away the dried leaves that
had accumulated at the base of the massive granite marker.
There'd been nothing fearful in this place with Gram.

Nothing fearful ever with Gram.

She'd been Laurel's rock.

Laurel sat down on the grass beside the graves. The
ground was damp. It had probably been watered early that
morning. She leaned forward and brushed her hand over
the small flat stones that marked each individual grave.

It had been so long since she'd visited. She should have
brought flowers or something. But Laurel wasn't particularly worried about her gram looking down on her with dis-
pleasure. She carried the woman with her in her heart
wherever she was. She didn't need to visit a grave to feel
close to her.

She'd learned that courtesy of Beau Golightly, who'd
been the one to suggest she write to her grandmother when
she'd been inconsolable after her death.

She lifted the canvas journal she'd brought with her. "I
shouldn't have stopped, Gram. Seems like life was so much

clearer when I was still writing to you. I've been rereading all the journals. Five years' worth. And I remember writing it all, I remember living it all. But I still can't remember that night, Gram, or the nights that followed. I still can't."

On the other side of her grandmother was Laurel's mother. And beside her lay freshly turned earth.

Her father. She hadn't come to the cemetery for his burial. No one had. That had been his request. Just another way of pushing her away, she felt.

She looked across the road, away from the family plot.

"I was going to get married, Gram. Of course, you know that. And you know what happened." She drew in her feet and rested her cheek on her bent knees. Her vision blurred, wet. "I really tried. Martin is a…a dear man. We'd been friends for years. Then a few months ago, he proposed. And I accepted. But I just couldn't make myself go through with it."

"Why not?"

The voice was not a ghostly whisper of her grandmother's spirit.

It was deep. Slightly drawling. And indescribably male.

She didn't lift her cheek. Didn't want to draw attention to the fact that now, here, at her grandmother's grave her tears had found their way to the surface and were slowly creeping down her face.

"Are you following me, Sheriff?"

She heard his footsteps. His legs—jeans again and boots probably shined up for Sunday—entered her field of vision as he came up beside her. "I've got people in this place, too," he said.

Of course he did.

Holly. The stepmother who'd been the only mother who'd mattered to him.

She turned her head, brushing her cheeks across her knees as she did so. She stayed huddled. "Shouldn't you be at church? Or your office or something?"

"Even sheriffs get a day off now and then. And Beau expects me only when he sees me." He hunkered down beside her. "Grass is damp. You're getting your butt wet."

"It'll dry."

Shane had no comment to that. He just crouched there next to her, studying the family marker. "Lucille was a great lady," he said after a while. He remembered the woman well, even though she'd died when he was a teenager. "She never had an unkind word for anyone, but she sure did manage to express her opinion, whether positive or negative, about the antics folks got up to around here."

"Sort of like your father." Laurel finally lifted her head, cutting off his view of her long, slender neck when her silky ponytail slid over it. She seemed to be staring at her father's fresh grave.

"You're very lucky, you know. To have been raised by a man like that."

Shane took off his hat and slowly turned it in his hands to keep them busy and out of trouble. Her shining hair was just as beckoning as her soft neck. "Being a preacher's kid isn't necessarily a walk in the park. Folks put their clergy on a pedestal. Expect the families to live up there with them. Fact is, we're all just human like everyone else. Full of fallibility."

"And full of goodness." Her voice was barely audible.

He slanted his gaze from the crown of his hat to her face. Her cheeks were wet.

Pointing it out to her wouldn't win him any favors, he figured.

He wasn't used to being presented with situations where he didn't know which direction to step. The law, well the law was pretty black-and-white. He was comfortable in that sort of environment. He'd already proven that fact with his one foray into commitment. But even when he'd called off his engagement to Denise, he'd been comfortable with the decision. It, too, had been clear cut. Maybe not easy. But clear, all the same.

Laurel Runyan though, was an environment unto herself.

And he wasn't as young as he used to be. His knees were killing him, crouched down the way he was.

He finally just sat down, and as he'd expected, the damp grass immediately started soaking through his jeans.

"You'll get wet," she said.

"I'll dry," he drawled.

She shook her head a little, then rested her cheek on her knees again, looking sideways at him.

He knew she was thirty years old, but just then she looked about as old as a teenager.

"You needn't babysit me, Shane. I'm sure you have better things to do with your time."

Shane. Finally.

He dropped his hat over his knee. For once her voice hadn't been tight or defensive. "Not right at the present. Unless you really want to be alone." He'd give her that. For now. Here in this place.

Her eyes were the wet, warm color of amber hit by sunlight. "No. I don't want to be alone." The admission seemed to surprise her more than it did him, and she looked away, propping her chin on her knees once more. A sigh lifted her shoulders, bare except for the wide straps of her pink sundress and the light tan that coated her supple skin.

His fingers flexed.

"It's like a pretty park here," she murmured after a moment. "I've always thought that, but it's even more so now, what with the stone benches and the new plants."

"Doesn't bother you that it's a cemetery?"

"No. It used to annoy my mom when I'd want to come out here and sit with Gram. Mom *didn't* like it here. Said it gave her the willies being around so many departed souls. When did you decide you wanted to be a cop?"

He slid a glance her way again. She was still looking ahead, giving away none of her thoughts. "Same year I quit seminary."

"That tells me a lot."

"The year after that summer," he elaborated, knowing she'd have no desire to delve further into that bit.

He was right. Sort of.

She placed her palms on the grass behind her, leaning back a little as she stretched out her legs. The folds of her dress fell softly around her calves. "Was your dad terribly disappointed?"

"He'd have been more disappointed if I'd continued seminary without really feeling the call."

They'd sat on the grass almost this same way that long-ago summer. Only, they'd been at the school fields, stuffing themselves on fried chicken, corn on the cob and icy watermelon. And later that night they'd watched fireworks.

And he'd kissed young Laurel Runyan for the first time.

"Why law enforcement? Your bachelor's was in psychology, wasn't it?"

He nodded. But going into his reasons for such a career shift was not going to lead anywhere good. And just then, he didn't particularly want to start an argument with Laurel on whether or not her father had gotten away with murder.

Naturally she believed one thing. He, however, believed

the other. And the fact that he'd gone into law enforcement to do his part in keeping such travesties from occurring wouldn't make things between them any easier.

"Evie's bound to have a pot roast going for Sunday dinner," he said instead. "She'll nag me for a month of Mondays if I don't get you there."

"Is it that time already?"

"Gettin' there."

"I didn't know I'd been sitting here for so long." Her forehead wrinkled.

"No crime in it, Laurel. No curfew's been set limiting time spent sitting on wet grass."

Her expression smoothed. She looked at him. "My dress is cotton. It'll dry about five minutes after I stand. You, however, are wearing denim jeans. You're not going to be so fortunate."

Seeing that faint smile curving her lips generated enough heat that his jeans ought to dry instantly. "Been through worse."

Her lips twitched. "I'll say. Remember when your truck stalled out by the creek?"

He hadn't stalled. He'd run out of gas because he'd been too damned preoccupied with keeping his hands off the pretty girl who'd been with him and had made some fool excuse about engine trouble because he hadn't wanted to admit the truth. They'd been spending every moment together when he wasn't working for Calhoun. They'd laughed and talked and fished and sometimes just sat quietly together, watching the summer clouds drift. But aside from a few kisses, he hadn't *really* touched her. "I wouldn't have fallen in the creek if it weren't for you," he countered.

Her eyebrows rose. "That's not the way *I* remember it.

You were standing in front of the truck with your head buried under the hood and when you stepped back to close it, you went right down the bank of the creek."

"I didn't know you were wearing a bikini under that dress of yours." Seeing her stretched out on the ground sunning herself in those minute scraps of fabric had knocked him for six.

She rose suddenly, brushing at the folds of her current dress. "The swimsuit was Jenny's. She was a little… smaller than me."

"Suppose you returned the suit to her."

"What? Yes, I imagine I did."

"Too bad."

Her eyebrow peaked. "Why?"

"I have fond memories of that bathing suit."

Her cheeks went pink. Then red. As red as they'd been that day when he'd tugged the strings loose on that bikini top and she had made no attempt at stopping him.

She swished her hands briskly down her dress. "Well, I, um, I have things to get to. And you've got Sunday dinner waiting."

"*We've* got dinner waiting."

She blinked. The riotous color in her cheeks faded, but only a little. "Oh, I really don't think—"

"Beau will be disappointed if you don't go."

Her lips firmed a little. "Do you regularly use your father to obtain what you want?"

He pushed to his feet, smiling a little. "Whatever works, songbird."

Her pupils widened. She blinked suddenly, as if she were coming out of some spell. "I'm sorry. You'll have to give Beau my regrets. I really do have things to do." Her voice had that tone again. The tight, defensive tone. The one that warned him to stay well clear of the invisible boundary she held around herself.

"What things?"

Her posture had always been perfect, but her shoulders went back a little more at that. "If it's so important that you know my business, Sheriff, I have an appointment with Mr. Finn this afternoon."

"What time?" He knew for a fact that Jack Finn played golf every Sunday afternoon, weather allowing. He wouldn't be finished until four at the earliest.

Her lips firmed. "Six."

"Giving you plenty of time to eat, put up with my dad's kibitzing and even have a little nap if you choose."

"I'm not three. I don't need a nap!"

She was as beautiful as ever, but a person would have to be blind to miss the dark circles under her golden eyes.

He wasn't blind.

He'd seen the lights that burned every night—all night—in her father's house.

The fact that the location of the light had changed almost hourly had told him that she hadn't simply fallen asleep with the lights on. She'd been awake. Moving around the house. Flipping on and off lights as she went. That, combined with the dark circles now, told him plainly that she'd slept poorly, if at all.

He made himself shrug. "Suit yourself. But Evie's turned into a mighty fine chef."

"For heaven's sake. I'm not going to starve if I'm not sitting next to you for Sunday dinner. I *am* capable of fixing a meal for myself."

"You cook?"

Her hands flopped. She started walking toward the road. "Of course I can cook."

His long stride more than kept pace. "Like what?"

"I don't know!" She shot him a look. "Are you wanting evidence to prove my claim or something?"

"Is that an invitation to supper?"

She stopped at her car. Uttered a short laugh and rolled her eyes. "You need no invitation, Sheriff. You've got a plate already waiting for you at Evie's. And somehow I think you're not likely to starve in this town even if your sister weren't a fine chef."

He grinned a little. It was true. People around Lucius were always pressing food on him. But not everyone in Lucius cooked as well as his sister did.

His hand brushed hers as they both reached for her car door. She drew back quickly, avoiding his gaze.

He opened the door—not locked, but there was no need in this place—and she slipped in, gathering up the floaty folds of her dress before he closed it. He leaned over a little, studying her through the opened window. "Tiff's," he said. "Just in case you change your mind."

The edge of pearly white teeth sank into her soft lip, barely noticeable. She nodded and fit the car key into the ignition.

Shane straightened and stepped back.

Her ponytail drifted over her shoulder, caught by the faint breeze, as she started the car.

The car that promptly died.

She shot him a look, shrugging a little nervously as she turned the ignition again.

Nothing.

He stepped forward, heading to the front of the car. "Pop the hood."

She did so.

He lifted it, then stuck his head around so he could see

her through the windshield. "You don't happen to have a bikini on under your dress do you?"

She laughed abruptly, shaking her head.

He smiled and turned his attention back to the engine. But the sound of her musical laughter stuck in his head.

He tweaked a few cables, twitched a few wires. "Try it again."

She did. Still nothing.

He brushed his hands down his jeans and closed the hood. "Gotta be a fuel thing," he told her.

She looked stricken.

"Car's ten years old," he said as he opened the door for her again. "Little things happen often enough. Don't worry. It's not your fault."

She still didn't look particularly convinced. "I should probably arrange a tow truck or something."

He shook his head. "Just roll up the window. Leave the key under the mat."

Her eyes widened.

"Everybody in town knows this car is Beau's. Nobody's likely to steal it before I have it towed to Stu's garage."

She tucked the key under the mat and rolled up the window, then climbed from the car. Her feet didn't drag—quite—as she walked with him to his SUV he'd parked a short distance up the road.

He opened the passenger door for her, but she nearly jumped out of her skin when he touched her elbow, helping her up inside.

He closed the door a little harder than necessary and went around to the driver's side.

The drive through town took longer than necessary only because of the after-church rush disgorging from Poplar Avenue onto Main. And he was perfectly aware of Laurel's small start of surprise when he drove right past Tiff's without slowing.

He kept on driving until he reached the Runyan place. But instead of turning in her driveway, he drove past and went up the graded drive that led to his own house.

At that, she did give him a sharp look, her eyebrows lifting.

"Decided I don't want to sit through dinner with my jeans sticking like wet glue to my butt."

That made her laugh briefly.

He parked behind the house where he usually did. She didn't wait for him to open her door, but slid off the high seat before he got around to her side. Her gaze traveled over the back of his house, comprised almost entirely of windows, then moved to the landscape which they overlooked.

"This is the view you meant," she said after a moment.

The creek meandered in the distance, close enough to be easily visible through the stand of trees that lined its banks.

It was idyllic.

"Yeah. Sunrises are pretty spectacular." He held out his arm. "Come inside."

The edge of that row of teeth was nibbling at her lip again. "I thought—"

"I know." He knew what she'd thought. That he'd set himself up as Roger's watchdog. And maybe he had. "Forget it."

She didn't look as if she was going to do any such thing, but she stepped forward and accompanied him up the sweeping wide steps that spanned the width of the sitting porch stretching across the back side of his house. "You have a pet?" She nodded her chin toward the empty food bowl.

"I have a cat who visits occasionally," he corrected. "Speck isn't anyone's pet. Beneath his dignity."

"I think Speck and I have already met," she said, remembering the cat she'd spotted when she'd first arrived in town. "Who designed the house?" Her palm lingered on the door.

"I did." He tossed his keys on the granite counter separating the kitchen from the great room where he spent a good deal of his time when he wasn't in the front of the house watching for the nightly traveling-light show within the Runyan house. "Make yourself comfortable," he said.

She smiled again, a trifle weakly, he thought.

There was only one chair in the great room. That, and an enormous television.

The rest of the room was all but empty.

He headed to the staircase. She perched on the arm of his big black leather recliner, looking as if she were going to bolt down the hill to whatever haven her father's house provided the second his back was turned.

He rapidly exchanged his clothes for dry ones and went back downstairs. His white shirt was still untucked, but he figured if he gave her two extra seconds, she was gonna head for the hill, literally.

She was still sitting on the arm of his chair when he went back downstairs, boots in hand, and started to rise when she spotted him.

He waved her back and grabbed one of the two iron bar stools from the counter, perched on it and shoved his foot into first one boot, then the other.

"How long did it take you?"

He was fairly certain she wasn't referring to the production of pulling on his cowboy boots. "About three years, start to finish." Though *finish* was a relative term, since there were projects he was still tweaking. "I moved in a few years ago."

"Going for the minimalist approach when it comes to furniture?"

Boots in place, he leaned back against the counter. "Been waiting to find things I want to fill the house with." He wasn't necessarily referring to furniture.

"That's an enormous kitchen behind you," she observed after a silence that stretched a little too long. "How often do you give Evie a break and do the Golightly Sunday dinner thing here?"

"They'd all end up in the hospital. Only cooking I do comes out of the microwave or off the grill."

"At least that's honest."

"I'm the sheriff. Supposed to be honest."

Her lashes swept down. "Well, I guess you're changed and dry again, so…"

He stood. Opened the door. She rose, too, giving another sweeping look around the interior as she joined him. Almost as if she wanted to memorize the sight.

Then they went outside and he drove down the dirt driveway and stopped in front of her father's house. "Are you really going to help with the kids' choir?"

"I told your father I would. We'll start rehearsals tomorrow evening." She reached for the door handle. "Tell Beau I'm so sorry about his car."

He wasn't surprised that she still intended to decline the dinner invitation. "Not your fault," he assured. "You need a ride tomorrow before Stu's got it running again, just give a shout."

She nodded, but he figured there was about a snowball's chance in hell of her actually asking for help from anyone, unless her circumstances were dire.

"Thanks." She quickly climbed out of the truck, slamming the door shut and hurrying around the back of it toward the patch of brown grass that surrounded her house.

He waited until she'd disappeared inside.

Interesting that she hadn't made any noise about getting out of the SUV and going to her house *before* he'd driven up the hill to his place.

Maybe she'd been as curious to see it as he had been to see her in it.

## Chapter Six

Dear Gram,
The Fourth of July picnic is coming up soon. There's the dance and fireworks and stuff, same as always. Dad says I can go with Jenny and her family. I'm pretty sure the Golightlys are going to be there, 'cause Mom has been helping Mrs. Golightly bake the stuff they'll sell at Tiff's booth at the picnic. I hope Shane will be there, too. I ran into him yesterday at the dime store. He'd just been over at the Luscious for lunch with Stu. He's so perfect looking, Gram. I always thought guys with dark hair were the best-looking ones, but Shane is blond and nobody is better-looking than he is.

He told me that he liked the solo I sang at church on Sunday. It wasn't anything fancy. The solo, I mean. Just a few lines. But it was pretty nice of him to notice, I think. I sure miss going to church with you, Gram. Mom is always working on Sundays, or sleeping it off if she's not, and Dad, well we both know he never steps foot in a church. Personally, I think he's afraid the walls might fall down around his ears or something if he did…ha ha. Not really funny, though, when you think about it.

Anyway, I'm hoping to see Shane at the picnic. So what do you think I should wear? My cutoff shorts? Or I could wear my red sundress, even though that's getting a little short. Mom says I've grown at least two inches in the past month, and I'm thinking she might be right. Pretty soon I'll have to start packing up everything that's in good condition to take with me to college. Can't believe it's coming so soon, but I got a letter just the other day from the college of music about a special summer program. Can't go to it this summer, because it costs too much, but it's exciting all the same. Gotta run now, Gram. Love, Laurel.

If she hadn't spent so much time reading about the past Laurel would have probably been done with her latest attempt at home repairs by the time she saw Shane coming.

It was easy enough to see his approach, considering that she was perched on the roof. She even sent up a rather futile prayer that he might not notice *her.*

Some prayers, though, just weren't worth the Big Guy's time, and that one was definitely one of them.

She settled herself a little more comfortably on the shingles and dipped her trowel into the awful, thick black sticky stuff that the hardware clerk had assured her would work to patch up her collection of leaks since reroofing was out of her budgetary question, then daubed it on the roof.

From the corner of her eye she watched Shane park his SUV presumptuously on her lawn. Or what would be a lawn if the grass were still living.

She dipped and daubed again and told herself there really weren't butterflies dancing around inside her.

The slam of his truck door was a solid crack in the hot afternoon.

She dipped again. Wiped a trickle of sweat where it was creeping down the back of her neck. The faint breeze the day had held earlier had long gone. It was Tuesday afternoon, and she hadn't seen him since Sunday.

"What the *hell* are you doing up there?"

She glanced down. Shane stood in the yard, his boots planted, his fists on his hips.

"Fixing the roof." She stated the obvious, not entirely certain why he was bristling.

"You don't need to be up there doing that yourself!"

She gaped when he started up the ladder propped on the side of the house.

"I'm perfectly fine up here," she told him when his head appeared above the roofline. Butterflies grew to the size of hummingbirds. "And I got all the instructions I needed on how to do this, first from Jack Finn when he was out here the other day, *and* at the hardware store." She swallowed. "I'm not incompetent, you know," she tacked on.

He stepped onto the roof, casting a look of aspersion over the roof. "You'd be better served taking a wrecking ball to this roof than trying to patch it. *That's* something Jack Finn should have told you."

He had, which she didn't see was any of Shane's business. "It only leaks in a few spots," she defended and slapped more goo in place. Thank heavens she was wearing thick rubber gloves. If she weren't, she'd never have gotten the sloppy stuff off her skin. "And I'm assured by experts that this glop will fix them."

He sighed noisily and crouched down beside her. "Glop. Is that a technical term now?"

Oh, she didn't want him to amuse the hummingbirds flapping away inside her. "Don't come any nearer. You might get some on your clothes and this stuff is lethal."

"Exactly. Why do you insist on doing this crap yourself?"

She sighed just as noisily as he had. "I can't *afford* to hire this out. Okay?"

"Hire." His voice dismissed the notion. "You've got people around here who are willing to *help.* If you're so bloody stubborn that you won't listen to reason about doing any of this work, then why the hell won't you accept help when it's offered?"

"Stu is helping me with the wiring in the kitchen," she said defensively. "I've already talked to him about it. He's coming out as soon as he has a chance to." She loosened her death grip on the trowel that he hadn't tried to take from her as she'd feared. It would have been embarrassing to have to wrestle him for it. But her claim at competence would have probably required some defense.

"Well, that means he'll be arriving any minute," Shane muttered.

She shot him a look, but the sunlight was half blinding. "He's been very generous. And *he* doesn't think he needs to tell me what to do."

"I'll bet he doesn't."

"What's *that* supposed to mean?"

"Don't get too cozy with my brother. He's not known for his longevity when it comes to women."

She could hardly believe what she was hearing. "I beg your pardon?"

"I wouldn't want you to get hurt."

She let go of the trowel. The handle fell against the goop and stuck. "You mean hurt like I was with *you?*"

His lips tightened. "No, that's not what I meant."

She shifted, planting the rubber soles of her tennis shoes a little more firmly against the shingles. She badly wanted to stand, but her legs weren't up to it. Better for him not to know just how badly he shook her. "Then just what *did* you mean, Sheriff?"

"Dammit, Laurel. I have a name."

"And maybe if you didn't act all…high and mighty all the darned time, I might use it more often!"

He frowned. "Don't you know how dangerous it is up here for you? How many roofs have you climbed around on?"

"One." And she didn't like it, at all. But she was determined to do what was necessary.

"One." Clearly disgusted, he rose.

And his boot heel slipped.

His foot skidded a good twelve inches, knocking into the can holding the roof patch.

Laurel gasped, horror engulfing her as she grabbed for him, instinctively wrapping her hands tightly around his legs.

He swore loudly as his boot slid again. He leaned forward, nearly right over her, to catch his balance. His head was two inches from hers. She was still latched on to him like a limpet.

"What the hell are you doing?"

"Keeping you from falling off the roof!"

"Jesus, Joseph and Mary." He pressed his forehead to her shoulder for a moment. "You're lucky you didn't send us both off."

She realized her arm was wrapped rather…high…around

his thighs. If anyone had been able to see them, it would have looked as if they were preparing to get horizontal on the rooftop. Her heart was charging in her chest, making her breathless. "I was only trying to help."

He'd bent one knee when she'd unbalanced him. Unfortunately, he'd planted it directly in the roof patch. Now, he looked down at the mess and shook his head. "Hell," he muttered.

"I'm sorry." She tried leaning away from him.

He made a rough sound. "Just...don't move, okay?"

She winced. What was he irritated with *her* for? She hadn't asked him up onto the roof; hadn't asked him for anything, for that matter. "What are you doing here, anyway? I was perfectly fine, so there was no need for you to come charging up here in the first place—"

His head angled, his gray gaze slamming into hers, and her voice dried up as surely as the day's breeze had.

"Stu's got the car fixed. I brought the key."

She realized she was staring at his lips and didn't realize that she'd moistened her own. "Um, thank you."

He eyed her for a moment, then closed his eyes, uttering a half laugh. "Laurel, honey, you're killing me."

She let go of him as if he'd jabbed her with a hot poker. "What are you talking about?"

He exhaled and disentangled himself the rest of the way from her. One leg of his jeans was sticky with thick black glop. He twisted around and sat down on the roof.

He didn't look inclined to explain his comment.

He had roof patch on his boots, too. And a roughly hand-shaped stain on his hip.

She swallowed, looking down. The heavy gloves she'd been wearing were too big, and were now too heavy with patch. It took only a gentle shake of her wrists and they slid off her hands onto the shingles.

They sat there for a while, side by side, silent.

Eventually, her hummingbirds and butterflies quieted.

And there was nothing but the warmth of the sun on her shoulders through her Clover Elementary School T-shirt, and the solid presence of Shane Golightly next to her.

The comfort of it sneaked in, seductively, and that was a danger all on its own.

Even if she could trust Shane after what had happened in the past, she couldn't trust herself. "Shouldn't you be out keeping the peace or something?"

He cast her a sidelong look. "Even in this hotbed of crime, I get a lunch hour now and then."

A lunch hour he was now spending sitting on her roof. "Is that a hint for a peanut butter sandwich?" She knew it wasn't, but she felt absurdly self-conscious all of a sudden.

The corner of his mouth kicked up. "Man oughta get something in return for hazardous duty."

She huffed softly. "And what is ever hazardous around Lucius?"

He looked at her for a long moment. Then his lids drooped a little, hiding the expression in his eyes.

But she'd seen enough.

Her mouth ran dry. Her lips tingled.

He was going to kiss her.

It was written on his face. In his body. Those wide shoulders angling her way, his elbow—where his hand was pressed flat against the roof—bending slightly as slowly, so slowly, so deliberately, he leaned—

"Yo, Shane."

Laurel's spine snapped straight, her first indication that she'd been leaning toward Shane, as well. She stared blindly down from the roof, hardly taking in the sight of the familiar-looking vehicle that now sat at the curb or the brawny man who stood beside it.

Shane seemed less startled by the interruption, as he looked down, as well. He shifted, propping one wrist over his bent knee. "Stu," he greeted blandly.

A small pickup truck pulled up behind the car.

Stu remained well back from the house so he could see them. He tilted back his battered ball cap. "Working on your suntans up there?" His voice was full of laughter. As if he knew exactly what he'd interrupted.

*Nearly* interrupted.

"He was helping me with my roof leaks," Laurel said hurriedly. She pushed to her feet, feeling unsteady in a way that had nothing to do with her sheer nervousness of being up on a roof at all. She swiped dust off the seat of the decrepitly old jeans she'd found in a drawer in her bedroom. "You brought the car."

Stu folded his arms across his wide chest. "Figured the spare key my brother there took off Riva's hands would do more good if you had something to put it in."

It seemed so elementary that Laurel felt foolish for not having thought it herself.

"I was gonna take Laurel by the garage," Shane drawled.

"Who's Riva?" Laurel asked Shane.

"She keeps the garage running for my inferior twin, there."

"Her?" Laurel nodded toward the pickup truck idling at the curb. She could just make out a sheaf of dark hair—maybe auburn—through the windshield.

"No. Riva's about 150 years old," Shane murmured. He rolled to his feet, far more comfortable with their perch than Laurel. "That's Freddie Finn's truck. She gives Stu a ride now and again out to his place on those rare occasions when they're speaking to each other." He closed his hand around Laurel's upper arm when she gingerly took a step in the direction of the ladder. "Watch your step."

She couldn't really watch anything when she was so excruciatingly aware of the brush of his knuckles against the side of her breast. But the toe of her tennis shoe brushed against the pail of roof patch, nudging her out of her stupor.

She crouched to pick it up, thankfully breaking that disturbing hold of his. But when she tried to pick up her gloves, she found they were stuck firm as concrete to the shingle where she'd dropped them. "Well, fudge," she muttered, and reached for the trowel.

It, too, had made itself a permanent attachment to her roof.

"Just leave 'em."

She looked up at him. "Don't you laugh."

"Wouldn't dream of it," he assured smoothly.

She narrowed her eyes. "Shane—"

"Your face is getting sunburned," he said. "You need to get out of the sun for a while."

She needed to have her head examined again is what she needed. She picked up the pail by its wire handle, and Shane took it from her, then waited for her to work her way past him to the ladder.

She stopped a foot away from the edge of the roof.

Going down looked a lot worse than going up.

And she hadn't much liked going up.

"Here." Shane took the pail from her. "I'll go first." His voice was soft. Gentle.

"Gonna stand up there all day?" Stu inquired. He'd moved around the house and stood at the base of the ladder.

"Ignore him," Shane murmured.

Laurel sank her teeth into her tongue when Shane's

hand slid up from the small of her back to curl around the base of her neck beneath her ponytail.

"Just take one rung at a time and don't look down," he added.

"It's not the rungs, it's getting *to* the rungs," she admitted.

"Just turn yourself around and step down." He moved to the ladder, putting action to words. "Not so bad." He easily stepped down a few more rungs, but his head was still above the roofline. "Okay. Come on. I'll be right here."

She swallowed. How could she have been so stupid as to come up on the roof without being absolutely certain that she could make her way back down again? "Just, um, just take the pail of goop down. I'll be along."

He gave her a look assuring her he knew she was putting off the inevitable. "Okay. Sit down. Scoot to the edge and put your feet on the top rung. Sit there, relax a little, and don't look down."

"Maybe you ought to call out the firetruck," Stu said humorously. "They could send up the basket."

"Shut up, Stu."

But Laurel didn't take offense. It was true. She was acting like such a ninny. And Stu was trying to make it easier in his way, the same as Shane. She sat down and gingerly inched her way toward the edge.

Shane nodded, went down the rest of the way, dumped off the heavy pail, and started up again. He stopped, still several rungs down, but still high enough to put his hands on either side of her legs where they dangled off the roof's edge. "Ready? Unless you prefer Stu's method and having it get all around town how you had to be rescued off your roof?"

She rolled her eyes.

His lips twitched a little. "Didn't think so. Just scoot

around until you're facing the roof instead of me. Your feet have plenty of room where they are on the rung."

And when she did what he said, she'd be sticking her rear practically right in his face. But if she asked him to give her more space, she was going to be right back in the fix she'd been in all along. Feeling as if she was hovering on the edge of a chasm with no support around her at all.

She slowly turned. Shane's hand went from the roof to her hip. Her waist.

It was a terrible irony that he made her feel secure enough to step down to the second rung, yet could still make her feel shaken right down to the core of her in the same breath.

"Doing okay?" His voice was near her ear.

She could feel the entire length of him protecting her from behind. She nodded.

His fingers squeezed her waist, approvingly. "Ready for more?"

*Ready?*

"Yes," she managed.

Step by step, they descended the ladder.

It was too bad that Laurel wasn't certain—even when they safely made it to the ground—if Shane had been referring to the ladder rungs any more than she had.

"Good grief, Stu, what's taking you so long?"

Laurel's uneasy thoughts stumbled at the impatient voice drifting around the side of the house.

"I told you I was expecting a call at home, and…oh." The leggy redhead rounded the side of the house and stopped short at the sight of them clustered around the base of the ladder. "Hello," she said, looking from Laurel to Shane to Stu. "Got a problem?"

Laurel felt her face flush. Undoubtedly Freddie Finn, who was the brains behind her family's towing business, could have capably shinnied up and down the ladder a dozen times over. "Not anymore. I'm the worst kind of fraidy cat, I guess. Got up the tree, so to speak, but didn't want to come back down."

The somewhat tight speculation in the other woman's brown eyes eased. Freddie didn't look at Stu as she stuck out her hand toward Laurel. "You probably don't remember me," she said. "Freddie Finn."

"I remember," Laurel assured, shaking her hand. "I met with your dad a few days ago. Between making notes on this place, he could hardly stop talking about you and your brother, Gordon."

A hint of embarrassment leaked into the other woman's face. "Yeah, that's my dad, all right. My condolences on your father."

"Thank you." Guilt joined the swirl of emotions that were still bubbling inside her. She'd barely given her father a single thought that day. "I hear that you live in a converted barn?"

Freddie looked as relieved at the change of topic as Laurel felt. "Yes. Dad did a lot of the work, actually. You should come out and see it. Get an idea on the kind of things he could do for you." She flipped her hair behind her shoulder, glancing at Shane. "I guess you're not going to buy the property after all?"

A bubble of silence formed.

Laurel looked at Shane.

Stu finally huffed. "Nice one, Fred," he muttered, closing his hand around her shoulder and pushing her along. "I'll let you know when I can check your wiring, Laurel," he called back.

"What the heck's wrong with you," Freddie grumbled as they went.

A moment later she heard car doors slam, followed by the rev of the engine.

Laurel crossed her arms, still watching Shane. Waiting.

What more surprises lay in wait?

"It's nothing to get upset about," he said after a moment.

She figured she'd be the judge of that. "*You* wanted to buy my father's house."

"I still do."

Her gaze dropped to the roof patch staining his clothes. It was incomprehensible to her. *"Why?"* She waved her arm at the hill behind them. "You have a beautiful home already. What could you possibly want with my father's house?"

"Does it matter?"

Did it? "Why didn't you say something before now? You've had enough opportunities."

"Because you wanted to be here," he said flatly. "You never once came back to Lucius, Laurel. How could any of us have predicted that you'd want to be here, in this house?"

"Okay, but why hide it? If Freddie Finn knows you wanted to buy it, who else knows? Why not just admit it, Shane, or are you afraid the news might send me off the edge of sanity!" Her voice rose sharply, despite her efforts to control it.

"Would you quit blaming every single thing that you don't like about me on that? I didn't tell you because it didn't matter. You're here and no amount of persuading you otherwise is going to change it. Hell. Look." His arm swept out.

The ladder.

The roof patch.

The gallons of paint stacked nearby.

"You're bound and determined to work on this house no matter what."

"Somebody has to," she said thickly. Her mind was teeming. "Even if it were you."

His lips thinned. "Honey, the only effort I planned to put into this house would have been spent pulling it down."

Her throat went tight. "You only want to buy it in order to tear it down?"

"Yes."

"Why?

"So nobody would ever get hurt in this house again."

Shane's words hung in the still, hot afternoon.

Laurel pressed her hands together. He'd said that before, but she hadn't believed he felt so strongly about it nor did she know why he'd taken it so personally. Had she misread his feelings for her?

## Chapter Seven

"Thank you for helping with the, uh, the ladder," Laurel said, changing the subject. She stooped down and picked up the pail of roof patch. Her head spun when she straightened. "But I'm sure I've taken up enough of your time now. And I'm supposed to meet with the kids again this evening. They, um, they're quite good. Even Joey. He's got perfect pitch. He just needs to stand still long enough to finish a song."

He exhaled. "Dammit, Laurel."

"Anyway, I need to clean up and get to the bank before then."

He closed his hand around her wrist, halting her when she took a step away from him. "Stop running away from me."

She lifted her eyebrows. "I'm not running from *anything*."

"Not even the guy you were supposed to marry? The one you were talking about to your gram at the cemetery?"

Laurel snatched her hand away. "That is *none* of your business."

"Maybe I want it to be my business."

"For pity's sake. That's taking the sheriff business a bit far, even for you."

His lips twisted. "Believe me, Laurel, it'd be better if it were sheriff business. Then I'd have these great, clearly defined lines to follow. Instead, I've got—" He broke off, shaking his head, muttering an oath under his breath.

"You've got *what?*"

He breathed in with a hiss. "This." His hand caught her behind the neck again, only this time there was no comfort in the touch. There was only heat.

"This," he said again.

And, lowering his head over hers, he captured her lips with his.

She gasped, rearing back, but his hand on her neck held her in place. And still he kissed her.

His head angled. His thumb found its way to her chin and nudged, angling hers.

Oh, heavens. She'd forgotten how he tasted.

No. She remembered the Shane he'd been. The thoughtful, kind young man before he'd left her.

This…this…was…

Her mind went blank.

She barely realized she'd let go of the pail. It fell to the ground with a rattle. Her fingers opened. Closed. Empty. But that was solved when she pressed them to his chest. Felt his surging heartbeat through the shirt he wore. "Shane," she breathed against his mouth.

He tore his lips from hers. Pressed his forehead hard against hers. "No clear lines," he muttered.

She was shaking.

"Who's the guy?"

When had she ended up pressed back against the side of the house? Sandwiched between Shane's tall, hard body and peeling, weathered siding? "What guy?"

His hands slid down her shoulders, her forearms, her wrists. He tangled his fingers through hers and pulled her left hand up. "The guy whose ring you don't wear anymore. The one you didn't marry."

Laurel's head fell back against the wall. She closed her eyes against the sight of Shane, but his image was still burned into her mind. "A good man," she whispered. "A *really* good man."

"But you chose to be here. Staying in this dump."

"This *dump* was my father's home," she countered, but without the heat she would have preferred.

"Do you still love him?"

"I'll always love Martin."

Shane let go of her hand. Stepped away.

And even though the sun was angled over them, hot and dry, she felt chilled.

"What are you doing here, then? Waiting for him to chase after you?" His voice was low. Silky.

As dangerous as his kiss had tasted.

"Martin would never do anything of the sort." He had too much dignity. "I wouldn't want him to." When she'd ended it between them, it had been final and they'd both known it.

There was no point in trying to make their relationship something it wasn't.

"Martin," he said, obviously waiting.

"Martin Kellner."

Shane's eyebrows lowered. "Kellner. I remember that name."

Laurel pressed her fists against the wall behind her back. "He was on staff at—"

"Fernwood," he finished, looking disgusted. "He was your *doctor*."

"Therapist," Laurel countered. "And get that look off your face. Nothing unprofessional happened. Martin would never—"

"Of course not. The man was probably a saint. What did he do? Convince you he was your savior? Your only road to happiness? Keep you occupied all these years? Is *he* the reason you never came back to Lucius?"

Laurel's hand flashed out.

The slap sounded loud.

The silence afterward sounded louder.

Her chest heaved. The outline of her fingers was clear on his hard cheek, and her palm felt on fire.

Horror filled her, making her nauseated. She'd never struck another person. Not ever. "I'm sorry," she whispered. Dizziness was a swamp she couldn't escape. She leaned forward against the blackness, staring hard at the ground as her vision seemed to pinpoint. "I shouldn't have done that."

*I'm sorry, honey. Mommy shouldn't have done that.*

Shane barely caught her before she pitched forward in a dead faint.

He swore and swept her up in his arms. She felt clammy. Her skin was flushed.

He carried her around the front and inside the dimness of the house. It was cooler inside, but only slightly, and he lowered her carefully onto the couch, propping her feet on the arms so they were higher than her head.

She didn't stir.

But she was breathing.

He cursed the fact that his hands were shaking. He pulled her shirt loose from the waist of her jeans. Flipped open the button at the waist, even though they weren't the slightest bit tight. There was nothing else she wore that was the least bit constricting.

He tapped her cheek lightly. "Laurel, honey. Come on. Wake up."

She didn't move.

He hissed out a breath and dragged out his cell phone, calling 911. Assured that help was on the way, he tossed the phone down and strode into the kitchen. There, he doused a towel in the sink, then returned to Laurel, pressing the dripping cloth to her arms. Her face. Finally just spreading it over her chest to soak through her dark-blue T-shirt.

He felt her pulse. It was fast but strong.

Heat was coming off her in waves.

Heat exhaustion, he figured. She was sweating, which was a good sign that it hadn't escalated to heatstroke.

He could hear the siren approaching and felt only marginally better.

He lifted her hands. Pressed them to his mouth. "Come on, honey. Open those eyes. Wake up."

She didn't stir.

The siren grew louder, cutting off abruptly when the ambulance arrived. Moments later Palmer Frame charged into the room. "What happened?" He set his enormous field kit on the floor beside the couch, taking Shane's position beside Laurel.

Shane told him. Palmer nodded even as he checked Laurel's vitals. "Temp's only one-oh-two, but she's definitely dehydrated," he said. He flipped off the wet towel and whipped up Laurel's shirt, attaching leads for his cardiac monitor. "How long was she in the sun?" With barely a pause, he began an IV.

Shane could only guess. "She was up there for a while before I got there. Maybe two, three hours."

"Any vomiting? Other injuries?"

Only arguing.

"No."

"Is she eating regularly?"

"Far as I know. She's got some groceries in the kitchen. An empty plate in the sink."

Palmer grunted. "IV's going. She should've come around by now. Noah," he looked over at his driver, who was waiting at the doorway, prepared to assist however Palmer needed. "We're gonna transport her."

Noah nodded and disappeared. Moments later he returned, pushing the rolling stretcher ahead of him, and the two men carefully loaded Laurel's limp body onto it.

Shane could only stand there feeling useless.

He hated it.

Palmer finished strapping Laurel in place, attaching the cardiac monitor and the IV bag to the gurney beside her, and they began maneuvering her to the door. "Does she have kids?" he asked suddenly.

Shane shook his head. "No. Why?"

Palmer jerked his chin toward the dining room. "My kids do that. Make forts underneath the dining room table with sheets and pillows. Just wanted to be sure we didn't leave behind some kid." He kept up with Noah as his assistant guided the stretcher down the plywood ramp.

Shane eyed the bedding. It wasn't fashioned into a fort. It was folded neatly atop a stack of two thin pillows and sat right beneath the dining room window.

What the hell was Laurel doing sleeping in the dining room?

He heard the slam of doors and hurried out to catch the ambulance. "I'm riding with you."

Palmer shrugged. "Get in the back."

Shane did, climbing in behind the other man.

The gurney was fastened down on one side of the ambulance. Shane sat on the other empty one, out of Palmer's way. He felt the vehicle turn in a sharp U, then frowned when the siren came on, nearly deafening him. It wouldn't take long for the ambulance to make it to the hospital, though.

He raked his hands through his hair. He'd forgotten his hat somewhere.

"Don't hit me."

He jerked upright. Laurel's eyes were still closed. Her head slowly turning against the stretcher.

He met Palmer's grim look and crouched down beside her. "Nobody's gonna hit you, honey." He carefully folded her limp fingers in his hand. "You're safe."

And he damned Roger Runyan to hell, all over again.

"Well, this was a warning for you, young lady. You can't be in the sun for hours the way you were without drinking plenty of water. Heat exhaustion is nothing to mess with. The IV will take care of your dehydration this time, but next time it'd just be easier to drink a few bottles of water, don't you think?"

Laurel nodded, feeling foolish, as the emergency room doctor, Dr. Carmichael, lectured her.

"I'd like to see you put on a few pounds, too," he went on. "And you either see your own doctor in a few weeks for a blood pressure check, or you come back here. Your body's showing all the signs of extreme stress, Laurel. You need to deal with it before you start experiencing more permanent consequences."

She frowned down at her hands. She'd wakened up in the hospital. Been put through a battery of tests.

Shane hadn't left except when the doctor had insisted on it, and now he was leaning against the wall, listening to every word the doctor said.

There was probably some law being broken by that, but she just didn't have the energy to insist he leave.

"Can I have my clothes back?"

Dr. Carmichael nudged his round glasses up his nose and smiled faintly. "Don't like our cutting-edge fashion, eh?"

The hospital gown she wore was pale blue with little flowers on it. It was also humiliatingly thin against Shane's gray gaze whenever he looked at her.

Which was often.

She could just imagine what he thought now.

He'd probably blame her entire state on "the house."

As if it were cursed or something.

"The nurse will help you get dressed again," Dr. Carmichael assured her. "She'll be here in a few minutes. You'll have a few forms to sign, and then you can go home. To rest and to eat. Understand?"

"I'll make sure of it," Shane said before Laurel could even get a nod in.

Her fingers slowly curled and she felt ill again.

She'd struck him.

There was never a reason to strike another person. Certainly not because he'd kissed her silly, then misunderstood everything about her relationship with Martin.

Her heart started racing and she closed her eyes, concentrating on her breathing, on slowing her pulse.

She did *not* need to have a panic attack here.

She flexed her toes. Concentrated on the movement. Ignored the activity around her in the curtained-off room. Flexed her foot. Released it. Tensed her calf muscle. Released it.

Her heart calmed.

Her breathing evened.

She hadn't even needed to get up to her thigh muscle.

She let out a long breath and opened her eyes, only to find her gaze landing immediately on Shane, who was watching her closely.

She lifted her chin a little.

She wouldn't be ashamed of a panic attack, not when she'd managed to stave it off more effectively than she'd done the last time she'd had one.

Then she'd been wearing a white wedding gown and had felt as if she were going to have a heart attack.

"Okay, Ms. Runyan." A nurse slipped around the curtain and approached the bed. She handed over a clipboard with an assortment of forms attached. "Some instructions from the doctor on avoiding heat exhaustion and heatstroke. Your insurance statement and a release form. Sign by all the red *X*s and the sheriff here can take you back home again."

Laurel scribbled her name where she was supposed to, took the pamphlets she was meant to keep and handed the clipboard back to the nurse.

"Okay, Sheriff. Outside the curtain again." The nurse shooed Shane, then turned back to Laurel. "That's one fine-looking man," she said under her breath, "but I figure you can get dressed with a little privacy here." She plucked a plastic bag out from a rack beneath Laurel's bed and plopped it beside her. "Now, if you wanna throw off your clothes again the second he gets you alone, that's your business." She grinned wickedly.

Laurel flushed. "It's not that way between us."

"Hmm. Didn't look that way to me. The sheriff was beside himself when they brought you in. You know, there are a lot of women around Lucius who would trade places with you in a heartbeat. Give a shout if you need some help."

Laurel didn't doubt there were plenty of women around who were interested in Shane. Even when he was a teenager, he'd drawn women like bees to pollen.

She'd been no different, either.

She quickly exchanged the hospital gown for her clothing, frowning a little over her shirt. It was definitely damp.

As if he'd been able to see right through the opaque curtain, Shane poked his head back inside the moment she finished zipping up her pants.

She quickly tugged the hem of her shirt down, avoiding his gaze as she reached for her tennis shoes.

He slid one out of her hand and hunkered down in front of her. "Push your foot in."

"I can put on my own shoes." She pushed her foot in.

"You can," he agreed, and tied the laces. He grabbed the other shoe, waiting.

She sighed. Slid her other foot into it. Then he straightened, picked up the paperwork the nurse had left and wrapped his hand around her upper arm, guiding her off the high bed.

"We're stopping for supper at the Lucius," he said evenly as he accompanied her out of the emergency room.

The sun was nearly set.

She hadn't realized so much of the day had slipped by. "I have food at the house." If she were quick, she wouldn't be late for the choir practice.

"Food you're evidently not eating enough of, according to the doc."

His SUV was parked blatantly in the No-Parking zone outside the door. Perks of the job, she supposed, as he practically lifted her into the front seat.

He got behind the wheel, flipped down the visor and found the keys tucked there, then drove out of the parking lot. Minutes later he parked in front of the café. He'd barely tooted the horn when the waitress Laurel recognized from the other day trotted out, a big bag in her hand. She handed it to Shane through the window, then trotted back inside.

Shane set the bag on the seat between them. "Fried chicken. I *know* you like that."

"I thought you meant you wanted to stop there and eat."

"Figured you could use a day or two before you have to stand up to all the gossip that'll be flying. Everyone in town knows you passed out and were taken to the hospital today."

She hadn't thought of that.

"They'll be speculating for weeks on the reason." Shane slid a look her way.

"What's that supposed to mean?"

"Watching to see if you're pregnant."

She flushed. "You heard the doctor."

"I heard him. Nobody else did."

"I'm *not* pregnant."

His gaze seemed to slide over her body, and she felt herself flush even harder. She'd have had to sleep with a man to get herself in that state. And even though she'd been engaged to marry Martin, she'd never slept with him.

The last man she'd been intimate with, the *only* man, had been Shane.

There was an identical sheriff's unit still parked in front

of her house when they arrived and Laurel frowned. "Your SUV is still here?"

"We've got three units for the department." He got out, carrying the food, and opened her door for her. "Watch your step."

She no longer felt in danger of collapsing with each step. "I'm fine."

His lips merely tightened. "Yeah, you looked real fine when you were out cold and Palmer Frame was hooking you up to a cardiac monitor."

The front door was still open and he went right in as if he already owned the place. "Sit." He dumped the bag of food on the coffee table, pushing aside the knickknacks she still hadn't bothered to pack away.

She didn't want to sit.

But the truth was, the chicken smelled mouthwatering, and she was feeling suddenly famished.

So she sat.

He went into the kitchen, returning with plates and silverware. She silently set out the food.

They ate.

And even when Laurel was full, she made herself finish a second piece of chicken if only to keep him from voicing the order to eat more, which was clearly written in his eyes.

Fortunately, the amount she did manage to put away must have been satisfactory, for he said nothing when she finally dropped her napkin on the plate and sat back from the coffee table.

He merely gathered up the plates and took them to the kitchen. Threw away the trash. Wiped up the few crumbs.

Laurel watched him. She knew what was coming. She just didn't know how to argue against it.

And when Shane finally stopped playing waiter and

stood at the end of the couch, determination carved in every line of his hard face, she knew the time had come.

"You're not up to directing the choir."

The base of her neck tightened. "Did I ever tell you how little I like being told what to do?"

"They'll survive without going to the festival this year. You're not up to it. You shouldn't even be here alone." He waved at the dining room. "It looks like a damn linen closet in there. You're sleeping on the floor, aren't you?"

She winced. "Maybe it's just my laundry."

"You never could lie worth squat, songbird. Now, you can pack, or I can do it for you while you call Evie and she can call the parents to cancel the choir deal. Your choice."

"I am *not* leaving and I'm *not* going to disappoint those children. You cannot force me to change my mind!"

"I wish I could *force* this place to be condemned," Shane bit out. "Then you'd have to leave." He was sorry for the words the minute they hit the air.

What was it about this one woman that sent his control right out the window?

She'd risen and moved behind the couch, as if she needed to put some distance between them. Her expression was brittle. Definitely *not* what Carmichael had advised, and Shane was only making matters worse.

"Laurel," he began again, determined to get it right. "You heard the doc. You can't go on like this." His cell phone chirped, and he ignored it. "Go pack. Please. You can go to Tiff's. Maybe with enough rest you'll be up to directing the kids for the festival," he coaxed. The phone chirped again and he yanked it off his belt. He wanted to throw it against the wall just then, but he couldn't. He had a duty to the people who'd elected him.

"I can't afford Tiff's." She leaned over and flicked her fingers against the pink and yellow papers from the hospital that were lying on the couch. "I can't afford *that*. Not if I'm going to have anything left over to make the repairs here."

"For Pete's sake, Laurel. *I'll* pay for your room if you're so worried about it!"

His phone beeped again.

Laurel lifted her hand in a futile gesture, turning away. "You don't understand at all," she said tiredly.

Understand? She was the one with her head stuck in the ground like an ostrich. He put the phone to his ear. *"What?"*

"Whoa, Nelly. Don't shoot the messenger." Carla's voice was tart. "Got a break-in at the Tipped Barrel. Manager just called it in. Said he arrived to find the office safe standing wide open."

"Send Tony," he said impatiently.

"He's not on," Carla reminded him. "His daughter's swim meet over in Billings, remember?"

Shane grimaced. How could he have forgotten? He'd signed the vacation-day request. "Fine. I'll take care of it." He'd also pay for barking at Carla for a month, no doubt.

He hooked the phone back on his belt.

Laurel hadn't moved.

"I'm just trying to—"

"Protect me. I know. I know." Her smile was thin. "Everyone has to protect Laurel, because, goodness knows, she can't seem to protect herself."

"I didn't say that."

Her eyebrows lifted a little. "Your entire attitude screams it, Shane."

The damnable thing was he knew she was right. "Maybe I need to protect you now because I didn't protect you before."

Her eyes flickered. "I didn't need protecting then, either."

*Don't hit me.* Her soft words in the ambulance rang inside his head.

"Besides," Laurel continued, "we were kids."

"You were barely eighteen. I was well beyond it. And regardless of how old we were, I shouldn't have left you the way I did."

She pressed her soft lips together. "It was a long time ago."

"It was," he agreed. "So why do I have the sense you're no closer to forgetting it than I am?" Or to forgiving me, he silently added.

## *Chapter Eight*

As far as Shane was concerned, the Tipped Barrel could close its doors and he'd be the first one to raise a beer in celebration of it.

Not that he had anything against a good watering hole. He liked to have a drink and shoot pool just as well as the next guy. But the Tipped Barrel just naturally seemed to draw more than its share of trouble. There was hardly a week that passed without some incident there requiring action from the Sheriff Department.

Yet even though he didn't want to leave Laurel alone, he did, after eliciting her promise to cancel the choir practice just for that evening. He drove out to the bar, which would fortunately remain fairly empty until after the dinner hour. He took the report from the manager, and on his way back to the office, called Donny Hicks, who owned the place, to confirm a few facts.

Wouldn't be long before Donny Hicks realized he'd hired a thief to run his business.

He stopped at the office and picked up Carla, so she could drop him off at Laurel's place and take the extra vehicle back where it belonged.

He didn't expect to see another car parked in Laurel's driveway when they arrived, but there it was.

Evie.

He went inside, not bothering to knock, to find his sister and Laurel parked on the couch, a bag of chocolate Kisses and a quart of ice cream parked between them.

Laurel didn't look surprised at his intrusion. She'd expected him back, after all.

His sister, however, was another story. She looked at him, her eyebrows shooting up into her blond bangs. "Ever heard of knocking, brother dear?"

"What are you doing here?"

She waved her hand at the treats. "Gorging ourselves on chocolate and ice cream," she said patiently, "while we go over details for the festival trip. What are *you* doing here? Or need I even ask? Everyone in town's been talking about the fact that you've staked your territory."

"What?" Laurel snatched her legs from the coffee table. "That's ridiculous." Her cheeks were pink.

"Is it?" Evie eyed him, mischief clearly evident in her gaze. "Don't think I'd put any bets on that, Laurel." She deftly unwrapped a chocolate and popped it in her mouth. "I came out to make sure Laurel's not suffering any consequences after her afternoon at the hospital. And to bribe her into helping me again," she admitted, tucking the chocolate in her cheek, making her resemble a blond chipmunk. "I need more help manning my booth at the July Fourth picnic in a few weeks."

"No."

"Think that's Laurel's choice," Evie drawled. "And she's already agreed. We've already got her working with the junior choir, and then there's the Lucius Ladies' Association, and—"

"She *needs* rest."

"*She* needs people to stop talking about her as if she weren't here," Laurel inserted. She picked up the ice cream container and stuck her spoon in it as if she wished she were stabbing something—or someone—else. "And as Evie said, I've already agreed to help at the picnic and that is that."

"She needs a room at Tiff's."

Evie shook her head. "Can't. Yesterday I could have, but not today. Booked full up for the next three weeks." Her eyes were merry. "Seems like you've got empty rooms going begging at your place, though. Of course, unless you've gone furniture shopping lately and haven't mentioned it to the family, I recall you having only one bed. In your bedroom."

Laurel's cheeks were red and he felt a strong desire to throttle his sister for embarrassing her.

The image of Laurel in his bed had been stuck in his head since the day she'd been in his house. He didn't need Evie's suggestions to breathe it to life when it was hale and hearty all on its own.

"Where are the kids?"

As a distracter, it worked only too well. Evie's merriment dwindled. "It's Charlie's night to have them."

"They don't spend the night, do they?" After Evie left Charlie, he'd remained in their small house while Evie and the children had moved into Tiff's.

"No. He'll bring them back before bedtime. He missed the last two weeks."

One of them, because he'd been locked up in a jail cell, Shane knew, for being drunk and disorderly. Too bad Shane hadn't been able to keep him there. "Kids would be better off if he missed every week," he muttered.

"They still need a dad, Shane." Evie's voice was practical. "And speaking of bedtime, I'd better get. One of my guests is planning to move to Lucius, Laurel. He's about your age. Single. *Very* good-looking. Change your mind and come to Sunday dinner and I'll introduce the two of you."

He caught the glance Evie slanted his way and ignored it even though the notion of his sister setting Laurel up with another guy annoyed the hell out of him.

"Invite Stu," he suggested. "She can have a real choice then."

"Stu's hung up over Freddie Finn," Laurel said abruptly, missing the look Evie gave him.

"Not a chance. They can't exchange five words without getting into an argument."

Laurel just lifted her shoulder as she gathered up the remains of the ice cream and chocolate and put them back in the bag in which Evie had brought them. "Whatever. Evie, thanks for coming by." It had been a surprisingly nice surprise to find the other woman at her door.

She'd known it couldn't have been Shane returning when she'd heard the knock on the door, because *he* didn't seem to feel a need to knock at all.

Evie had helped knock out the phone calls to the choir parents and had been just as concerned about Laurel being up to helping with the festival as Shane had been. Only in a nicer way.

"I'll see you at choir practice tomorrow."

Evie waved off the bag when Laurel tried to hand it to her. "Pop that in the freezer," she suggested. "We'll finish it another time. One way or the other we're going to get you permanently back in the swing of life in Lucius."

Laurel squelched the warmth that tried to curl inside her. What would happen if she *did* find her fit in the fabric of Lucius again? Was there any hope of making it actually last?

Ignoring Laurel's lack of a resounding agreement, Evie slipped past Shane, patting him on the cheek. "Be good, Mr. Sheriff."

Then, as abruptly as she'd appeared, she was gone.

There was only Laurel and Shane now.

She swallowed and went to the kitchen, stowing the desserts—bag and all—in the old-fashioned freezer. There was barely enough room since the tiny freezer desperately needed to be defrosted.

"Is there something wrong with your bed?"

Laurel shook her head. "You're like a dog with a bone," she murmured. "*No,* there is nothing wrong with my bed."

"Then why don't you sleep in it?"

"I just don't. I…don't like sleeping upstairs. And yes, I realize that makes me sound just as crazy as you seem to think I am."

"Dammit, woman, I *don't* think you're crazy!"

She jumped, more stunned that he'd raised his voice than at his words.

He raked his hair back. His shoulders rose and fell in a deep sigh. "You don't have to be afraid of me."

Shock had a bitter tang as it settled inside her. "Why would I be afraid of you?"

"You keep jumping like a rabbit."

"I do not," she dismissed.

He took a step toward her.

She jerked, her foot sliding a few inches back.

His lips thinned. "Really."

Never before had she been so despairing of her fair skin as she felt the ever-ready flush rise hotter than ever. "I'm *not* afraid," she insisted.

Admitting that he made her nerve endings jump just from his presence wasn't exactly something she was raring to divulge, however.

"I'd never hurt you, Laurel. It's important that you believe that."

She hesitated, wariness adding yet another prickle to her overactive nerves. "What…exactly are we talking about here?"

"I don't hit women."

She tucked her arms together tightly. "I never suggested that you did. Or would." She'd been the one to strike him. "I don't know what came over me earlier." Her voice trembled. "I never should have slapped you."

"I deserved it."

Her eyes burned suddenly. When she wished for tears, they wouldn't come, yet when she didn't, they were all too ready. "Nobody deserves it. No matter what the provocation, physical violence is never an answer."

Oddly enough, his lips curved faintly. "Is that what you tell your third-graders?"

"I…not in those words, but yes. I do."

"Beau would be proud. He *does* use those words. Almost verbatim."

"Your dad is a wonderful man."

"Sainted as they get."

She couldn't quite tell if he was being facetious or not. But she knew he had a good relationship with his father. "He's very proud of you, too."

"I'll stay here tonight. Will that help you sleep better?"

She stared. "Is that on the regular menu of sheriffly services?"

"No," he said evenly. "And you don't have a lot of choices, Laurel. You have to sleep. You can do it here, with me—" he tilted his head, looking amused when she made a sound at that "—on the *couch*," he elaborated. "My place won't do. You've seen it. There is no couch. Or you can go to Beau's. He's got a spare room."

"What about Stu?" Her voice was a little tart. "You're ready to farm me out to any one of your family. Evie's full up, so you'll just work your way down the list?"

"Stu doesn't need any encouragement. And as you'll remember, I offered to stay here first." He scrubbed his hands down his face, looking like a man struggling with dwindling patience.

And finally, Laurel looked beyond her own discomfort and managed to see his.

He was exhausted.

His eyes were dark. Bloodshot.

There were lines in his cheeks that weren't ordinarily there.

It was nearly midnight, and he'd been on duty since just after dawn. She knew because from her impromptu bed beneath the window, she'd watched the headlights of his SUV bounce down the steep road from his house. Then, hidden in darkness behind the front screen door, she'd watched him head past her house toward town.

She'd watched until the red glow of his taillights was no longer visible.

"You work too hard."

He looked at her. "Trying to divine the way your mind works, songbird, could keep a man busy for a lifetime."

No man had ever wanted to spend a lifetime with her.

Not even Martin, who, dear as he was, had included an escape clause in his proposal plans. They'd get married. Travel the world. Enjoy life together. If the marriage didn't seem to be working for them down the road a few years, no harm, no foul. They'd still be friends. And if it were working, on they'd go. Still together.

Not the proposal of one's dreams, she supposed. But he'd meant it in the best of ways. There simply wasn't an unkind bone in Martin's body.

So why couldn't she love him?

Why couldn't she have looked at him while her nerve endings popped and crackled like crispy cereal, making her long for things she'd barely ever known?

"The couch has a broken spring somewhere in the middle," she said abruptly. "You won't like sleeping on it. I managed it only the first night I was here."

His gaze focused on the couch. A muscle sprang to life in his jaw, flexing rhythmically. "Then I'll take the floor."

"There are two bedrooms upstairs. And," her voice faltered a little when his gaze slanted to her face, "and you could use…one." She sucked in her lower lip, moistening it.

Just because *she* couldn't seem to find any peace in the one room she'd even entered, didn't mean he wouldn't.

Since he was so set on staying, that was.

"I could use one," he repeated. "I'm not going to mistake that for an invitation to share." He lifted his hand as soon as the words were out. "Don't worry. That deer-in-the-headlights look of yours is answer enough."

"I—" She sank her teeth into her tongue, hastily stopping its wayward tendencies.

"You…?"

"My old bed is twin-size," she finished hurriedly. Was she simply doomed to embarrass herself around him at least once an hour? "You're so tall, you might not be very comfortable."

"And your dad's room?"

"I, um, I…you're welcome to check it out and decide for yourself." How could she admit the truth? That she hadn't had the stomach for doing something so simple as opening the door to her parents' bedroom.

Something in his expression sharpened. "You haven't gone in there?"

She shrugged. "Don't be ridiculous."

"Laurel."

*She* felt ridiculous. "Okay, so I haven't gotten to that room yet. Want to arrest me for it?"

Shane watched the parade of emotion crossing Laurel's face. He had no desire whatsoever to sleep in old man Runyan's bed.

He had *every* desire to sleep in Laurel's. But that wasn't going to happen now. It probably wouldn't happen ever, not after the way he'd treated her all those years ago.

Didn't stop a man from wanting the impossible, though.

He went up the stairs. Stopped at the top and looked down at her.

Small prisms of light refracted off the colored beads hanging from the old lamp on the end table, casting little bursts of fireworks on the cracked and peeling walls. "Ever wish you could turn back the clock, Laurel? Turn a different way, take a different path?"

She closed her arms around herself again as if she were chilled from the inside out. She didn't answer for a moment, and when she did, it was no answer at all. "That sounds odd coming from you."

"Why?"

She shrugged a little. "I don't know. It's something you might have said before. But—"

Before, he knew, was *before*. Before he dumped her with all the grace of a rhinoceros. Before her mother died.

Before.

"But now?"

"You're the sheriff," she said simply.

"And in your world, sheriffs don't ponder philosophy? The twists and turns of fate or choice?"

"The only time sheriffs have *been* in my world was when Sheriff Wicks questioned me about my mother's accident, and I only know he did that because I was told he had." She dropped her arms and moved away from the golden circle of light cast by the lamp. "It happened there, you know." She pointed to where he stood. "That's where she fell from."

The head of the stairs, in front of her parents' bedroom door.

"At least that's what I read," she added after a moment. "In the news archives when I needed to know such things."

Wicks had hammered her to admit what she'd witnessed, Shane knew. He'd read the case file when he'd joined the department, though he'd heard enough of the story from Beau and Holly.

Laurel had had no attorney present during Wicks's questioning, and only Beau's intervention had stopped the futile inquisition. He'd insisted that Laurel be seen by a physician as she was obviously in shock. Shock was the least of it. Within a month she'd been moved from the county hospital and placed at Fernwood for psychological care.

When she was released nearly a year later, she didn't return to Lucius.

The gossip around town at the time, according to

Holly, had been that she refused to return because of her father's guilt.

"Wicks was voted out of office," he told her. "There was a recall election, in fact. Caused quite the uproar."

"Because he couldn't make the charges against my father stick?"

"A woman had died, Laurel. People wanted—" for her benefit, he kept himself from saying *Roger* "—someone to be held accountable for it."

Her head lowered. She sat gingerly on the edge of the worn, tapestry rocker. "I should have been able to clear him."

"It wasn't your responsibility. No one blames you for being unable to corroborate the charges against your father."

"My father blamed me for being unable to corroborate the facts. He wouldn't have had suspicion hanging over him the rest of his life despite the dismissal of the charges if I'd been able to make a statement."

"And so you stayed away."

"He didn't want me here," she clarified, her voice thin. "He made that abundantly clear."

"Laurel—"

"Don't come home ever again, Laurel," she intoned in a macabre mockery of her father's voice. "Every year, he said the same thing. Don't…come…home." She tossed back her head. Her walnut hair shimmered in the lamplight. "If that doesn't prove he blamed me, I cannot imagine what would."

Shane wrapped his hand around the old-fashioned iron doorknob on the bedroom door. The white paint had long ago been nearly worn off, and it felt rough under his palm. The paint on the door itself was thick and ridged with too many years and too many coats.

He took his hand off the knob, turning away from the

room, and went back down the stairs again. He stopped in front of Laurel. Crouched down until he could see her face.

Her eyes were wet.

"Then he was a fool," he told her softly. "For not appreciating the one person who still believed in him."

"And you think *I'm* a fool, because I did believe in him."

He wished he could deny it. More than wished. He'd have given his right leg just then if he could have, to believe Laurel's faith in her father wasn't severely misplaced.

He stroked his hand down her hair.

Her lashes fluttered, her eyes nearly closing. She exhaled, a shaking sigh that reached down inside him and twisted him into an even tighter knot.

He wanted to hold her against him and make everything bad disappear.

He might as well try spreading a piece of the moon on a cracker.

He wasn't good at personal relationships. He'd failed Laurel years ago. He'd failed his fiancée and her son not so many years ago. So what made him think he had a chance in hell of doing any better now?

"Go over there to your bedroll," he said gruffly. "Get some sleep."

"You're leaving, after all?"

He shook his head. "I'll sleep on the side of the couch that doesn't have a broken spring."

She pressed her lips together softly. Then gave the faintest of nods. "You're even more stubborn than I remembered," she murmured.

"That'd be me." He took her hands and pulled her to her feet, and then she went over to the mound of pillows and sheets and sank down on them.

He reached for the lamp and switched it off.

Maybe it was his imagination, but, despite her assertion that she wanted to be left alone, her eyes had shown nothing but relief when he'd told her he was staying.

## Chapter Nine

"I do *not* need this right now." Laurel pushed back her hair from her face and glared up at Shane. "We need to leave or we're going to miss our flight from Billings to Spokane."

It was early Friday morning. The choir members were already loaded up in the school bus for the trip to Billings, along with the three parent chaperones. After the past week of almost manic rehearsals, everyone was set—anxious—to depart.

Only Shane the Sheriff stood in Laurel's path. "You're not up to this," he said for about the fiftieth time.

She could feel the top of her head starting to lift off. She'd spent the past week working toward this trip, and the past several nights trying to pretend that she wasn't sleeping through the night only because of his presence under her roof.

He'd arrived late each night and left before she'd awakened, but she'd certainly known he'd been there.

Every night.

She'd been as grateful as she'd been disturbed.

Now she was just infuriated. "I'm a big girl." Her voice was as tight as her scalp felt. "I can handle a choir of twenty kids even without the help of three other adults. But having all of their faces pressed against the windows of that bus over there while you lecture me isn't going to help me any."

"You don't look any better than you did Tuesday when you passed out." His voice was just as tight. Just as quietly furious. He shot a look to where Beau was ambling toward them. "I can't believe *you* haven't put a stop to this," he told his father when he joined them.

Beau's brows rose a little. He lightly touched Laurel's shoulder, a little gesture of support for which she was profoundly grateful. The only reason she might have looked shaken was that she'd had no expectation of seeing Shane come barreling up to the church in his official vehicle as if he were set on stopping the next great bank robbery. She'd seen his silent, flashing lights and had expected some sort of disaster.

Instead she'd just gotten a dose of overbearing censure.

"Why would I do that?" Beau asked curiously. "Laurel's willingness to temporarily step in with the choir is a godsend."

"For the choir maybe," Shane countered. "Look at her." He waved his hand toward Laurel. "She looks like a stiff wind would knock her over."

There wasn't an inch of skin on her body that wasn't burning, and there was nothing remotely pleasant about it. "Just because you've set yourself up as my…my *nightlight*—" which had obviously been a huge mistake "—it gives you no right to dictate what I am or am not capable of doing!"

She couldn't even bring herself to look at Reverend Golightly, she felt so humiliated. She darted around Shane and strode to the bus. At least, she hoped she strode. A good, sturdy no-nonsense stride.

As she jumped up the steps, she feared she'd probably just run, and looked as ridiculous while she was about it, as she felt.

She slid into the first seat, behind the driver. "Let's go."

"But—"

"Let's *go!*"

The driver shrugged. He got paid whether they left on time or not.

The silence inside the vehicle was palpable as the bus slowly lumbered out of the parking lot.

Laurel refused to look at Shane or his father as the bus drove past them.

In minutes, the bus was out on Main and heading toward the highway. She exhaled silently and tilted her head back against the seat.

They were on the road. They had a long trip ahead of them, but they were on their way.

Everything was going to be fine.

It would be fine—just so she could put that fact in the sheriff's face—even if it killed her.

Everything *wasn't* fine.

They arrived at the airport to find the flight was delayed nearly an hour. The news was A-okay with their twenty excitable teens and preteens. But *fine* wasn't the word Laurel would have used to describe the way she felt when she realized that there was one glaringly absent suitcase among the dozens of backpacks and assorted luggage that was slowly being fed through the security machines.

Her own.

She knew just where she'd left it, too. And why.

Sitting on the hood of her borrowed car, parked in the lot at the Lucius Community Church. Sitting there, because she'd been too anxious to get away from Shane before she did something foolish.

Like leaving behind her only suitcase?

At least she'd packed all of the music and her binder containing the trip details in the book bag she'd already loaded onto the bus. She could deal with not having her own toothbrush and a few changes of clothes. Leaving behind their music would have put a major crimp in things.

Joey Halloran was trying to climb onto the conveyor belt for the X-ray machine. His father, Tom, grabbed his belt and pulled the boy back off. Tom and Louise Halloran were two of the chaperones, though as far as Laurel had been able to tell, it took most of Tom's undivided attention keeping his son out of mischief.

And speaking of Louise, Laurel hadn't seen the woman for a good twenty minutes. She'd looked punky on the drive from Lucius, but Louise had insisted she was just feeling queasy from the bus ride. She sent Sophie, one of the older girls, to check on her. "She went to the restroom a while ago," she told the girl who nodded and set off down the wide corridor. A moment later, Sophie was standing in the doorway of the restroom, waving frantically toward Laurel.

"Here." She handed Alan her bag of music. "Tell everyone whose luggage has been cleared to gather by those chairs right there. I want to hear '*It's Good.*'"

His eyebrows shot up. "We're gonna sing here? In the airport?"

Singing was the one thing she knew would keep every single child—including Joey—occupied. "Yup." She waited a moment, just long enough to see that he was successful in getting everyone's attention, before she headed toward Sophie.

The sight of the tall, long-legged man bearing down on her from the opposite direction nearly stopped her in her tracks.

Shane had so little faith in her that he'd tracked her all the way from Lucius?

She didn't know whether to stomp her feet or bawl her eyes out.

She did neither. She turned into the restroom, ignoring Shane's approach, and patted Sophie's arm.

"She's been puking like crazy," Sophie whispered, none too quietly.

Laurel herded the girl toward the door. "Don't worry. Go back to the others."

Sophie looked only too glad to escape.

Laurel entered the white-tiled room. Louise sat huddled on the floor by the sink, her back against the wall, looking positively green.

"I'm sorry, Laurel," Louise muttered. "I don't think I can make it."

Laurel hushed her and grabbed a handful of paper towels, dampening them under the faucet. She crouched next to the woman and pressed the compress to her forehead. "You're burning up. Do you think you have the flu?"

Louise groaned. "Don't even say the word. My sister-in-law was sick with it for a week."

Laurel sat back on her heels. "You certainly can't travel like this."

"Tom will insist on driving me home."

Laurel had already come to that conclusion herself. From what she'd seen of the man, he did nothing without his wife, and vice versa. It was utterly sweet.

But right now, it was a problem.

Without both Tom and Louise, there would not be enough adult chaperones to make the trip. The church's stipulations on the traveling conditions had been strict and perfectly reasonable. Twenty youth required four adults, minimum.

"Shane Golightly is here," Laurel said. "Maybe he could drive you home and Tom could still go with us."

Louise looked doubtful. "He was only going because I insisted." She drew in a slow breath. Let it out even more slowly. "I'm beginning to think this trip is jinxed. That the choir simply isn't meant to go to Spokane this year."

"Don't say that."

Louise looked at her sideways. "Nancy eloping and leaving us with no choir director? Now this?" She pressed the wet cloths to her flushed cheeks, then to her throat. "Joey is going to be fit to be tied. The only reason he's been behaving this past week is because of this trip."

*Behaving?* Laurel wisely kept her mouth shut on that one. "Nothing is jinxed," she assured her. "Do you think you can make it out to Tom now?"

Louise reached up and closed one shaking hand over the edge of the sink. "I can guarantee you that Tom won't be coming in here to get me. He'd be mortified."

Laurel tucked her hand under Louise's arm, helping her.

"It'll be a miracle if the entire choir doesn't come down with this," the woman muttered as they shuffled out of the restroom. "Cooped up the way we were on the bus, I've exposed everyone. You'd be better keeping your distance than helping me."

"Your fever is making you delirious. Everything is going to be fine."

"Yeah, if you can talk my husband into going to Spokane." They made it to the corridor. "Oh, listen to them. They're singing. Don't they sound sweet?"

Laurel didn't have to catch Tom's attention. He spotted his wife and immediately headed their way. His usually florid face was so pale that his freckles stood out as if they were measles.

His hands reached out for his wife. "Honey, what's wrong?"

Laurel left them to it and swallowed down the knot in her throat as she headed toward the choir. She'd like to think they were being so diligent with their singing all on their own, but she suspected their orderly behavior had more to do with the presence of their sheriff standing nearby. His cowboy hat was dipped low over his forehead, his boots were planted firmly, and he definitely did not look like a man to be messed with.

She went up to him. "You had no business following us from Lucius," she began, trying not to sound nervous and failing miserably, "but since you're here, you might as well do some good. We need a chaperone. And you, Sheriff, are elected."

For once, she seemed to have surprised him. He thumbed his hat back. His eyes narrowed. "Don't recall that particular vote."

"Only one needed to vote. Me." She nodded toward Tom, who was hovering outside the restroom. Louise was noticeably absent again. Didn't take a genius to know where the woman had gone. "Louise can't possibly make it. Tom isn't likely to leave her side. That leaves me one adult short in the chaperone department, and since you're here…" She clamped her hand around his unforgivingly hard forearm and dragged him as far from the singers as she could. "If you refuse, those kids are going to miss the festival for certain. Do you really want that on your head, Shane? Be reasonable. You have deputies. You can leave Lucius for a few days, can't you? Come with us and you can also have the perverse pleasure you seem to take in playing watchdog where I'm concerned."

His gray gaze slid over her face, then flicked to the choir. "It'd be easier to cancel this whole deal."

She crossed her arms and gave him a severe look. "Since when is easier more important than giving children an opportunity to experience a trip like this?"

The crease in his cheek deepened. For some reason he'd obviously found her statement amusing.

"When I was eleven, *I* went to the Spokane Festival," she said tartly. "It's an experience I never forgot. Dozens of choirs. Competing, yes, but there's this camaraderie among all the children. Growing up in Lucius, most kids don't have that opportunity!" She grabbed his arm, squeezing it. "Please. Just…just do this. Do it for Alan, if for no other reason. He's your nephew."

The youth had sung through at least three versions of "It's Good" and of their own accord had begun singing another piece—a modern arrangement of "Ave Maria." A crowd had begun to form as travelers stopped to listen.

"I'm not really any good with kids."

She dismissed that with a soft huff. "Look at them, Shane. They're marvelous. Maybe playing watchdog brought you after me, but you're here. And we need you."

Shane looked down into Laurel's earnest face. "I wasn't playing watchdog," he said after a moment. Not entirely. "Here." He leaned over and plucked a suitcase from the shrinking collection that was readied for the security personnel. "Figured you'd need it."

"You came here to bring me my suitcase?"

He dumped the plain black suitcase among the others. "You're welcome."

She nibbled at her lip.

Silence fell between them, broken only by Joey's solo. The boy was positively lapping up the attention he was getting.

Shane had no business thinking of leaving Lucius for three days. But he'd known he was toast the minute Laurel set her pleading amber gaze on him and asked him for help.

"Fine," he said shortly.

She stopped nibbling, and her lips stretched into a brilliant smile.

"I might not be able to get a ticket at such short notice," he warned.

"We won't know until you try." Her hands pushed him toward the short line at the ticket counter. It was sort of like a scrappy little terrier pup launching herself at an ornery old bull. "The flight could be called at any time."

Hiding the grin that wanted to tug at him, he went.

"I knew everything would be fine," Laurel said seven hours later.

The choir had duly checked in at the festival site. They'd sat through an hour-long welcome session, and now they were packed into three large tables at a pizza joint next to their hotel.

Shane looked over their group, who displayed varying degrees of exhaustion. Alan looked as if he was as likely to drop his nose into the slice of cheese pizza he held as he was to taking a bite out of it. No matter how much Evie had been a proponent of the trip, if she'd seen how exhausted her boy was, she'd have probably come unglued.

There were twelve girls and eight boys and as far as

Shane had observed, there was little evidence of the group separating along the lines of gender or age, which spanned from fifth to eighth graders. They were an interesting group, actually. And even though Laurel had been a last-minute addition, there was no question that she was in charge.

It would have been more logical for either of the other two chaperones—Jana Waters or Katy Foster—to assume that role since they'd been involved in the planning of the trip from the beginning. But both of them seemed perfectly content to leave the task to Laurel.

And Laurel, with her notebook of schedules and agendas and emergency medical paperwork, seemed perfectly at ease with it all.

He didn't know why it should be so surprising. He knew in his head that she was a grown woman. That she was educated, that she'd obviously found a career for herself.

But witnessing her easy competence with his own eyes *was* surprising.

The question was, Why?

He was no closer to an answer when Laurel started bustling everyone into finishing their meals while she paid the check. Twenty kids and four adults ought to have been damned chaotic, he thought. But there was also little chaos as they all trooped across the parking lot to the hotel.

In the lobby, Laurel flipped open her binder and began doling out room keys to the chaperones. "The rooms are all connecting," she reminded. "Visiting between rooms is okay until 10:00 p.m. Then everyone better be in their own room, or you'll deal with me."

Nobody quibbled.

Not even Shane.

Their fingers brushed when she handed him his key.

"You're in a two-bedroom suite," she told him, staring fixedly at her neat little lists. "The hotel wouldn't be thrilled if they knew there are eight boys in there with you, but given the circumstances, that's the way it has to be."

"Guess I'll probably survive," he said wryly.

She smiled faintly and turned to the group. "Okay, everyone. Ten o'clock is lights-out. Breakfast is at 6:00 a.m." She ignored the groans that announcement was met with, and continued. "We have to be at the conference facility by eight. Anyone I have to personally wake up is going to regret it. Okay? Okay. Be off to the elevators, then."

En mass, the youth trudged out of the lobby, dragging backpacks, favored pillows and suitcases.

More than once Laurel had reminded them that they were responsible for their own gear.

They seemed to have that fact down pat, now.

He hung back with Laurel, waiting until the last of the last was ahead of them. He tilted his head. "How would I regret it?"

She blinked, flipping her binder closed as she looked up at him. "Pardon me?"

"If you have to personally wake me at 6:00 a.m."

Her cheeks went red. "I'll make sure you're sitting next to Joey on every bus and every plane we take between now and Sunday evening," she said primly, and grabbed the handle of her own rolling suitcase and headed after the others.

Shane laughed and followed. Yeah. That would be something to regret, all right.

They went up to their floor in batches, and Shane had barely unlocked the men's assigned room before the boys bolted inside, wanting to explore every nook and cranny of the suite.

When Joey started poking around the minibar, Shane cleared his throat and shook his head.

Joey made a face but redirected his exploration.

He let the boys sort out their preferred sleeping arrangements and wished for the freedom to pop open one of the beer bottles in the minibar. Instead he made himself comfortable on one end of the enormous couch in the common living area and grabbed the remote control for the television.

Joey hung over the back of the couch. "What're we gonna watch, dude?"

Shane lifted his wrist, glancing obviously at his watch. "*We're* not going to watch anything, dude. You've got fifteen minutes before lights-out."

"Nah. Not really. We're the men, man. We don't have to do what the girls do."

Shane saw Alan roll his eyes as his nephew opened the connecting door to the room beside them, and three of the oldest "E" girls practically tumbled inside. Tiffany, Ashley and Emily were their names. Shane couldn't keep them straight though. Not when they seemed to have adopted some sort of like-one-like-all look. Each had their hair pulled back into the exact same ponytail, with identical pink ribbons hanging from it. Even their clothes seemed designed as one unit. Short little skirts and tiny little T-shirts that—if he'd been one of their fathers—he'd have vetoed before they stepped out the front door.

He tuned out their high-pitched chatter and focused harder on the baseball game showing on the tube. He figured he had about twelve minutes left before he had to start shooing teenyboppers to their own rooms. But he was surprised, yet again, when, just before ten, they bounced their way back to their rooms, grinning cheeky little grins at him. "Good night, Sheriff Golightly," they chirped in unison.

Odd how they didn't seem to speak separately, yet they could sing in three-part harmony without turning a pink-ribboned ponytail.

He pulled his boots off the glossy magazine he'd stuck between them and the glass coffee table and went to check the two bedrooms under his watch. In both cases, there were two boys per double bed and one on the floor since they'd all determined that surface was more comfortable than the roll-away beds the hotel provided. In the second room he eyed his nephew, making his nest on the floor with pillows and blankets between the two beds. "What'd you do? Lose the coin toss?"

Alan grinned and shook his head. "Won it." He waved at one bed. "Mark snores. Matt's feet stink." Then he jerked his head toward the second bed. "Ryan ate anchovies on his pizza so you know what *he's* gonna be like all night. And Ben," Alan shook his head in mock sympathy at his friend. "And Ben is just stuck."

Boys were boys, Shane figured, amused, and flipped off the light and closed the door.

The minute he did, he could hear an assortment of snickers and snorts. But within a half hour, sounds from both bedrooms had finally ceased.

He raked back his hair and rubbed his palm down his face. He might have delivered Laurel's luggage to her, but he was not similarly equipped. He had no change of clothes, no razor, no toothbrush.

Well, he was in a hotel. Toiletries were the least of his worries.

He pulled off his shirt and hung it over the back of the swiveling bar stool at the small bar and tossed the two pillows that he'd confiscated from the two bedrooms to one end of the couch. Then he sat down again, tugging off his boots.

The couch was a damn sight more comfortable than that horse-hair episode at Laurel's place.

He stretched out with a deep sigh and turned down the volume on the ball game. It was then that he heard the soft tapping on the door.

Not the connecting door. Not one of the bedroom doors. The outer door.

He pushed his tired muscles into motion and went over to it, pulling it open immediately when he saw Laurel through the peephole.

"What's wrong?"

Her lips tightened a little. "Why does something have to be wrong?"

He looked over his shoulder into the suite. The bedroom doors were still firmly closed. "It's after ten. Aren't you supposed to be guarding your quad of girls?"

"They think I'm doing the official bed check." In the soft light of the carpeted hallway, her cheeks looked flushed.

He looked at the plastic shopping bag she held. "What do you do? Confiscate their CD players and headphones if they're not sleeping?"

She smiled a little, though she still looked flushed. "No. This is for you." She extended the bag toward him. "I, um, I had to guess at the sizes, but hopefully everything will suit you. If not, the hotel gift shop opens again in the morning at ten and you can exchange anything you need to."

He thrust one hand into the bag, encountered fabric, and dragged it out. "What is all this?"

She tugged at her earlobe, looking down the hall. "Just a pair of sweatpants and a few shirts. Nothing much, but maybe you'll be more comfortable than being stuck in the same clothes all weekend long."

"You shouldn't have spent your money on me."

"I didn't. It came out of the funds for the trip, same way dinner did." She moistened her lips and looked up at him. A quick, glancing little look that nevertheless managed to heat something inside him. "I really do appreciate this, Shane. I know it was a lot to ask. And you really *didn't* have to agree."

"Could have fooled me," he drawled softly. He dropped the dark-colored T-shirts back into the bag.

Her gaze flicked upward again. She swallowed and nodded, and chewed on her lip.

The teacher in command was nowhere in sight.

There was only an amber-eyed woman wrapped in a long-sleeved blue T-shirt and loose-fitting matching pants who reminded him far too much of the girl he'd made love to on blanket-covered straw about a lifetime ago.

As if she knew exactly where his thoughts had gone, her eyes widened a little, and she pressed her lips together. "Well. I'd better get back to my room." She rocked on her feet but didn't really go anywhere, and he realized she was barefoot, as well.

Hell. He'd been sleeping under her father's godforsaken roof for several nights, but he had managed not to see her wearing anything looking like sleepwear. He was thirty-damn-five years old. He'd seen women's bare feet before. He'd seen *Laurel's* bare feet before.

He felt like knocking his head against the wall if only to knock out the image of her, padding barefoot and soft in her cute little blue pajamas, toward him.

"I, um, meant to tell you that you don't have to hang around with the choir all day tomorrow or anything. Once we get to the conference center, you can go sightseeing or do whatever you want."

"I know. I heard Jana and Katy talking about their plans for tomorrow."

"Shopping?"

He nodded. "I'll happily leave them to it."

She smiled a little. "Well, anyway. I just wanted you to know. You're not an indentured servant or anything. We just have to have four adults when we're traveling and at night and stuff."

He wondered what she wore under that soft blue knitted stuff. Not much, he guessed, when she suddenly crossed her arms, a self-conscious, protective gesture if he'd ever seen one.

"Better finish your bed check." Get her going. Get her moving. If she didn't, he was going to put his hands on her shoulders and pull her to him.

And canoodling between the chaperones was probably one of those verboten items listed on the first page in her handy-dandy binder.

"Right." She curled her toes against the carpet. Her toenails were painted red. She took a step away. "Don't forget. Breakfast at six."

"I won't forget."

Her lips twisted, the dimple in her cheek appearing. "No. Forgetting is *my* gift."

He caught her wrist. Felt the jump in her pulse beneath his fingers. "No, songbird. Your gift is a lot more complicated." Then, because he couldn't help himself any more now than he could when he'd been twenty-something and stupid as hell, he leaned over and pressed his mouth hard against hers.

When he lifted his head, she swayed a little.

"Go."

She moistened her lips, hesitated long enough for him to nearly have a heart attack, and then with a quick nod, she turned on her bare heel and quickly walked down to her room.

He could see her fumble with the room key, give him a look over her shoulder that he couldn't read from this distance, then disappear inside.

He let out a long, long breath.

And he closed himself in his own room.

It was going to be a long, *long* weekend.

## Chapter Ten

"Why did you say you weren't very good with kids?"

It was Sunday and they were on the flight home. If Shane had thought the kids were excitable before the festival, it was nothing compared to their ebullience on the way home.

The choir had taken third place in their division, and the flight could have been fueled along by the lively energy pulsing in the rear portion of the plane where their group was sitting.

He couldn't imagine they'd have been more excited if they'd won first place.

He was sitting next to Laurel, only because he'd slipped into it when Sophie—assigned the seat—started doing hip-hop in the aisle with the "E" girls.

"Shane?" Laurel prompted.

He shrugged, not really wanting to think much about his

near brush with parenting in the past. Not that Denise's seven-year-old son would have considered his mother's engagement as giving Shane any sort of parenting rights. The kid had detested Shane.

Unfortunately, though it certainly hadn't begun that way, the feeling had ended up being mutual. No matter how hard and how many times Shane had tried with the kid, both before and after his relationship with Denise ended, his efforts had been futile.

"Don't deal with them much," he told Laurel truthfully. "And when I do, it's because they're in trouble with the law."

"Evie's kids adore you."

He shrugged again. "Julie likes to come to my place so she can skate around on my empty hardwood floors in her stocking feet. Mostly, they relate better to Stu. He's more like our dad. Friendly."

Laurel made a noise.

"What?"

She just shook her head. Her hair slid smoothly over her shoulder. "Please. You are *so* much like your father."

He'd never really thought so. Not even when he was planning to go into the ministry. "Beau has a gift with people. I mostly intimidate them."

"And that bothers you?"

"Better not." He grinned a little. "Handy thing when you're the sheriff."

She made a soft little "mmm" sound and looked out the oval window beside her. An announcement crackled over the speaker that they were beginning to near Billings and the passengers should prepare for landing.

The dancing in the aisles didn't even falter, and Shane could see two of the flight attendants heading their way, purpose in their strides despite the smiles on their faces.

He stood and let out a short, sharp whistle, and the revelry ceased, almost comically. A dozen young faces turned his way. "Seats."

They all began tumbling into their seats as he sat down again. Sophie, he noticed, didn't quibble, taking the seat he'd had earlier.

"Dad's gonna want you to be their choir director permanently."

She shook her head. "Nancy Thayer might have something to say about that when she returns from her honeymoon."

"You helped them win third place."

"No, my presence just made certain that they met the requirements for competing. Nancy is the one who's worked with them as a choir. Not me."

"Nancy's been taking the youth choir to the annual festival for three years. This is the first year they're returning to Lucius with a trophy. Believe me. The parents and kids are going to want you."

"Well, I don't want anything of the sort!" Her cheeks flushed and her gaze darted around, but the noise of the engines did a good job of preventing voices from being carried.

He was more interested in her vehemence than whether she was overheard, though. "Why not?"

"I haven't even decided whether I want to stay in Lucius," she said abruptly. "Once I deal with my father's house—" She broke off with a shrug. "I don't know." She looked out the window again.

How could he have gotten so accustomed so rapidly to the idea of her staying in Lucius? Roger's funeral had barely been a week ago. "The school you teach at in Colorado expects you back in the fall, of course."

She mumbled something, but with her facing away from him and the noise of the plane, he couldn't make it out. He covered her hand where it clutched the armrest between them and felt the way she nearly jumped at the contact. He kept his hand there, though, until she looked at him.

"I...don't have a job there anymore," she finally said. "I quit because I was expecting to be married to Martin by now and he planned to do a lot of traveling."

He *really* didn't like the idea of her coming so close to marrying that other guy. "So there's no reason not to stay in Lucius," he said logically.

She didn't answer that. Merely tugged her hand out from beneath his and leaned over to fumble in the carry-on bag she had tucked under the seat in front of her. When she straightened again, the flight attendants were making their final rounds before the plane landed.

Laurel kept her attention fixed out the window, but she saw nothing. Not when there was only one thing filling her head, engulfing her senses.

Shane.

He hadn't gone sightseeing the day before while the choir was busy all day. He'd stuck to her side almost like glue, fading out of sight only when their choir was on deck or competing. He'd been there, wearing his jeans and that ridiculous Experience Spokane! T-shirt she'd found in the gift shop for him. Except, the shirt hadn't looked at all ridiculous with the way it clung to his broad shoulders.

She still wasn't sure if he'd hung around that way because he figured she was likely to keel over from exertion or not. In the end, she supposed it really didn't matter. He'd filled the need for a chaperone, the kids had their trip, and now everything could get back to normal.

Not that she knew what normal was for her, anymore.

The plane landed and the passengers in the rows ahead of their group deplaned—undoubtedly happy to no longer be cooped up with twenty over-excited youth. Laurel waited until the kids were moving off the plane before she followed. As she went, she was eyeballing the seats to make sure nothing had been left behind by her charges, only to realize that Shane, immediately behind her, was doing the same thing.

She nabbed a worn teddy bear. He found a portable CD player. From the plane they boarded the school bus waiting for them, and then they headed back to Lucius.

Some of the stuffing was starting to leak out from the kids' stores of energy by the time they arrived. Parents were already waiting in the parking lot, including Evie and Tom and Louise Halloran—who was obviously feeling better. Shane, Jana and Katy were out, helping to sort belongings. Laurel stopped long enough to thank the bus driver for his service, then she too stepped off the bus.

The sun was just beginning to set.

Evie rushed over, pumping Laurel's hand in hers. "Alan called from Joey's cell phone. Third place! Oh, drat, but I wish I could've gotten away to be a chaperone. Please tell me you got lots of pictures."

Laurel nodded and laughed when the woman pulled her in for a tight hug. It was only one of many. It seemed that every single mother felt a need to squeeze the daylights out of Laurel. By the time the parking lot was finally clearing and there was only Shane's SUV and Laurel's borrowed car sitting there, she felt oddly teary.

"Told you," Shane said as he picked up her suitcase and stowed it on the front seat of her vehicle. "They're going to want you to take the job permanently. Evie's already on a harangue about it. She won't rest until she gets what she wants."

Laurel climbed behind the wheel. "Then she'll be pretty unrested."

He hooked his arms over the door before she could pull it closed. "Speaking of rest. Where are you going to sleep tonight?"

Alone, sadly.

Her face went hot as the thought sneaked in. "At my father's house," she said calmly. "And you don't need to play night-light. I'll be fine. You were with me the entire weekend. Surely I've proven my own competence by now."

"It has nothing to do with competence."

"Spoken like a man who's never had his mind picked apart by psychiatrists." She realized her hands were squeezing the steering wheel too tightly, and deliberately loosened her grip as she started the car, then tugged the door closed. "Good night, Shane. Thanks again for your help." She drove off before he could respond—positively or negatively.

She was vaguely surprised when the sight of his SUV didn't appear in her rearview mirror as she drove back to her father's house. Surprised but not disappointed.

No. *Not* disappointed.

She tried to shrug off her odd mood as she went inside the house. It was a far sight tidier than when she'd first arrived, but still it seemed close and confining.

She dragged her suitcase up the stairs straight past her parents' closed bedroom door and tossed it on the narrow bed in her bedroom. She unpacked, exchanged her wrinkled traveling clothes for a comfortable knee-length T-shirt dress and went downstairs and back out to the car.

She drove out to the cemetery where she sat near her gram and watched the sun set. She went to the grocery store and stocked up on a few essentials. She passed the sheriff's office and figured she was in some trouble when she was able to recognize Shane's usual SUV—which ought to have been identical to the other ones the department possessed—parked on the street there.

She returned to the house again, scrambled an egg and fixed toast for herself, then collapsed on the makeshift bed under the dining room window.

No, she didn't need Shane there just to get some sleep under her father's roof.

But as she lay there for a long while before finally dozing off, she was honest enough to admit to herself that— even if she'd convinced him his presence was no longer necessary—she missed him.

Taking a long weekend off meant Shane played catch-up at the office all day on Monday, and he was glad to knock off when suppertime rolled around. He drove home, fully intending to drive right on past the Runyan place.

But the sight of his sister's car parked in the street caught his curiosity. The sight of Laurel, standing in the yard surrounded by painting equipment as she talked with Evie, caught at more than his curiosity.

He pulled up and parked behind Evie's car.

Laurel had smears of something on her bare arms and a white cap on her head.

He shifted in his seat and watched the two women through the side window.

They knew he was there, since they'd both glanced his way when he'd driven up. But the smile spreading across Laurel's face didn't dim.

She was beautiful.

He looked down at the thick file he'd been studying for most of the day. Roger Runyan's file held nothing that Shane hadn't already known, but he still was going through it again with a fine-tooth comb. Now he slid it under his hat on the seat and got out of the SUV and walked up to the women.

The painter's cap had Lucius Hardware printed in dark-green lettering on it. And the paint smears, when he got close enough to see, were the color of buttercups. "Tired of your arms being flesh colored?"

Laurel brushed at the spatters on her arms. "I know. I'm a mess." She grasped one of the stir sticks stacked on the ground and stirred the paint slowly. "I tested it a little, there by the front door. I think it'll be a nice change from white."

Evie was nodding.

He had no desire to take the smile off Laurel's face by stating his opinion on the practicality of painting a house that would have been better demolished. "It's a nice color," he agreed.

"Oh, high praise, indeed," Evie said. She suddenly fumbled with her pocket, pulling out a tiny cell phone that was quietly vibrating. "Excuse me." She turned and walked a little distance away as she answered her call.

He was glad Stu had given him a heads-up earlier that afternoon on the amount of work Laurel had accomplished that day. That he'd had enough time to conquer the urge to bolt out to her place and remind her that the last time she'd done some repairs—on the roof—she'd passed out from exhaustion. Still, seeing the muscles in her slender arms flex as she stirred the contents of the huge paint bucket, he found it hard to keep his thoughts to himself. "How much do you plan to do today?"

She lifted her shoulder. "As much as I can. There are still hours of sunlight left. So…" The edge of her teeth sank into her lower lip as she concentrated.

The paint was surely the most well mixed in the county, judging by the attention she was giving it.

"What made you decide to paint the outside first?"

"Had to start somewhere." She didn't quite look at him when she finally stopped stirring and picked up a metal paint tray. She dropped it on the ground next to the paint pail and crouched down next to it, as if she fully intended to muscle it up and pour a measure into the tray.

He nudged her hands away. "You're liable to dump the whole thing in the dirt," he told her. He scraped the excess paint off the stir sticks into the bucket and handed them to her, then lifted it and poured a stream into the tray.

"Show-off," she muttered. But she didn't look unduly upset as she swiped the edge of the pail when he set it back on the ground. "If you're that set on showing me how it's supposed to be done—" she gestured at the equipment stacked on a flat piece of plastic "—then grab a paint roller."

There was a hint of challenge in her voice.

He wondered if she was aware of it.

Then he saw the gleam in her eyes as she lifted the paint tray and carried it up the plywood ramp and set it on the porch.

Oh, she knew all right.

She figured she had him pegged right down to his boots. He thought she was wasting her resources on the house, and she knew it.

Evie neared again, looking a little frazzled. "You know the architect I consulted about adding on to Tiff's? He was going to be in town tomorrow, but he's over there right now, waiting. Says he has only an hour before he has to return to Billings. Shane, I hate to ask, but could you keep an eye on the kids for me? They're inside Laurel's. This guy is harder than wet soap to get ahold of. I don't want to miss him."

"They can stay here," Laurel offered easily, "even if he can't. Slave labor is *always* welcome."

Trevor poked his nose out the screen door. He'd obviously been listening. "I wanna paint."

Alan soon appeared after his little brother. "Me, too."

"You don't know what you're getting into," Evie warned Laurel.

"I survived the festival trip, didn't I?"

Evie laughed at that, nodding. "More than some could say, probably. Okay. Alan, you make sure Trev behaves. I'm not worried about Julie. She won't go near the paint, probably. Too fastidious." Evie was already heading to her car. "I won't be long, I promise." She climbed in and drove off, her hand waving out the window.

Laurel looked at Alan. "You really want to paint?"

He nodded.

"Well, all right. But you need something to cover up your clothes a little. Don't think your mom would appreciate it too much if she comes back and you look like this." She swept her hand down, gesturing at her own paint-spattered jeans and T-shirt. She looked at Shane for half a moment then quickly went inside.

Shane could hear Trevor's young voice piping along that he wanted a paint shirt, too.

He stared at the house.

How many times had he envisioned it being torn down? How many times had he looked forward to that day when there was nothing remaining of the place where Laurel had been so devastated?

He rubbed his hand down his face. Muttered an oath and went to his truck. When he turned up the drive to his house, his tires spun a little on the gravel, spitting stones out behind him as he went.

\* \* \*

Through her bedroom window upstairs, Laurel saw Shane drive away as if the hounds of hell were chasing after him.

Disappointment felt heavy inside her, but she put a smile on her face, anyway, as she surveyed the young males wriggling in front of her. Julie was sitting primly on the couch downstairs, paging through a magazine that Laurel had picked up along with her other supplies. She couldn't help but wonder how long inexpensive home decorating ideas would hold the girl's interest.

"Okay. Here you go, sir." She handed Trevor an old button-down blouse from her high school days. It was white and fairly devoid of female details and wouldn't be so huge on him that he would be unable to function. "And for you, Alan, I think something larger is in order."

She knew the boy was nearly eleven, and a fair-size youth he was, too.

"Do you still have something?" Worry lurked in the boy's blue eyes that he might not find suitable attire. "Mom'll skin me if I get something on these."

Laurel swallowed. "I definitely have something." She went up the hall toward the stairs.

The two boys trooped behind her.

Her heartbeat sounded more loudly in her ears with each step that took her nearer her parents' bedroom door. Hardly able to breathe, she closed her hand over the iron doorknob and threw the door open.

No ghosts came rushing out.

No remembrances came rushing back.

There was nothing but a stuffy, unoccupied bedroom.

"Miss Runyan?"

Laurel blinked a little. Alan stood beside her. "Call me Laurel."

And she stepped into the bedroom, going straight to the closet door, looking neither left nor right. She pulled out the first shirt her hand encountered and turned back around, stopping short.

Again the boys had followed her.

Trevor was bouncing his rear end experimentally on the end of the quilt-covered bed, and Alan was looking at the dresser next to the door. "You got more pictures than my mom even."

Laurel hurried from the bedroom, aware of nothing more than the profusion of photograph frames cluttering the top of the dresser. "Come on. Paint is waiting."

They clambered down the stairs behind her. Laurel handed Alan the brown plaid shirt she'd grabbed.

Julie was still sitting on the couch. Laurel stopped next to her. "Are you sure you don't want to come out with us? You don't have to paint."

Julie shook her head, studying the open magazine on her lap. "I'm okay," she insisted shyly.

"All rightee. Come out if you change your mind, okay?" The girl nodded. She turned the page.

Laurel wasn't sure whether to smile or sigh.

The article on painting concrete indoor floors was probably *fascinating* to an eight-year-old.

But she wasn't going to push Julie to do anything she didn't want to do. This wasn't a classroom, after all. So she went outside, organizing the boys with paintbrushes and small containers of paint and instructions, as if she were oh-so experienced in the finer details of painting the outside of a house, when the only things she'd painted were crafts for school projects.

"Where'd Uncle Shane go?" Alan asked after a moment. He was working more or less beside her, his tongue generally caught between his teeth as he concentrated on his assigned portion.

Laurel shook her head, determined to ignore the hollowness inside her. She'd survived her dash in and out of her parents' bedroom. She'd survive the fact that Shane had left, too. "I don't know. He probably had something he had to do."

She ran the loaded roller up and down around the front window. She could see Julie inside, but the moment the little girl realized she was being watched, she quickly looked back down at the magazine and flipped a page.

It took less time than Laurel expected to finish covering that short section of wall, and she moved the boys around to the side of the house. "All right. Keep the paint on the house, not each other. I'll be right back."

She carried the empty paint tray back to the big bucket. Tipping it still proved too heavy and awkward. She didn't want the money she'd spent on the paint just ending up in the dirt.

Too bad Shane wasn't still around.

Annoyed with the thought, she went inside and found a plastic bowl in the kitchen cupboard. Muscle wasn't everything.

She started for the door again, tapping the bowl against her leg.

"Miss Runyan?"

Oh, success, please. She stopped and looked at Julie. "You can call me Laurel."

"It's very messy, painting."

"Well." Laurel spread her hands looking down at herself. She had a fresh new set of spatters. "In my case, I'd have to say so. But my skin will wash and my clothes are work clothes anyway, so it's okay. Are you sure you don't want to come give it a try?"

The girl looked torn.

"I can get a shirt that'll cover you from your neck to your toes. And I even have plastic gloves that you can wear, if you don't want to get it on your hands."

"I just don't wanna get my dress dirty."

"It's a very pretty dress. I wouldn't want it to get dirty, either." It was so clear that the shy girl wanted to join her brothers. "How about if I grab another shirt and leave it with you just in case, and you can decide?"

The girl twined a strand of long, blond hair around her finger. Finally she nodded.

Laurel grinned. "Be back in a flash."

She went up the stairs again, not giving herself a chance to hesitate as she went through the still-opened door of her parents' room. Another shirt in hand, she turned to go downstairs and caught a glimpse of her reflection in the dusty mirror over the dresser.

She looked a fright.

No wonder Julie was so skittish.

She shoved her hair back more smoothly beneath the cap, but wiping at the smudges on her face only spread more paint since her fingers were fairly coated with it.

Her gaze fell on the collection of photographs. Dozens and dozens of simple frames in an assortment of sizes.

Her gaze sharpened, racing over the items.

*So* many photographs.

Her throat tightened with each one that she looked at.

So many, and *all* of her.

She leaned closer, holding the shirt and her hands well away. Elementary school pictures. High school pictures. Candid shots of birthdays and Christmases. Of her sitting on Gram's lap. Of her graduation.

She straightened like a shot.

Her *college* graduation.

Despite her messy hands, she grabbed the picture frame. It was a small photograph. But there was no mistake.

It was her all right, in her cap and gown, standing near the entrance to the student union where she'd met up with classmates following the commencement ceremony.

How on earth had her father gotten a picture of her when he hadn't *been* there?

And why did he have it at all?

"Are you all right?"

She looked up from the photograph.

Shane stood in the doorway. He wore a ragged gray T-shirt with the collar and sleeves torn out, and a pair of threadbare jeans that ought to have gotten him arrested in a few particularly conservative states.

"What are you doing here?"

"Julie told me you were still up here. But what *you're* doing seems more the point," he countered quietly. "You opened the door."

She pressed her lips together for a moment. "Shirts," she managed. "For paint wear."

His gray eyes that missed nothing were unbearably soft. "Are you okay?"

Was she?

"He had this." She held out the photo. It wavered.

He took the photo with one hand and closed his fingers around her shaking hand with the other. "You were graduating," he said, looking at the photo. "Hold it. That's not Lucius High. Is this your college graduation?" His hand tightened on hers. It steadied her, that hold, but it also made her eyes burn deep inside her head.

She nodded.

His thumb brushed over the photo, lightly tracing her image. "Prettiest coed I've ever seen."

It was the absolute last thing she expected him to say. She let out a sudden burst of laughter even as the burning behind her eyes turned liquid and spilled past her lashes.

"Ah, baby. Don't cry."

She shook her head, blinking, but the tears didn't stop. "How did he get that photograph? He wasn't there. He was never there!"

He pulled her against him, and he felt solid and warm and strong. His hand closed over her neck, smoothed down her tangle of hair, stroked up and down her back. "Honey, either he *was* there, or he sent someone in his place. And he cared enough to save the photograph. Saved a lot of photographs, looks like."

Her fingers tangled in his shirt. "I don't understand him." She pulled in a shaking breath, desperately trying to collect herself. She peeled her fingers away from his shirt and swiped them over her cheeks. "I'm sorry," she whispered.

He gave her a few inches of space, but when his big palm slid against her cheek, she nearly lost all the control she'd gained. He tilted her head back.

She swallowed. Her vision blurred all over again.

"Sometimes not everything has to be completely understood," he murmured. "Just accepted."

His lashes were inky black, almost startlingly so around his gray eyes. She could feel herself sinking into his gaze. "Like faith." Her voice was little more than a breath.

"Like faith. Love."

Her chest ached.

His thumb stroked slowly over her cheek.

She could feel herself slipping further into his mesmerizing gaze. As if she were leaving the solidity of herself behind.

He lowered his head and brushed his lips over her forehead. Her temple.

She could feel herself trembling.

His thumb moved again. Lightly chafed her bottom lip.

She dragged in another ragged breath. Exhaled his name.

His mouth drifted again, and slowly, so slowly settled over hers.

## *Chapter Eleven*

It was the giggling that finally penetrated the spell cast by the taste of Laurel.

Still, Shane took his time breaking the kiss. He waited until Laurel's soft lashes fluttered open, until the satisfying haziness in her eyes cleared. "We have an audience," he murmured.

Nothing else could have cleared the dregs of desire more efficiently. Her eyes widened. A flush flirted with the delicate lines of her cheekbones.

She stepped away, focusing anywhere but on him. "Here." She hastily picked up the shirt, which had fallen to the floor at some point, and handed it to Julie who, along with her two brothers, was goggle-eyed and still giggling.

Julie took the shirt.

"We need more paint," Alan said.

"Right. Of course you do." Laurel cast him a somewhat

desperate look over her shoulder as she hustled the children back down the stairs.

Shane took a little more time joining them.

But when he did, and the lot of them—including his finicky little niece—were brushing, rolling and generally swabbing paint on a house he hadn't figured was worth the effort, he felt something unroll inside him that he hadn't felt in a very long time.

Contentment.

Evie took longer than she'd expected, phoning Shane at about the time he'd made his way around to the rear of the house, that she was going to be a while yet.

He didn't mind. The kids were occupied, and Laurel had a smile on her face, one that stayed there even when she'd catch him watching her.

The smile was good.

The fact that he'd heard her singing softly to herself as she'd painted was even better. Even at the festival, he hadn't once heard her sing a single note.

He assured his sister that her children were being well entertained and to take her time. Then he went around to the other side of the house where Laurel was working, the children scattered around her.

The sight jarred him for a moment, seeming to imprint itself on his brain where he thought he'd never be able to completely remove it. He'd seen her in what he considered her teacher mode. But just now, she seemed…maternal.

He didn't know why that fact tugged at him so. When he'd been engaged to Denise, her young son had been a total bone of contention between them.

"What do you think," Laurel called to him, gesturing at the finished wall. "I'll still have to paint the eaves and trim, of course. I figured a sort of dark mossy green would look nice, but I wasn't entirely sure, which is why I didn't purchase the paint yet."

He nodded, barely seeing the house. "I think it's time for pizza. What do you guys think?"

The children nodded. Alan had his tongue between his teeth as he drew the paintbrush along the house's foundation. Julie was busy with the hose, swishing it over the paint on her bare legs. Trevor had lost interest in painting the house and was, instead, sitting on the ground making drawings in the mud with one of Laurel's paint sticks. "I'm *starving,*" he said.

Laurel looked stricken. "Good heavens. I should have stopped and fixed them all sandwiches."

"Yeah," Shane drawled, looking at the kids as he came up behind her. "They look pretty mistreated to me, Miz Runyan." He kissed the back of her neck, making her jump, and set the kids giggling all over again. "You have paint on your ear," he murmured against the ear in question.

She cast him a look over her shoulder. "You're just feeling superior because *you* are not as messy as we are." A sudden dimple flirted in her cheek. "Yet."

He barely had time to back away before she'd turned and run her paint roller right down the front of his shirt.

"Oh, whoa. She's gonna get it now," Alan predicted.

"Julie. Bring me the hose."

Laurel's eyes widened, but they were sparkling. Her lips parted, but they were still curved into a smile. "Oh, no you don't."

"Maybe I just want a drink of cold water."

"Right. And I'm the Queen of England."

He held out his hand and took the hose from his niece. "Your Highness." He bent over and took a drink from the steady stream of water. Then he straightened and sprayed the water straight in Laurel's face.

She screamed, laughing, and ran away toward the hill behind the house, dropping her paint weapon along the way. "This is not, oh!" She darted the other way, trying to evade the water. "This isn't dignified behavior for a sheriff," she sputtered.

The kids were laughing and screaming, too, whether to protect Laurel or simply to get their dose of water spray, he wasn't sure. He grinned and sprayed it over them, too, but while he was doing so, Laurel charged him, low and fast, grabbing his legs.

He gave a bark of laughter as he stumbled and righted his balance. "Nice try, songbird." He grabbed her around the waist, tipping her upside down.

Her legs kicked, but he held her fast. The kids were laughing so hard they could barely stand.

She squirmed. "You're going to regret this, Shane," she promised breathlessly, when he renewed his grasp on the hose. "Really, *really* regret this."

Regret seeing her laugh? He shook his head. "Don't think so." And turned the hose directly against her stomach.

She squealed and wriggled and laughed so hard they wound up in a tangle of legs and arms and cold, running water.

"Dog pile!" Alan crowed. Then the children bounced on them, too. Shane laughed, turning his back to the kids, protecting Laurel from the worst of it.

She was shaking beneath him, water dripping from her hair, her eyelashes spiked with it. "You are a nut."

Julie squirmed between them. "Are you gonna kiss again?"

He caught Laurel's gaze with his. "Not yet."

His hand was on her bare waist where her wet shirt had twisted up, and he tightened his hold for a moment. Her pupils dilated.

Then he let her go, tipping the children off. "First one cleaned up gets to choose the pizza."

In a flash they were running hell-bent for the house.

He grabbed Laurel's hand and pulled her to her feet. Miraculously, they had managed not to spray mud or water on the side of the house, though the paint roller she'd been using was full of dirt.

He lowered his head and pressed a hard, fast kiss on her lips. "Better make sure Trevor doesn't win the race," he advised, turning her toward the house and giving her a gentle push. "He's the only one who likes anchovies."

She smiled as she walked away from him. "Maybe I'll make sure he *does* win," she countered. "I like anchovies, too."

To Laurel's amusement, Julie won the clean-up race, and the pizza—when it was delivered from the only place with decent pizza in town according to Shane—was a nice, tidy pepperoni and mushroom, which the little girl ate with a knife and a fork.

Evie arrived before they were finished, and she hurried them along as she chattered a mile a minute about her frustrating meeting with the architect who'd nixed her idea of expanding Tiff's existing structure. When she finally wound down and hustled the kids out, the house felt decidedly quiet.

And Laurel and Shane were decidedly...alone.

Rather than sit there across the dining room table mulling that particular point to death, she rose, quickly collecting up the used paper plates and napkins.

Too quickly, she realized, when, barely a minute later, she and Shane were still decidedly alone, and she had nothing to occupy her nervous hands.

When the phone rang, she very nearly jumped right out of her skin.

The corner of Shane's lips twitched, and she wanted to just disappear under the floorboards as she went to answer the phone.

She was thirty years old, for heaven's sake. Not eighteen.

She picked up the phone midring. "Hello?"

"Miss Runyan? This is Marian Smythe. I'm a member of the Lucius School Board. Do you have a moment to talk?"

She blinked in surprise, casting a look at Shane. "Yes, Mrs. Smythe. How can I help you?"

"Well, I'm sure you're aware of our need for teachers and Rev. Golightly gave us your name. I hope you don't mind me interrupting your evening."

"Of course not."

"Perhaps you'd be willing to meet with the other members of the board and me this week? We're sorely in need of three teachers, you see, and the search committee is just about at their wits' end."

Laurel listened as the woman went on. Shane had picked up the last slice of pizza and carried it with him out to the porch. Through the window she could see the back of him where he stood outside. "I'll be happy to meet with you," Laurel finally agreed. "But I really haven't decided if I'll be staying in town or not."

"I understand," Mrs. Smythe assured. "The reverend said as much, but I'm hoping that we might be able to convince you. So, the day after tomorrow? At 10:00 a.m. at the library at the elementary school."

"I'll see you then." She hung up the phone only to stare at it pensively.

With his usual unerring sense of timing, Shane came back inside. "Here. Your mail was sitting on the rocker out front."

Laurel glanced through the envelopes. Two "occupants" and one addressed to her. From Martin.

Feeling the weight of Shane's gaze, she set the mail aside.

"He's probably begging you to come back."

Of course, he would have seen the return address printed on Martin's envelope. "No. He's not."

"How do you know?"

"Because he understood perfectly when I told him I couldn't marry him."

"Then he's a damn fool."

"First he's a saint, now he's a fool. Well, if you must know, I wish—" Her back teeth closed hard on each other.

"Wish what? That you *had* married him?"

She flopped her hands to her sides. "No. I didn't—I couldn't—oh, never mind! I don't want to talk about it."

"Or read about it, evidently." He flicked the edge of the linen envelope with his fingertip.

"That is just a check," she assured. "He bought my car for his son. Nothing more."

"You *sold* your car."

"Yes."

"But you claim you're not sure you're staying in Lucius."

"I haven't decided."

His gaze slanted pointedly to her palm where she was smoothing down the bandage he'd produced from the first-aid kit he kept under his trunk seat when he'd seen the blisters forming in her hand. "You're doing all this work on the house because you haven't decided?"

"That's right." She stopped fiddling with the bandage.

"What are you afraid of, Laurel?" His voice was quiet. Patient.

So patient that her immediate rejection of his question died. She frowned. "I don't know," she finally said instead. "Too many things to list, I think."

"Is staying in this house going to help that?"

She thought about her parents' room. The photographs on the dresser that she'd never known were there until that afternoon. "I'm afraid if I don't stay here, I'll never know the answer to that."

The phone rang in her kitchen again and she picked it up even though there wasn't a soul she wanted to talk to.

But it was for Shane.

"It's Carla Chapman," she told him and held out the phone.

He automatically patted his belt, where his cell phone ordinarily was. Only, he wore no belt. Merely the pair of cargo shorts that he'd exchanged his muddy, painted jeans for before they'd eaten. He took the phone and Laurel slipped out of his way.

"Whatever it is, have Tony handle it," he said to Carla.

Laurel scooted the metal chairs into the table and went into the living room, wincing a little when Shane muttered an oath in response to Carla's answer.

When he finished his call, she was picking up the old games she'd found in her closet for the kids from the coffee table. Pick-up sticks and a box of marbles. Hardly the latest in electronic games, but they'd occupied the threesome simply out of novelty.

"I have to take care of something." He stopped beside her. Any semblance of patience had disappeared from his expression. He looked grimly annoyed. "It shouldn't take me long."

She wasn't certain how to take that.

Did he think they'd crossed some invisible threshold back into the land of kisses and caresses?

*Hadn't they?*

So she simply nodded. "Okay."

He looked as if he wanted to say something more. But he didn't. He merely headed for the door. Seconds later his headlights flashed across her front window as he turned toward town.

She clutched the box of marbles to her chest, exhaling slowly.

Then she carried the toys back upstairs and put them away.

Every muscle in her body was tired from the day's activities. She took another hot bath, scraping again at the bits of paint she'd missed the first time. The water felt good on her muscles, but only seemed to make her more tired. Yet trying to sleep held little appeal.

She slipped into a clean gown, picked up the journal that was sitting on the desktop, and carried it to the bed. She curled against the thin pillow and pulled up the knitted afghan her grandmother had made for her when she was little.

She flipped open the book near the front.

> Dear Gram,
> I graduated from high school today. Hurrah! Now it's on to college. Mom says I'm nuts for wanting to study vocal performance. Says its completely impractical. As usual, Dad didn't say anything, but at least he doesn't tell me I'm nuts. Love you.

The screen door at Laurel's place was shut when Shane returned from hauling Charlie, drunker than a skunk, out of the Tipped Barrel and home again. He'd left the guy sprawled inside his front door.

He wished he'd had cause to lock the bum in a cell again, but Charlie hadn't been driving this time. He'd had his keys on him, all right, but he'd been hugging a whiskey with one hand and an annoyed waitress with the other when Shane interrupted the festivity.

Shane peered through the screen into the brightly lit house, expecting to see Laurel inside. "Laurel?"

There was no answer.

He pulled open the screen and went inside. He'd have to give her his spiel on safety. Yeah, Lucius was a safe place to live. But she was on the edge of town, and there was no such thing as being too careful.

She'd moved the pile of linens out of the dining room before they'd ordered pizza, calling the pile laundry when Alan asked. It was all still sitting undisturbed where she'd left it at the base of the staircase.

The car his father had loaned her was sitting in the driveway. It hadn't been moved.

He started up the stairs. Past her father's room. The door was still open.

He'd loathed Roger Runyan, and nothing Shane had found out by looking over the man's case gave him reason to change his opinion. But he could acknowledge that the guy must have had some feelings for his daughter. What else could explain all those pictures of Laurel? Particularly the one from her college graduation?

The floorboards creaked loudly as he went down the narrow hall. The bathroom door was open; the room dark. He continued a few more feet.

Laurel's bedroom.

He stuck his head around the doorway. "Laurel?"

The bed was small, and she was curled up, barely occupying half of it. Asleep.

He stepped closer, grimacing when the worn floorboards there creaked just as badly as the hallway had.

But she didn't stir.

Her hair was damp, streaming around her on the pillow. He carefully untucked the canvas-covered book she was holding from her lax fingers and set it quietly on the desk. Then he drew the pink and purple afghan up to her shoulders.

She sighed a little, seeming to sink even further into the pillow.

He started to smooth her hair away from her face but didn't. "Sleep tight, songbird," he whispered.

Carefully avoiding the boards that had squeaked before, he left the room. Downstairs he shut off some of the lights and quietly let himself out the door, locking it behind him.

The next day Laurel went through the door of the office at Golightly Garage and Auto Body and nearly swallowed her gum, a feat considering she wasn't chewing any.

The woman sitting at the counter just seemed to inspire that sort of response. Laurel was positive she'd never seen anyone with hair quite that shade of purple or with eye shadow quite that shade of green. Not outside of a Halloween dress-up contest at any rate. The woman was eyeing her in return, too, as if Laurel presented as unexpected a sight.

"Help you with something?" The woman held up a bottle of nail polish and shook it violently.

She was so petite and wrinkled it was a wonder the shaking didn't send her right off the stool where she was perched.

"I was hoping I could see Stu," Laurel said. The woman must be Riva. The woman who helped Stu run the garage.

"And you'd be Laurel. Heard you'd be dropping by soon." The woman tipped her half-glasses up her nose for a studying moment, then shoved them even higher until they were stuck in the middle of her forehead, where they seemed to magnify the penciled eyebrows that hovered a solid inch above her natural ones. Her teeth—blinding white and seeming two sizes too large for her tiny face—flashed. "I'm Riva. Been working with Stu since he was in short pants. You gonna date him?"

"Stu? We're just friends."

"Hhmphf. Friends. That boy needs t' stop being just friends with every pretty girl he meets and find himself a wife before he's too set in his way for takers. But I meant the sheriff, hon. You gonna date *him?*"

Laurel nearly choked. "Is, um, is Stu around?" she persisted.

She hadn't seen him in the service bay when she'd parked near the opened door.

"Well, yeah, he's around. His garage," Riva said patiently. "You're a good-looking girl. What's wrong with either the sheriff or Stu?"

"Hell, Riv, would you just shut up?" Stu rambled in from an interior door, a greasy red shop rag in his hand. "Hey, Laurel, come on back. Shane said you might come by. Got a car perfect for you back here. Just been giving it a once-over. Think you'll be happy with it, but if you're not, there are a few others I can recommend."

Laurel gratefully escaped Riva's arch look and followed him through a doorway into the enormous garage area. There were two cars up on lifts. A third car, the one Stu headed toward, had its hood up, and he popped it shut as he passed by.

"The engine's solid," he said, opening up the driver's

side door of the little red sedan, and gesturing with his hand for her to take a look. "Tires are new, did the brakes just last year."

She'd told Stu she was ready to look at cars to buy, but now that she was actually *doing* it, nerves were creeping in. "Why's the owner selling it?" She slid into the driver's seat, looking around the interior. It showed hardly any signs of wear.

Laurel glanced up at Stu when he didn't answer. He was staring at something outside, and she looked over her shoulder to see what so fascinated him.

A tow truck was pulling up in the parking lot. It parked behind one of the upraised cars, and Freddie Finn slid out of the cab. She lifted a hand and shouted something Laurel couldn't quite make out, then began lowering the bed of the tow truck.

Laurel looked back at Stu. He was twisting his red rag as if it were a snake he needed to dispatch. "Go help her," she suggested. "I'll just check out the car a little more." Try to convince herself that taking this step—this mark of permanency—wasn't a mistake.

"Freddie doesn't want my help. Never has." His lips twisted. "Stubbornest woman I ever met. She doesn't need to be hauling cars around all day," he said under his breath.

Laurel bit her tongue to keep from smiling. "What *does* she need to be doing?"

He shrugged, looking red around the ears. "She ain't getting any younger. Getting married. Having kids."

Laurel couldn't help her grin then. "Just exactly what every woman over thirty wants to hear."

He looked chagrined. "Aw, Laurel. I didn't mean any offense."

She laughed a little. "None taken. You really like her that much, then, that you think marriage and babies around her?"

Horror darkened his eyes. "Hell no!"

She just smiled wider and shook her head. "Again, a lovely and welcome reaction any woman would be happy to see in the man they're interested in."

"She's not interested in me."

"The same way you're not interested in her?"

He cast Freddie a speculative glance. The woman was completely preoccupied with unloading her cargo. "She's always going out with other guys," he finally said.

"Well, have *you* asked her out?"

He looked even more chagrined, and she knew that he hadn't.

"Oh, Stu," she murmured. "You've gotta get on the stick here. After all, *you're* not getting any younger."

He glared at her. Then chuckled. "Yeah, yeah. So, what about the car? Think she'll do you for?"

Laurel nodded, ignoring the nervousness clutching at her stomach. One step at a time. Small achievable goals. She could do this. "Can I write the owner a check, or do you think they'd prefer cash? I have a bank account here in town now."

"Check's fine. You can leave Dad's car here when you take this one. I've been wanting to flush the radiator, anyway."

"Hey, Laurel." Freddie sauntered into the garage and flipped a small set of keys toward Stu. "Owner's name is Reeves. Wants the engine rebuilt. Said you were expecting the car."

Stu caught the keys easily. "I am. Thanks. Town picnic's next week," he said suddenly.

"Yeah, so?" Freddie's voice tightened a little.

Laurel quickly leaned over, busying herself peering into

the glove box. She hummed a little under her breath, trying not to listen. But it was hard, when the two were standing right beside the car.

"Just seeing if you're going."

"What? You think I can't get a date?"

"I didn't say that. Hell, you're *always* on a date." Stu's voice turned annoyed.

"Which makes me some sort of tramp?"

"Did I say that?"

Freddie made a disgusted sound. "You sure sounded that way. I'd rather have plenty of dates than be as antisocial as *you* are. I suppose you can't be bothered with the town picnic at all."

"Then you'd be wrong, right, Laurel?"

She sat up warily. "Pardon me?"

"Oh, I'm supposed to believe that *you* are going with Laurel."

"Why not?" Stu asked evenly.

Laurel wanted to disappear. She caught the flash of dismay in the other woman's eyes, before it was quickly hidden.

"Well," Freddie said blithely, focusing her gaze somewhere in the vicinity of Laurel. "Everyone in town knows she's Shane's territory. But I hope you'll have a great time. Maybe we'll see each other there." Her smile had a brittle edge as she strode out of the garage and climbed into the truck.

"Sorry," Stu said when Freddie's truck roared out of the parking lot. "Didn't mean to use you like that. But you see what she's like?"

*Shane's territory?* How could she have forgotten so well what living in a small town was like? "Set Freddie straight, Stu. She didn't like the idea of you taking someone to the picnic. That means something, you know."

"Yeah, it means she thinks I'm an antisocial clod." He

slid the keys to the car in his lapel pocket. "Make your check out to Phil Boyle," he said as if the matter were closed. "He's already signed the title, so you can take the car with you now if you want."

She took out the temporary checkbook the bank had given her until her own checks could arrive, and made it out. Moments later she had the signed-over title in her hand. And a fresh set of butterflies in her stomach. "This is by far the easiest car purchase I've ever made."

He tipped the brim of his ball cap, grinning crookedly. "We aim to please, ma'am."

There was just no way she could ignore his niceness. It went down to the bone, just as all the Golightlys did, and she leaned forward, hugging him. "Thank you, Stu. And don't give up on Freddie. She'll come around."

He patted her shoulder and accepted the key to his father's car. "Don't mind if I don't hold my breath on that, will you?"

She laughed a little and leaned back, looking up into his face. He was so like Shane, yet he was ever so much…easier. Like a comfortable teddy bear. "Faint heart never won fair maiden," she reminded him.

The strident honk of a horn brought their attention around.

Shane's SUV sat in the parking lot. His hat was pulled low over his brow as he eyed them through his windshield.

Stu's arms fell away from Laurel. "What's got his shorts in a knot?" He headed toward the vehicle.

Laurel followed.

She hadn't seen Shane since the night before. She knew he must have returned, though, while she'd slept, because he'd left her with a box of bandages and her front door had been closed and locked when she got up that morning.

Only Shane would have done that.

"Have to drive to Billings this afternoon," Shane said when she reached the side of his truck. "Won't be back until late."

She couldn't interpret the expression in his eyes, but she knew that something about it set her teeth on edge. "Drive carefully."

"Thought maybe you'd like to go along. But I see you're busy." His voice was silky.

Definitely on edge. "I *beg* your pardon?"

His gaze flicked over Stu. "Make sure she eats her dinner," he said.

Stu settled his cap a few inches back on his head. "Figure she's a big girl, bro. Doesn't need someone telling her when she's hungry."

Laurel bristled. She didn't know what was going on between the two brothers, but it *surely* couldn't be over her. She held up her new set of car keys, shaking them by the plain metal ring holding them together. "I bought a car," she said. And hoped she hadn't made a monumental mistake. At least she hadn't called a moving company to transport the rest of her stored belongings. "And I'd like to drive it home if you'd be so kind as to move your SUV out of the way."

What had she been thinking? Just because Shane had been, well, wonderful lately, didn't mean that it was bound to last.

She hadn't held his interest for long the *last* time, after all.

She climbed in the car. Turned the key and revved the engine a little harder than necessary.

The moment the SUV had moved enough to give her an inch to spare, she zoomed past it.

Just because they were twelve years older, had she expected anything to change?

## *Chapter Twelve*

Laurel sat bolt upright, nearly knocking her head on the edge of the dining room table.

Seven nights in a row since the one she'd spent in her own bed upstairs.

Seven nights when she'd barely been able to sleep again, this time wondering what was wrong with her that she'd let Shane Golightly, of all people, disturb her so badly.

She hadn't seen him since he'd come upon her and Stu at the garage.

Fine with her.

Just because she'd kept a surreptitious lookout for his SUV driving up or down his steep drive didn't mean anything.

He'd said he was only going to Billings for the day. So what had kept him away for seven?

For a moment she sat there in the dark, her heart thudding heavily.

A glance out the dining room window up the hill told her nothing. His house was dark as a stone.

It wasn't the sound of his SUV driving past that had wakened her. It wasn't anything in the house—or her mind—that had wakened her. It was the squeal of tires on the road outside.

Headlights swept over her head, strobing eerily as they traveled across the walls.

Somebody driving too fast around the curve on the road in front of the house.

Happened all the time.

She started to lie back down, bunched the pillow more comfortably for her head, only to sit up again when there was another shrieking tire squeal. She pushed to her feet, went to the front door and pulled it open, peering out through the screen.

A car was doing doughnuts around and around on the curve in the highway.

"Idiot," she breathed.

And then, even as she watched, another car approached.

Her heart rate ratcheted up to the top of the scale, and she could only stare in horror as the cars headed directly for each other. She was running for her phone even before she heard the crash.

Her fingers shook. The 911 operator took her information, and she cursed the fact that her father had never bothered to replace his old-fashioned phone—the only one in the house and it hung on the wall in the kitchen next to the refrigerator.

"Emergency services is already responding ma'am," the calm voice assured her. "Are *you* hurt?"

Laurel heard the wail of a siren. "No. I'm fine. Thanks." She hung up and ran for the door again and was halfway down her plywood ramp before she thought to go back in and pull on something more substantial than her shortie nightgown. She yanked on jeans, tucking in the nightgown as best she could as she shoved her feet into her tennis shoes and ran out of the house.

One of the cars lay on its side in the middle of the road. She could smell the sharp stench of gas from her porch, but what struck her cold was the high-pitched wail of a child crying.

She ran across the yard, nearly plowing into Shane, bent low over a woman lying in the street. He barely glanced at her. "She's in shock. Bring a blanket."

Where had he come from?

Laurel didn't pause to question him but turned on her heel and ran flat-out back to the house. She grabbed a blanket from her impromptu bed on the dining room floor and raced back to him with it.

He began tucking it around the woman. "Ambulance should be here in a few minutes," he said tersely. "I need to check the other vehicle."

Laurel crouched beside the unconscious woman. She took over with the blanket. "Go."

He headed to the other car. It was facing the opposite direction, but it was still sitting upright on its four wheels. Laurel saw him bend down, check on the driver, then he was running back across the road toward her and the car that was hemorrhaging gas.

Laurel saw the first car's door open, and the driver got out, lurching around.

Drunk, she realized, disgusted. But it figured, given the way he'd been driving in circles right in front of her house.

The woman on the ground moaned, and Laurel carefully settled her hands on her shoulders. "Shh. You're safe. An ambulance is coming."

"My…son," she whispered.

"He's safe, too," Laurel assured her, seeing Shane carrying the crying child away from the wreckage.

The woman's eyes closed.

The ambulance screeched to a stop, pulling right up on Laurel's yard to make room near the vehicles for the fire engine that was hard on its tail.

Laurel scooted away from the woman as the EMTs took over. She stood to one side, well out of the way, hugging her arms tightly. Going inside her house was out of the question, so she continued standing there, watching and wishing she didn't feel so useless.

"Here." Shane appeared at her side and thrust the child at her. "Palmer is the EMT in charge. He'll check the boy out in a few, but only thing wrong as far as I can see is a scrape on his foot. Keep him occupied until then."

Laurel didn't quibble. The boy's wails had ceased and now he was staring, his eyes wide and fearful. He couldn't have been much more than four, she guessed.

Over his head, Shane met her look. His eyes were like ice. It was the only indication he gave that he was livid.

Unfortunately, she wasn't entirely certain that it wasn't directed at *her.*

She tucked the boy against her and rubbed her hand soothingly down his sturdy little back. He was clad only in cartoon-patterned pajamas.

"I want my mom," he whimpered.

"I know, sweetie." Laurel turned so he wouldn't be able to see the workers huddling over their patient. "She's getting help right now, so we need to stay out of the way. I'm Laurel, and I live in that house right there." She pointed and was grateful that she'd chosen to paint the exterior before tending to the interior.

It didn't look nearly as ominous as it might have only a week earlier. And it was a far more comforting sight than the road, where the flashing blue and red lights created a frantic circuslike atmosphere. The fire crew was spraying something over the road, presumably to deal with the pooling gasoline.

"Can you tell me your name?" She prompted gently.

Shudders worked through the child. She wasn't sure at first if he would answer. "Nathaniel Peters III."

"That is definitely an impressive name." She sat on the ground and took heart that Nathaniel clung to her neck, staying firmly in her lap. "Are you named after your daddy?"

"Uh-huh. And my goompa."

"You must be a very special young man to be named after *two* people. How old are you?"

He let out a hiccupping sigh. "Five."

"Are you in kindergarten?"

"Uh-huh. I wanna see my mom."

"Soon, sweetie. Where do you go to school?" She kept Nathaniel talking, trying to keep him as occupied as possible so he wouldn't take too much notice of the frantic activity around his mother.

Another truck had driven up—a tow truck this time. It parked, its loud engine idling, by the side of the road. An SUV identical to the one Shane drove had also appeared, and the man driving it had spread flares across the road to divert any traffic that might come along. He and Shane now stood together in the middle of the road and though the second officer wore a khaki uniform, it was very apparent that Shane—even in blue jeans and a half-fastened shirt—was the man in charge.

Mr. Doughnut was sitting on the far side of the road, his

back against the trunk of an ancient pine. Every now and then he moved, as if he intended to just get up and walk away, but each time he tried, Shane looked the driver's way and the man subsided.

Eventually Shane finished with his deputy and went over to the driver and hauled him to his feet. The other officer began talking on his radio, taking measurements of the road, making notes on a clipboard. The fire crew righted the car Nathaniel had been riding in, and the little boy cringed at the loud noise.

Laurel wished she dared take him inside her house, but she didn't want to agitate him any more than he was by moving him even further from his mother.

A second tow truck eventually arrived, and both vehicles were loaded up. Laurel easily recognized one of the tow folks as Freddie Finn. There was considerable debris littering the road, and a tall man from the second tow took an enormous broom to the task.

Shane handcuffed the drunken driver, and Laurel continued calmly chatting with Nathaniel as she watched Shane none too delicately shove his prisoner into the back seat of his deputy's SUV. She kept up her chatter, too, when one of the EMTs finally left the injured woman's side and approached them. He crouched down next to Nathaniel and introduced himself. The man was huge, but his demeanor was incredibly gentle with the child as he examined him.

"Good to see you up and around again," he murmured to Laurel. "Palmer Frame. Saw to you the day you fainted."

"Is my mom gonna die?" Nathaniel whispered, catching sight of the stretcher his mother was being transferred to.

"No," Palmer assured. He fixed a bandage in place over the raw scrape on the boy's foot. "But she needs some extra attention because her legs are *really* sore right now. But I'll bet you can see her in the morning."

"My daddy's on a trip."

"I know, pal. Your mom told us all about it. Don't you worry, though. We're gonna take care of both of you until he can get here. Okay?"

Nathaniel nodded. He had a stranglehold around Laurel's neck. "I'm not s'posed to talk to strangers," he divulged belatedly.

Laurel hugged him. "This time it's okay. Everyone here is just trying to help you and your mom. See that man?" She pointed at Shane. He was in conversation with his deputy and one of the firemen. "His name is Sheriff Golightly."

Nathaniel wrinkled his nose. His dark hair was rumpled, his cheeks flushed. "That's a funny name."

He was precious. "A little, but he's a really good sheriff," Laurel assured.

"What do you do?"

"I'm a schoolteacher. In a few years you'll be in the third grade and that's the grade I usually teach."

"I don't go to school here."

She didn't teach here, either, despite the efforts of the school board when she'd met with them. They'd offered her a job.

She'd agreed to consider it.

"What's your teacher's name?" she asked.

"Miss Henderson. She's pretty." Nathaniel lowered his cheek against Laurel's shoulder. "But not as pretty as my mom."

Laurel rubbed his back, rocking him slightly. Her eyes burned. She could remember being little and talking about how pretty her mother was.

\* \* \*

To Shane the nightmare seemed as if it would never end. And even when the ambulance had driven off to the hospital with the injured victim and there was nothing left but the road cleanup crew from Dewey—Lucius's neighboring town and even smaller than Lucius—Shane felt as though the nightmare still went on.

Laurel had been sitting on the ground in her front yard with the little kid clinging to her like a monkey for well over two hours. He could tell that she had the boy talking, that she was keeping him well distracted from the grim sight of his injured mother.

The woman would recover, but Palmer had told Shane that she had—at a minimum—broken both her legs and unquestionably had sustained a concussion.

He consciously relaxed his hands, which wanted to fist and pound the man who'd caused it all.

Good ol' Charlie Beckett.

Shane wanted the bum to rot in jail, but he knew he wouldn't. He'd get some time, all right, but nothing that would be punishment enough.

And what about *him?*

If he'd found some cause, some legality, he could have kept Charlie locked up and this nightmare would not be occurring. Instead, the last time he'd seen Charlie was when he'd hauled him home from the Tipped Barrel.

Charlie had probably not been sober since.

He swallowed down his anger, but he knew it was directed against himself as much as it was against Charlie.

"How're you doing, little man?" He hunkered down next to the pair. It was nearing dawn and the temperature had dropped. He hoped Denise made it soon. Her crisis center was in Billings, and it was the closest facility to house children displaced in situations like this.

"You're Sheriff Golightly," the boy enunciated carefully. "I wanna go see my mom."

He barely contained himself from brushing his hand over the kid's tousled head. Once again the sight of Laurel with a child was tugging hard at him.

"You can see her in the morning, after she's had some sleep. I promise." He knew the crisis center would take the boy to visit his mother daily while he was in their care. Which shouldn't be long, since Tony had told Shane the boy's dad was getting the earliest possible flight to Montana.

"Where do I gotta go?" Nathaniel's voice shot up to a squeak.

"Don't worry," Laurel murmured, pressing her cheek against his head. "You're going to stay somewhere very nice."

"In that house with you?" He pointed behind her.

"I wish you could," she said gently.

"I don't wanna go someplace else!" His face crumpled.

Laurel cuddled him. "He needs sleep," she told Shane over the boy's head.

Don't we all, he thought grimly.

He'd barely walked in his door after spending days chasing down old witnesses in the Runyan case when he'd heard the noise out on the road.

Headlights danced along the curve in the road followed shortly by the arrival of a tan sedan. "That'll be Denise Mason," he said. "She runs a crisis center in Billings."

Laurel's gaze slanted to the car that parked behind hers in the driveway.

He couldn't tell what she was thinking as she watched the woman approach. He straightened, feeling as if he'd lived about five years in the past few hours.

When he'd heard the crash up at his place, he'd somehow imagined Laurel in peril.

"Howdy, stranger." Denise walked up to him and kissed him smack on the lips. "We've *got* to stop meeting like this." Her voice was wry, and he had to give her credit for it.

Considering they'd once been engaged.

Laurel was watching them, her expression unreadable, and he felt his neck get hot.

Dammit. He was too old for this crap.

Denise was already moving past him to Nathaniel, her demeanor nothing but good cheer.

She was great with kids. Always had been. It was only in her own son that she'd refused to separate reality from love.

She stuck out her hand to Nathaniel. "I'm Denise. And you are Mr. Nathaniel Peters III, I hear."

His eyes widened.

"I talked to your daddy on the phone on my way here. He left a message for you. Want to hear it?"

He nodded and she pulled out her little cell phone, dialed a few numbers, then held it to the boy's ear. Whatever the dad's message said, it had Nathaniel both relaxing and getting teary again.

"But I don't wanna go somewhere else," he kept saying.

Shane wanted to look away but couldn't. Both Laurel and Denise knew that leaving the boy in Laurel's care might be the easiest thing at the moment, but it wasn't at all the legal thing.

With one hand he was clutching the ragged teddy bear that Laurel had produced and clutching Laurel with the other. Shane could see the distress in Laurel's eyes as she carefully separated herself from the boy.

Handing Nathaniel over to Denise was the right thing to do. Denise's center was one of the best in the state. Nathaniel's situation would be remedied within hours at most, just as soon as his dad could make it to town. His mother would recover from her injuries. The Peters family would be reunited.

Some families weren't.

The Runyans hadn't been.

Laurel had been barely eighteen when she'd been put into state care after Roger's arrest. Too old for a place like Denise's—had there even been such a facility in operation back then—and too young and emotionally devastated to be on her own.

It didn't take long for Denise to get what she'd come for—whether that was good or bad Shane couldn't quite decide given the wrenching separation between Nathaniel and the woman who'd given him comfort for a few hours—and he and Laurel silently watched the taillights of her car disappear around the bend.

He saw the surreptitious way she wiped her eyes and felt even worse.

"Sun'll be up soon," he said. "You ought to get back to bed." She was wearing her nightgown. It was tucked into a pair of jeans, true, but he could still recognize the thin white fabric for what it was.

She finally looked at him. "Your face is bleeding."

He touched his temple. Sure enough. Charlie's punch had drawn blood.

Too bad Shane didn't have leeway to punch Charlie.

"It's nothing."

Laurel got that prissy schoolteacher look of hers again and he was almost grateful for it, considering it was a damn sight easier for his conscience to take than that pinched look she'd had watching Nathaniel's departure.

She tsked. "You have a cut. It needs to be cleaned."

"I'll take care of it."

"When?"

"Later. Go inside. You should never have come out here in the first place."

She propped her hands on her hips. "I'm just supposed to *ignore* the fact that two cars collided practically on my front step? Why don't you just say what's been bothering you ever since I saw you at Stu's garage last week?"

"Nothing's bothering me," he said evenly. A monumental lie. "You want to try your hand with Stu, you're welcome to do so."

*"What?"*

"Just go back to bed, Laurel." He turned away and headed toward the gravel drive. He'd been so bloody panicked that, like some damned fool, he'd run the half mile down the hill rather than drive it.

Then, when he'd realized Laurel was completely safe, his anger had turned toward himself.

He'd known Charlie was a damn fool. A dangerous fool.

And look what happened.

"I'm tired of you ordering me around. And I'm not trying anything with Stu. For heaven's sake. He's your brother!"

That hadn't stopped Denise.

He kept walking.

"You need that cut on your head sewn up," she called after him. "Because I think your common sense is pouring out of it!"

He stopped. Wheeled around and returned to where she stood, nearly vibrating with emotion as she stared up at him. "My eyesight that day at the garage was just fine," he said tightly. "He was all over you."

"I hugged him. For the car. *You're* the one I was kissing. Just what kind of woman do you think I am?"

"You were ready to marry some other guy, what? A month ago?"

She flinched. "It doesn't mean I'm hopping from one bed to another. Martin and I never even—" She broke off. Waved her hand dismissively. "Oh, go away. Bleed all over yourself. Why should I care?"

"You and Martin never *what?*"

Her throat worked. Thin silvery light was beginning to fill the sky. "Never slept together," she finally said, her lips tight. "And I'm not remotely interested in your brother that way, either. Not that any of this is *any* of your business!"

"You were gonna marry Kellner yet you never slept with him?"

"*He* was a gentleman," she enunciated carefully.

"He was a damned fool," Shane countered bluntly.

Her lips parted. She turned on her heel and stomped across her yard, up the plywood ramp and slammed the door shut.

He stood there, considering the merits of going after her, and decided not to.

The mood he was in, God knows what he might do.

## Chapter Thirteen

Shane went up the drive and back inside his house. His cat, Speck, streaked around his legs the second he opened the door, bolting past him to disappear upstairs.

The beer he'd opened earlier was still waiting on the counter. He grabbed it. It no longer held any appeal. He tipped it down the sink and went upstairs.

A hasty shower did little to improve his mood, and he dragged on a pair of old sweats and went back to the kitchen. There were still a few hours before he had to be on duty, hours that he could spend trying to catch some Zs.

Instead, he reached for a fresh coffee filter and set the coffeemaker brewing.

The liquid was just beginning to stream into the pot when his door opened and Laurel stomped inside.

She made a face at him and stepped forward, dumping a large white first-aid kit that he immediately recognized on the counter. "I knew you weren't going to clean up that cut," she said.

"You took that out of my SUV." He still had the Runyan file in there.

"So?" She flipped open the kit. "Sit down and let me do this so I can get out of here."

"I can clean my own cut."

She cast him a pointed look. "Really." Her voice was arid. "And how many times have I said something to that effect that you've completely ignored?"

"And gotten pissed off whenever I did," he reminded. But he pulled out one of the iron bar stools and sat. "I thought you were pissed off at me *now*."

"I am. I need a clean cloth."

He pointed at a drawer. "I think there are towels in there."

"You *think?*" She tsked and pulled open the drawer. "Try again. Take-out menus for pizza and," she lifted one out, studying it more closely, "Chinese. Since when does Lucius have a Chinese food restaurant?"

"It went out of business a few months after it opened."

"Too bad. I like Chinese." She dropped it back in the drawer and opened the one next to it. "Struck oil." She pulled out a white dish towel and wet it under the faucet, then turned to him.

With him sitting on the bar stool, they were very nearly eye to eye. She seemed to hesitate for a moment, her gaze skimming over his bare chest.

Well, if she didn't like the fact that he was barely clothed, she shouldn't go around busting into his kitchen. He raised an eyebrow, daring some comment.

Her lips firmed. She briskly reached for his head with one hand, tilting it to suit her while she dabbed the wet cloth over his cut.

He jerked. "Ouch."

"Don't be a baby." She kept dabbing.

"You were way more gentle with Nathaniel."

"Nathaniel is a child. You're an extremely annoying… man." Her voice dropped a little. She turned away and rummaged in the first-aid kit. She pulled out a packet of antibiotic ointment and squeezed a dab over his cut.

"Dammit, woman, that stings!"

"Good." She slapped an adhesive bandage in place. "You want to tell me what's really eating you? Because I don't believe this is about me and Stu. What happened this week? Where have you been all this time?"

The rising sun sent golden fingers through the windows, and he could see straight through the folds of her thin nightgown. And he proved to himself just what a gentleman he wasn't when he didn't look away. "Nothing's eating me."

"Right." Her fingertip gentled as she ran it along the edges of the bandage near his eyebrow.

Charlie had rotten aim. He'd been going for Stu's nose.

"Every muscle in your body is clenched for a fight," she said. "So what is it? You might as well tell me. I'm not going anywhere until you do."

"When did you get to be so interfering?"

"I've been taking lessons from you." She stopped messing with his bandage and stepped back until she was leaning against the cupboards across from him. Out of the beams of sunlight. "Well?"

"I don't talk about the job."

"Well, how macho for you. But that at least tells me it *isn't* your ludicrous assumptions about Stu and me that has you so wound up."

He exhaled roughly. "It's not ludicrous. It's happened before. Stu. And a woman of mine."

Her lips parted. She blinked. "I'm not a woman of yours," she said faintly.

His jaw tightened. "Aren't you?"

She crossed her arms. "So, who was she?"

There was no point pretending he didn't know what she was talking about. "Denise."

"That woman from the crisis center? The one who kissed you?" Her mouth twisted over that last bit. "And here I thought she was just showing some odd professional behavior. Did you love her?" Her voice went thin.

"Loved her enough to think I wanted to marry her."

She paled a little. "Were you with her, then? In Billings?"

He rubbed his hand down his face. It would be easier to tell her he was than to tell her what he'd really been doing. "No."

She didn't look convinced.

"We were over a long time ago."

"Then what *were* you doing?"

Turning over stones from Billings to Orlando as he re-interviewed witnesses and finding nothing that could dispel Shane's belief where Roger was concerned. "Working," he said. "Didn't Beau tell you that when he came by to check on you?" His dad had agreed to go by every day.

She flushed. "Should have known those visits were *your* doing."

"I had little to do with it. Beau wants you to stay in Lucius. He wants you to direct his junior choir. Get active in his congregation. He's not likely to miss an opportunity to try to talk you into all that."

"Did you build this house with Denise in mind?" she asked doggedly.

"No. I started the house before we got serious."

"But then you broke up and you never furnished this place. Are you still in love with her?"

"Hell, no."

"Well, that was quick."

He wasn't so unaware of the female mind that he didn't realize he'd stepped right into a minefield. "She had a kid. Scott. Only seven but he was already a hoodlum. I knew it but she refused to see it. Despite her line of work, she couldn't deal with it when it was her own boy. The kid was heading down really nasty paths, but all she believed was that I wanted to drag my job into every aspect of our lives. No matter how many times I tried to get Scott involved in better activities, even counseling at one point, she thought I was overreacting because of *my* career. She turned to Stu, thinking he might be different, I suppose. He was, but he was no more into marriage than he was into taking tap-dance lessons. So she ended up getting hurt double measure."

"Well." Laurel crossed her arms again, effectively hiding the shapes and shadows that so tantalized him. "What happened with her son?"

"He's serving two years in juvenile detention for robbery."

Her lashes drooped. "Then I'm sorry for Denise. But she didn't look like she's letting that keep her from moving on in her life. The rock I noticed on her ring finger was at least several carats. I ought to know." She lifted her fingers, wriggling them. "I gave up one that was remarkably similar."

He frowned at the reminder that she'd come so close to marrying someone.

Someone *else*.

"You've been eating better," he said abruptly. She was still slender as a reed, but there was definitely more curve in her arms. And he could see, plain as the increasing daylight, that there was nothing wrong with the rest of her. He wondered if her nipples were still the color of new straw-berries. He couldn't tell, despite the near transparency of her gown.

"Is that supposed to be some polite way of telling me I'm gaining weight?"

"You're just looking…better." He was a dog. Pure and simple.

She frowned severely. "Fine. Thank you. Now stop side-tracking the issue. Or do you just generally behave like a missile ready to blow whenever a car accident occurs in your town?"

"Drunk drivers piss me off." He grabbed two mis-matched mugs from the mug tree on the counter—a gift from Hadley somewhere along the way—and splashed coffee into them. "Here."

She was watching him, her eyes the color of soft, melt-ing caramel.

He didn't want her soft gazes just then.

He wanted *her.*

He wanted to bury himself in her and shut off his mind to the crap in the world that he wasn't able to change no matter how much he wanted to. He couldn't stop all the drunks. He couldn't stop all the abusers.

He couldn't stop wanting Laurel.

"Talking *can* help."

"No. Talking *won't* help. Not this time. That woman is still going to be in the hospital for a good long while. That little kid is never going to be able to forget what happened to him tonight."

"But they *will* be fine, Shane. And none of it is your fault." Her fingers drifted over his forearm. Settled atop his hand fisted against the granite counter. "*You* weren't the drunk behind the wheel."

"No. I'm the guy who's supposed to make sure that drunk doesn't get behind a wheel."

She turned toward him. Her breast pressed softly against his arm. "And how are you supposed to do that? Are you the watchdog for the entire population? You're only one man, Shane. A…good man. But you can't—"

"This one I should have. Because it was Evie's scum of an ex-husband who was driving. I *know* he's a drunk, he's always been a drunk and doesn't have the spine of a flea to ever stop being a drunk. I knew what he was capable of and I should have prevented it. The guy should've been in jail."

"For what? Had he done something illegal? Last I knew being an alcoholic was a disease, not a legal offense."

"I knew what he was capable of," he repeated flatly.

"Which still doesn't make it your responsibility." She chafed her palm over his fist. "My mother drank. She hid it well, but she had a problem. I knew it when I was barely a teenager. It didn't mean it was my responsibility to keep her from…doing the things she did."

It was the first he'd ever heard of Violet being a drinker and it distracted him enough that he shoved Charlie to the corner of his mind. "What things?"

She just shook her head, her hair brushing his shoulder. "The point is that doing your *job* is surely as much about not abusing your authority as it is about exercising it." She settled her other hand on his back, sliding it down his spine. "Am I right?"

Whether she was or not was moot, because she might as well have set a match to a powder keg with the way her hand was stroking his back. "Why didn't you sleep with him? The ex-fiancé."

Her hand paused. Just sat there, burning a hole into him from the outside in. "We were talking about you."

He flipped his fist over, closing his fingers around her wrist as he turned toward her, pulling her against him.

Her eyes widened.

Some things just couldn't be hidden by a ten-year-old pair of sweatpants.

"Topic's changed. If you want to leave, now's the time, Laurel."

She drew in a quick breath. Her breasts lifted against him. "I…don't."

"Don't what?" He closed his hands over her shoulders, pushing her back until they no longer touched. It was like tearing out his own tongue. "Don't touch you? Don't want you?"

"I don't want to leave." Her admission was little more than a sigh.

It was enough.

He pulled her back to him, lowering his mouth, finding hers. "I'm not gonna stop," he breathed into her. "And I don't have patience."

Her hands caught his neck. Her fingers dragged through his hair. "And I *don't* need coddling." She arched against him, the low sound rising in her throat more intoxicating than any amount of liquor.

He slid his hands down her back, hesitated on the taut curve of her rear, pulling her harder against him.

She hissed in a breath. Her hands slid down his spine again, and along the edge of his sweats, maddening him.

He lifted her against him, his hands sliding under her thighs, turning and settling her on the counter. Sunlight angled over her, glinting gold on her skin. "Unbutton your nightgown." If he tried, he'd tear it.

Her throat worked. Her hands trembled. She slowly reached up to the modest neckline of the lightweight gown. She undid the first little round button. Then the next.

He could see her heartbeat pulsing against her throat.

There was a soft thud.

She'd toed off her tennis shoes.

Another button came free. Then the fourth.

The fifth.

The gown hung open down to where it was captured by the waist of her jeans.

He drew his finger from that beating pulse at the base of her neck down the narrow strip of bare flesh.

Against his shoulders, her fingers flexed. Kneaded.

He flipped the button on her jeans loose. Her eyes closed.

"Look at me," he murmured. "I want you to see me."

She moistened her lips again. Her hands tightened. Flexed again. Her knees hugged his hips. "I always see you," she whispered, but her lashes rose heavily. She shuddered when he slid down her zipper.

"Lift up."

She lifted and he pulled the jeans free. The tangled hem of her nightgown dragged along, falling over her thighs as he slipped them down her legs and tossed them aside.

The sleek curves of her legs beckoned. He pressed his mouth to them. Each one.

She shifted. Her toes curled. "Shane." Her voice held a new edge.

Her shin was warm. Smooth. Her knee was ticklish. Her thigh was velvet.

She leaned over him, dragging his head up to hers, covering his mouth, nipping at his lip.

He straightened, his hands sliding along her thighs, finding nothing but more velvety smooth skin along the way. His heart charged in his chest like a freight train. The need to plunder, to conquer was a live thing inside him.

He pulled her nightgown off her shoulders. It pooled, a drift of gossamer clouds around her hips on the smooth black-and-brown mottled granite.

Her breasts were fuller than his dreams remembered. Her tight nipples still the color of new strawberries.

And he was a starving man.

He leaned down, capturing one crest with his lips, the other with his fingers.

She jerked. Cried out softly. Arched into him as if she, too, were starving. "Shane."

He dragged his mouth up to hers, tongue against tongue. She writhed, her feet twining behind his thighs. Her fingertips dug into his back.

Cursing inside his head at his own raging impatience, his hand dragged over her breast, flattened against the jumping muscles in her smooth abdomen and slid down, finding the heart of her, heat and moisture unhidden despite the soft gauzy gown still draping her.

Her head fell back, breaking his kiss. Her breath was a whistling sob that drove his touch. She was shaking like a wild thing. He was no better. He closed his hand around her nape, pulling her against him, pulling her closer, chest to breast. He slowly dragged the nightgown aside.

She pressed her open mouth against his neck, muffling the cry she gave when his fingers met her. Parted her. Became part of her. Her legs tightened around him as she convulsed, nearly blinding him so great was his pleasure in hers.

Laurel sobbed against Shane, her lungs starved for breath, her body starved for more. So much more. She pushed at the gray sweatpants that barely hung on his hips until he finally just yanked them off with one hand. He was glad for the first-aid kit, then, as he dumped it with his other hand and found the condoms he'd added to the contents years ago when he'd learned being sheriff sometimes meant explaining the facts of life to overheated teenaged boys.

He was beyond overheating as he reached for Laurel again and pulled her forward off the counter. A low, feral growl escaped him as he sank inside her.

She winced, tightening her arms urgently around him.

But he'd stilled. "Did I hurt you?"

She shook her head, blindly pressing her mouth against the hard sinew of his neck. Her breasts tingled from the dark swirl of chest hair abrading them. "Don't...stop."

He lifted her against him, hard and full, so full, inside her. "You give me more credit than I deserve," he muttered, pressing her back against something—the refrigerator? "if you think I could." His arm held her weight as he thrust heavily into her.

She gasped, every nerve inside her tightening.

Something rattled softly. Glassware. Someone was moaning Shane's name, again and again. She knew it was her but couldn't summon the control to stop.

And maybe it didn't matter. He surged harder. Suddenly stretching his arm alongside her head, his palm slamming flat against the surface of the refrigerator. His arm tightened behind her back, an iron band. "Song...bird." He groaned sharply, and she cried out, her nerves spinning free as he jetted hotly inside her.

His breath was as ragged as hers was when her senses slowly returned. "I think...I've gotta...sit," he muttered.

She didn't have a solid bone or functioning muscle left in her body so she just hung on, resting her head on his shoulder because she didn't have the strength to lift it when he turned and slid his back down the wall.

She could still feel him pulsing inside her, and the pleasure of it caused ripples to work through her.

He stretched his arms along her back, looping his hands over her shoulders. She managed to peel open her eyelids enough to see his face.

His eyes were closed, his mobile mouth relaxed.

She shifted, bending her knees a little more comfortably, and inhaled sharply as her inner muscles flexed around him.

"Don't do that again," he warned. "We might end up killing each other." His hands slid down her back. Curved around her hips. Slid between them to cover her breasts, not caressing, but holding. "Perfect way to go, though."

She was draped over him like a blanket. Yet moving took too much energy and reminded her just how long it had been since she'd been with him.

He seemed none too anxious to move, either.

"Guess if I were a gentleman, I'd apologize for not making it to a bed at least," he said eventually.

"Guess if I'd wanted a gentleman, I wouldn't have bugged out on my own wedding to one."

"Mmm."

His hair had grown since she'd arrived in Lucius. It was starting to wave behind his ears. She stared at the heavy gold strands. "Did Stu really have an affair with your fiancée?"

His chest rose and fell. "Not until after she'd tossed my ring in my face."

Denise was probably the biggest fool on the planet despite the competent manner she'd displayed with Nathaniel. "Stu's just a friend to me, you know."

His thumbs dragged over her nipples. "He'd better be."

She sat up, wincing a little as unfamiliar muscles were tested. "Do you believe me?"

His eyes were slits of silver between his lashes. "I don't think you have what it takes to lie when you're naked like this." The crease in his cheek deepened. He slowly pressed his thumbs against her nipples, and they obediently rose, pressing back. "You're sore, aren't you. Every time I breathe, you wince a little."

Heat rose under her skin. "So?"

"You weren't with the gentleman. When was the last time you *were* with someone?"

She huffed out a breath. "When was the last time *you* were?"

He didn't even hesitate. "Earlier this year. Saw a woman who was working for the guy Hadley married. A private investigator. Her name was Mandy."

"Sounds…exciting." She was making every effort at seeming nonchalant and failing miserably. Mandy probably was six feet tall with legs to match.

"Mutually satisfying for a few weeks," he drawled.

Her lips twisted. "Bully for you."

His fingers gently toyed with her breasts. "Jealous?"

She lifted her head enough to give him a look. "Not in the least."

"I am," he said quietly. "Jealous of any man who's had your attention. Particularly *this* kind of attention."

She swallowed. "Then you'd only be jealous of yourself," she admitted after a long moment.

## *Chapter Fourteen*

He stared at her, not saying a single, solitary word.

"Well." Laurel could feel herself flushing again. "I guess I know what it takes to make *you* speechless."

His hands left her breasts. They settled on her waist. "You haven't been with anyone since me."

"I believe that's what I just said." Embarrassed, she turned her head, looking away from him.

"Oh no, songbird." He caught her chin in his hand and dragged it back around. "Why not?"

She wished the ground would swallow her whole. She wished she'd never admitted it. She wished that she weren't naked as the day she'd been born and still fused together with him, so she could escape. "Well, how many men should I have been with? What would be the normal number so you wouldn't look at me like I'm some sort of… of…feeble oddity?"

His lips tightened. He thumped his head once against the wall behind him. "None. Hell, Laurel, you think there's not some Neanderthal inside me who's pounding his chest right now? I just admitted that I didn't like thinking of you with anyone else. But I figured I'd have to get over it, because it was your life. Your business. Your right. And, geez. I took you against a bloody refrigerator." His voice was gruff.

Her heart clutched. She laid her hand on his chest, loving the prickle of hair against her palm, the deep, steady thump of his heart. "You probably ought to check that we didn't knock over the milk bottle inside."

His brows drew together. Then he gave a bark of laughter. He got to his feet, lifting her off him. "Come on. Upstairs."

The sun was fully risen now. There were no shadows remaining to hide within. And even though she tried not to stare, he was fully, gloriously nude.

"Don't, um, don't you need to go on duty soon?" She knew how early he went because she'd watched him drive to town almost daily.

"Yeah. But we've got time." He lifted her hand and pressed his lips to her knuckles as he headed toward the staircase, seemingly unconcerned that they'd left their only pieces of clothing behind in the kitchen.

"Time for what?" She padded up the stairs when he urged her to go before him.

"You'll see."

She bit back a huff of laughter. "If it's your etchings, I think I saw them downstairs already."

On the landing, he turned her toward the room at the end of the hall. "Better." He walked her through the open doorway. But they passed the ocean-wide bed, covered in a dark-brown comforter. "This," he said, nudging her through the adjoining doorway and waving his hand at the enormous oval tub. "It has whirlpool jets."

He let go of her and crossed the spacious bathroom, flipping on the faucets, located at each end of the tub. "Make yourself comfortable. I'll be back in a few." He brushed his lips over her forehead, closing the door behind him.

She stared at herself in the mirror.

Her lips were red and puffy. There was the distinct shape of a hand on her arm, the tender scrape of razor burn on her breast. And her eyes were practically glowing.

She looked, she imagined, like a woman who had been very well loved.

She pressed her palm to her chest where her heart seemed to lurch inside.

Making love did not mean being in love, she reminded herself. That was a lesson learned twelve years ago.

Unfortunately, when Shane returned a short while later carrying two mugs of fresh coffee, which he set on the side of the tub before sliding into the swirling water behind her, that reminder seemed woefully inadequate.

"Now," he murmured, kissing the tip of her shoulder as he scooped her back against him, "just relax. Have some coffee."

She could feel him, very much unrelaxed, against her. And she felt a smile on her face that she couldn't seem to remove. She caught his wrist, pulled his palm to her mouth and kissed it, then slowly drew it beneath the bubbling, churning surface of the warm water and pressed it to her breast.

She tilted her head back, looking up at him. "I'd rather see some more etchings."

His palm tightened on her. "Trust me, songbird. There'll be plenty of time for that. You're gonna want to wait a while longer—"

She reached behind her, closing her hand boldly around

him. "Trust me, Sheriff," she murmured. "I know my own mind, here."

He groaned a little, grabbing her hand, stilling it. "I see. Well, if you put it that way." He tilted her sideways and found her mouth with his. His hand stole along her thigh.

The coffee, when they finally remembered it, was stone cold.

For the first time in Shane's career, he called Carla and told her he wouldn't be in that day unless something urgent arose. She'd been full of questions, particularly since she knew some of what he'd been up to while he'd been gone. Questions that he'd ignored, but he knew the second he hung up that she'd be back on the horn looking for details of why.

Laurel was sprawled facedown across his mattress, the sheet gathered around her hips. She had one leg stuck out, and her hair was a tangle around her shoulders.

She was the only woman he'd ever had in his bed here in this house.

He stood in the window that overlooked Laurel's house down the hill.

Laurel's house. When had he begun thinking of it as hers, and not her old man's?

She'd finished painting the trim while he'd been gone and had, indeed, chosen a deep mossy green. Shane was honest enough to admit the house looked far better than he'd expected. But what was wrong with it went beyond a few coats of paint. It needed major renovations—not just a working furnace and fresh plaster—if it were going to be truly livable.

"You're looking very serious standing there." Her voice was thick with sleep.

He looked over his shoulder. She'd turned on her side, dragging the sheet up over her breasts.

He figured he was a pretty pathetic case when he envied the sheet.

"You did a nice job painting the house."

She bent her elbow and propped her head on her hand. "But?" She waited.

"That's all. Paint looks good."

Her lips curved softly. "Well, you did a good portion of it."

"How'd the school board meeting go?"

"Fine."

"They offer you a job?"

She nodded and shifted again, folding the edge of the sheet neatly against her.

"And?"

"And I'm thinking about it." Her lashes swept down. "You know, I think I'm starving."

He knew he was, and not just for some lunch. But it bugged the hell out of him that she refused to commit to staying in Lucius.

"I've got bread and peanut butter and not much else."

"And you lecture me on not eating well enough," she said lightly. Her pink cheeks belied her nonchalance as she threw back the sheet and walked into the adjoining bath, coming out a moment later wrapped in the robe Evie had given him last Christmas.

Beyond hanging it on the hook in the bathroom, he couldn't recall ever actually using it. On Laurel, though, the deep blue terry cloth looked pretty swell, since it was several sizes too large and the lapels kept parting no matter how tightly she tied the belt.

"We could go to the Luscious." It would seriously set tongues wagging when they showed up there together, what with him essentially taking the day off.

"Maybe I want to cook. I can, you know. I *am* capable." Her dimple flashed as she sauntered out of the room. "I can spread peanut butter with the best of 'em."

He heard the pad of her footsteps as she skipped down the stairs. His gaze slanted back to the window.

"Shane," her voice floated back to him. "You have beer and apples and that's it!"

"You're the brilliant chef," he called back.

Her laughter lilted up to him.

He found himself smiling.

*She* was what his house had been missing.

He slid into a pair of jeans and went down to join her, only to find her heading out the door, Speck twining around her ankles as if he wanted her to stay.

Shane eyed the cat. Who knew where he'd been hiding inside the house. "Where you going?"

"To get some food from *my* refrigerator."

"In that robe?"

"Nobody's going to see. I'll just run down and be right back." She suddenly came back in, almost tripped on the cat as she reached for the first-aid box still sitting on the counter. She'd obviously replaced the contents he'd scattered. "Silly kitty." She leaned down and scratched Speck's head. "Never would have figured you for a cat lover." Her gaze slid up to him.

Shane shrugged, deciding he enjoyed the sight of her, wearing nothing but her tennis shoes and his robe, petting the cat that had sort of claimed him. "He only comes around when he's hungry. Doesn't have much to do with me."

She straightened, tucking the kit under her arm. "Yeah, tough guy. You're the one feeding him. I'll be right back." She slipped out the door.

He pulled open the refrigerator door.

Sure enough. A few bottles of beer and a bowl of apples, and even they looked a little questionable. He didn't even have any leftovers from Evie's Sunday dinners. And the milk—

"Whoa." He held it away from his nose, hurriedly pouring it down the sink along with a strong stream of water. He shoved the carton in the trash, which was full of about a month's worth of used coffee filters and grounds and not much else. He quickly pulled out the bag and replaced it with a new one. Laurel already thought he was nuts for having practically no furniture. He didn't need her thinking he was a complete slob.

He took the bag out to the can behind the house and dumped it in, then rounded the side. Laurel stood next to his SUV, leaning in the opened passenger side.

"The first-aid kit doesn't always want to fit under the seat," he said, stepping up behind her. "Let's go to the Luscious. You can show off in the kitchen later." He didn't care *what* sort of gossip that inspired. The townspeople could get used to seeing the two of them together just as Laurel could get used to the idea of the two of them. Together.

Laurel stiffened when Shane slipped his arm around her waist. "The kit fit fine once I pulled this out of the way," she said, pushing at his arm and turning to face him. She held up a thick file, clearly labeled Runyan. "This was under your seat." She hadn't noticed it at all when she'd pulled the kit out in the first place. "What were you doing with this file?"

His lips tightened. "It's property of the Sheriff's Department. I'm the sheriff."

There was a dark pain swirling inside her. "It's my father's case. Old news. Why have it now?"

His hand closed over the top of the opened door. "I've been reviewing it."

"Since when?"

He hesitated.

"Since *when?*"

"Since we got back from Spokane."

Her stomach clenched. "Afraid I might follow after their footsteps?"

"Dammit, no. I wanted to see if I'd have done the same thing Wicks did. I wanted to make sure there hadn't been a mistake."

She looked down at the cover of the heavy-duty folder. "A mistake in dismissing the charges against my father."

"A mistake in making them in the first place," he corrected tightly.

"And?" She could barely force out the word for the hope suddenly congesting her system.

He looked pained. "The evidence was there. The charges were solid. Wicks was right when he made them, and wrong when he dismissed them."

How could she have forgotten how quickly hope could be dashed? She ought to have learned it when she was eighteen. "Is…is my statement in here?"

"Yes."

She felt ill. "What did I say?"

He slowly took the file from her. Flipped it open. Paged through several sheets, then pulled out a typed report and handed it to her.

The file was at least two inches thick, yet he'd found the page unerringly. He was obviously very familiar with the contents.

She took the sheet. The contents were painfully brief. "I didn't see her fall," she read. "That's all I said?" She hadn't defended her father, hadn't done anything but state that she hadn't seen the fall.

"Repeatedly." Shane took the sheet from her slack fingers and returned it to the file. "I'm sorry."

She looked past him, seeing nothing at all. "No wonder he didn't want me around. What good was I?"

"Don't." His hands closed around her face. "Don't waste your thoughts anymore on it, Laurel. The guy doesn't deserve it!"

"He deserved more from me than he got! I don't care what all that says," she flicked her hand against the file. "I know he wasn't capable of hurting her! It was an *accident*." It had to be.

"You know it because you want to believe it. That's your heart talking, not your head."

"Fine. I know in my heart that he didn't hurt my mother. Ever. Why can't you believe *me?*"

"Laurel, there's no point in getting into this."

"I think there is *every* point!"

He leaned past her, tossing the file on the seat. "You were the one who said it. *Don't hit me.*"

She frowned at him. "I never said that."

"Ask Palmer Frame. He heard it, too. You were just starting to come around in the ambulance the afternoon you passed out."

She hugged her arms close. The day was already warm. Why was she shivering? "And you always take seriously the ramblings of an unconscious person?"

"I always take *you* seriously. I always did. That's why you scared the hell out of me when you were only eighteen!"

Her eyes burned. "My father *never* hit me. He never hit anyone."

"Honey, it's his shame. Not yours."

"It's *not* his! It was my mother's." Her voice shook. "It was my mother who hit me. Never my dad."

He closed his hands over her shoulders, muttering an oath, but she shook him off. "And she only hit me once. She was drunk." Her chest ached. "She cried for the rest of the day afterward."

"Come inside."

"Why?" Her heart was pounding. Her head felt dizzy. She wanted to scream, to run away, just run away from the unreasonable panic swelling inside her. Go. Go. "Oh, God, not now." She leaned forward, gasping for breath and not finding it. Relax. Relax. She clenched her fist. Released it.

It wasn't working. She still couldn't breathe.

"Laurel." Shane hauled her up, lifted her onto the seat. He caught her face between his hands. "Look at me."

She wanted to still the shaking. His eyes, God, she'd always disappeared in his eyes. "You won't…believe…me," she gasped. "I'm…not…crazy."

He caught her hands, his gaze boring into hers. "Shh. Take a breath. Inhale. That's it. Squeeze my hands. Good. Let go. Exhale. That's it. We'll do it again. Together. Slower. Yeah."

His voice mesmerized her. The urge to flee began to fade. She could feel the edge of the file under her thigh. The sun shining warm and bright on them.

Tears burned from the corners of her eyes. Her panic dwindled, shrank, leaving exhaustion in its place. "He didn't do it, Shane."

"Shh." He pressed the backs of her hands against his lips. The concern in his eyes was clear. "We don't have to talk about it."

But she was afraid that they did. She pulled her hands free and tugged the file out from beneath her. She set it on her thighs. Her fingertips dragged over the edges of the papers inside.

"The first time I saw her hit him was after Gram died."

"*What?*"

She felt sick. "They were arguing. As usual. I don't know about what. And my mother hit my dad. Hard enough to knock off his eyeglasses. I, um, I ran into the room—their bedroom—and picked them off the floor. They were broken." Her voice lowered. "Dad grounded me for the weekend. As if I were the one who'd done something wrong." She plucked at the file folder. She'd faced the truth with the help of a *lot* of therapy from a number of therapists. But that didn't make it easy to discuss now. "My father wasn't the abuser, Shane. He was the *abused*."

Shane looked poleaxed. "There was no record of it, Laurel. No hospital reports of *his* injuries, but two of your mother's. A broken wrist. A laceration that required stitches."

"He didn't want anyone to know," she whispered. "Even me. But you can't hide everything from your own family in your own home. He always excused it. Blamed it on her drinking…and that was true. When she was sober, she was fine."

"Why didn't you *say* something? Tell someone?"

"They were my parents." She pressed her palms flat on the file folder. "I don't care what these papers say, Shane, other than that they *didn't* say enough to keep the charges against my father in place. He did not hurt her."

"Laurel." His voice was cautious again. That awful, horrible cautious that she hated. "All you've admitted only tells me he had a motive. If Wicks had known the truth, the charges could well have been lessened. Roger could have pled out. Instead, he was left to live with the fact that murder charges could have been brought against him at any time if new evidence ever came to light."

"Evidence like me remembering what I saw that day?"

Her throat felt raw. "Maybe Sheriff Wicks knew the truth but didn't care. Maybe he *wanted* my father to never have any sort of closure. Of resolution. Who *knows* what Wicks wanted?"

"He damn sure didn't want to lose his career," Shane said quietly. "He's living in Orlando now, working as a rent-a-cop. Believe me, if he could have done things differently, he would have."

"How do you know what he's doing now?"

His lips thinned. "Because I just spent the last week tracking him—and everyone else related to the case—down."

She blinked, slowly absorbing the shock of that. "Why didn't you tell me?"

He sighed. "What good would it have done? You don't want the truth. You want your faith in your father upheld no matter what the facts state."

She winced, feeling like she'd been kicked in the stomach. She wiped her cheeks. "Maybe the truth would justify my faith," she countered rawly. "I can't do this."

"Do what?"

"Be with you." And it was different than when she'd called off the wedding to Martin.

*This* felt as if she were ripping out her soul.

"Why? Do you think I'm going to pull the same stupid stunt? We're not kids anymore, Laurel. I'm not going to walk away from you again."

"Why?"

"Because I want you with me, dammit!"

She sucked in a hard breath.

"That house," he waved his hand behind him, gesturing at his home, "has been waiting for something for years. *You.* And now that you're here, do you think I'm going to just let *you* walk away?"

"You think I need...protecting. How can you want me with you when you don't believe in me? Not even enough to tell me the truth of what you've been doing this past week? If I hadn't found the file, would you have said a word about any of this?"

His expression tightened. "Probably not," he allowed. "But I don't think it's me believing in you that's the problem, Laurel. I *do* believe in you. Whether or not I agree with your opinion of what happened does not change that. I think you're the one who's busy doubting herself. That's why you're so damn quick to accuse me of it."

She stared. "You're wrong."

"Am I? You have a job offer from the school district you won't commit to. You have a friend in my sister, but only if she initiates it. You *know* you miss singing in church but won't go a step past what you did for the festival in Spokane. What are you waiting for, Laurel? You said you'd quit your job in Colorado. But you won't make a decision about staying here. Do you want to make a life for yourself, or do you just want to play at it wherever you are, never making a commitment at all because your brain just wants to protect you from the real memories of the night your mother died!"

She slid off the seat, pushing past him. "I should have just lied. Told you that I *saw* her fall. That my father was nowhere near her."

"I told you, Laurel. You couldn't lie then, and you can't lie now. Stop putting the past between you and the rest of your life."

His image wavered from the tears blinding her. "Stop *telling* me what to do. What to think. To believe."

"God Almighty." His voice rose. "I'm not trying to! I just want you to see that it doesn't have to matter. We don't agree on what happened. It doesn't have to come between us."

She shook her head. "It's been between us since the day I returned to Lucius," she said thickly.

Then, before she broke down completely, she turned and walked back down the hill, feeling as if she were leaving bits of herself behind with every step she took.

## Chapter Fifteen

Dear Gram,

Shane leaves for seminary in two weeks. I can't stand the thought of him going. I love him, Gram. So much. He's so funny and handsome. He treats me like a grown-up, too. He actually believes that I really *could* be a singer. For real. I sure dream about it a lot. (When I'm not dreaming about him, that is.) He promised to meet me after he's done with Sunday dinner with his family. I baked him an apple pie, just the way you taught me. He said we'd go somewhere and have dessert. I'm just gonna tell you, 'cause Jenny would blab to the whole town if I told her. But I'm gonna be with Shane this afternoon. With him. He doesn't know it, yet, but I just can't bear for him to leave and not…well. You know. I hope you're not ashamed of me, Gram. I need to get to church early this morning. I'm singing "How Great Thou Art." I know that was your favorite hymn. I'll sing it for you, Gram, and maybe if you are ashamed of me, you'll forgive me just a little. I love you.

"Mind if I come in?"

Laurel jerked, her heart leaping at the voice, only to settle just as quickly around her toes when she recognized the voice on the other side of the screen door as Beau Golightly's.

She shoved the journal behind the cardboard box that was half-filled with knickknacks and went to the door. "Of course I don't mind." She pushed it open, stepping back for him to enter.

His eyes, so like his son's, took in the collection of boxes sitting haphazardly on top of the furniture. "Looks like you're moving," he murmured.

She couldn't even make *that* decision. "Just boxing up stuff for donations. There's a truck coming on Monday."

"Always nice to contribute to a good cause." He settled on the arm of the couch. "Weren't you supposed to be helping Evie over at the picnic this afternoon?"

She wouldn't have thought she could feel any lower, but she did. "I…didn't want to run into Shane," she admitted, feeling raw.

For the past two days she'd been feeling raw. Wincing with every sound outside her house, expecting him to be there. Not sure if she felt better or worse that he never was.

"Having a disagreement?"

She twisted newspaper around the base of a lamp. If she hadn't started reading her old journals again, she'd have been done with the packing-up chore. "He didn't tell you?"

"Shane stopped confiding in me years ago," Beau told her gently.

She pushed the lamp base into a box that she'd have no hope of sealing with packing tape the way she'd done the others. "Do you believe what everyone thought?" Her voice was abrupt. "About my father?"

Beau took his time framing his answer. "I believe he was a very private man and he loved you."

She'd boxed up the contents of her father's bedroom first. Only the photographs had been left untouched. "That's not an answer."

Beau stood. He cupped her shoulder, squeezing gently. "It's not what everyone else thinks that matters, child. It's what you believe."

Believe. She picked up the tape gun, even though there was nothing for her to tape. "Shane doesn't believe me. He thinks it's just…wishful thinking on my part that my mother's death was an accident."

Beau let out a sigh. He looked at the staircase. "It was an accident, Laurel. A tragic accident."

She felt something inside her loosen. As if she'd been waiting a lifetime for someone to just say the words she knew in her heart had to be true. "Then my father did talk to you about it."

"No." He squeezed her shoulder again. "Let it go, Laurel. Your father—right or wrong—thought your absence from Lucius would ensure that you could let the past go."

"He was wrong," Laurel whispered. "Because I can't seem to let anything go."

"Ah." He smiled wryly. "You must know my take on that."

She shook her head.

"Get yourself back in my church on Sundays and maybe you'll remember," he chided. "I believe the biggest messes we make in our lives are when we think *we're* the ones in control."

She managed a smile.

"You and Shane will find your way if you both want it badly enough," he predicted. "In the meantime, you and I are probably the only residents of Lucius *not* at the picnic. Your grandmother would be appalled at us both. She was on the town council back when they started having a town picnic, you know."

Laurel shook her head. She hadn't known, and she wasn't entirely certain that Beau—reverend or not—wasn't padding the facts a little. "I'm not dressed for it."

"Then go throw on a pretty dress. I'll wait. The Golightlys are known far and wide for their patience." He slipped the tape gun out of her hands, pulling loose the tape where she'd nervously stuck it over her palm. "Go on. You know you want to."

She wasn't sure of any such thing.

But she went.

Mindful of the increasingly late hour, she dashed a brush through her hair, splashed water on her face and pulled on the first thing her hands came to. If Beau's approving expression was anything to go by when she returned downstairs, she supposed the red sundress suited the patriotic theme of the day.

He ushered her out to his waiting vehicle, and they headed into town.

When she'd been little, the Independence Day festivities had been held on the fields that the junior high shared with the high school.

Now there was a lovely town park where it could be held. Beau parked as close as he could get, and they walked the rest of the way, passing carnival-type rides and games of every sort before they reached the collection of food booths serving up everything from watermelon slices to fried wontons.

"I knew you'd make it," Evie said when she spotted Laurel. "Here." She pushed an apron at her. "You're not going to want to get chili spattered on your clothes."

Laurel took the apron and slipped it over her head, tying it behind her. "I'm sorry I'm late." Late? If it weren't for Beau, she'd have been a complete no-show.

Shame weighted her down.

"Forget about it. You're here now."

Evie was a whirlwind. Filling empty containers of pastries to display, greeting people as they went by. It was hard not to be swept along in her energy.

"Stu was looking for you earlier," Evie said when she had a chance. "Wants to show you off around Freddie, I imagine."

Laurel waited until her chili customer walked away from the booth. "There's nothing between us."

"Oh, sugar, I know. Here. Toss that in the trash barrel behind you, would you please?" She handed Laurel an enormous empty foil pan.

Laurel stuffed it in the barrel.

"Heads up," Evie said in a low voice before she turned around. "Lawman at eleven o'clock, heading this way."

Her mouth dried.

"Oh, geez. Don't look like that." Evie smiled, talking between her teeth. "His ego is healthy enough as it is. Hey, there, Shane," she turned, greeting her brother. "I have a peach cobbler with your name on it."

"Maybe later. Hello, Laurel."

She dared a glance at him. Nearly did a double take. She'd never seen him before in an actual uniform. Sharply pressed khaki from head to toe, badge on his chest catching the dwindling rays of sunshine.

He was impressive. "Hello."

He didn't waste any time over *her* appearance, though.

"Keep an eye out for Billie Whittaker, would you?" He asked Evie. "Heard he's been visiting the keg a lot at the Tipped Barrel's booth. He'll be looking for trouble same as every year, no doubt."

"Tony already said to keep a look out."

He didn't give Laurel so much as another glance as he turned and strode away.

"Take a breath," Evie advised dryly.

"I've never seen him in uniform."

"He wears the khaki-badge-deal to things like this. Most people around Lucius know him no matter what he wears, but we get tourists for events who sometimes need to see the whole package. Reminds them to mind their manners while in our fair town." She made a face as she discarded yet another empty container. "Of course, then there's my former spouse who doesn't know how to behave properly in *any* town." She straightened again. "He's lucky he didn't kill someone that night."

"On the way here, your dad told me that Mrs. Peters was transported to a hospital back in Helena where they live. And Nathaniel is back home, too. He spent only a few hours at the crisis center."

"All's well that ends well, I suppose." Evie shook her head. "I don't know what's happened with Charlie. He never used to be so reckless."

"Alcohol can change a person," Laurel murmured.

Stu was approaching and his attention noticeably dragged on Freddie Finn and her date where they sat together at a round, plastic table covered with a red, white and blue cloth. Freddie looked glorious in scarlet shorts and a matching halter top, and the man with her was clearly appreciative of the fact since he could hardly keep his eyes off her. "I suppose you knew Denise," Laurel asked suddenly.

"Oh, sure. But you don't have to worry about her. She and Shane were over a long time ago."

"And Stu?"

Evie's eyebrow lifted. "You heard that bit, too?" She finally paused, resting her hands atop the wooden plank that served as a countertop for the booth. "Denise is a smart cookie, but she had a seriously blind eye when it came to her son. That whole thing was constantly between her and Shane. Unfortunate. Shane could have helped Scott if Denise hadn't been so stubborn. I don't know if she turned to Stu with the idea that Shane wouldn't want to lose her to his own brother or not, but regardless, she managed to completely ruin things for good with Shane, and made Stu even more distrustful of women."

She knew she ought to correct Evie's impression that Laurel was in any position *to* worry about Shane's past love. And she wasn't blind to the fact that, essentially, she was doing a similar thing by pitting her belief in her father against Shane's belief in the so-called facts.

Evie dished up a bowl of chili and exchanged it for a handful of change from a customer. "It wouldn't have worked between them even had it not been for her son. Maybe you've noticed that Shane likes to keep control, particularly when it comes to work, which he never discusses with anyone outside the department. Denise liked to run the show, too. And she blew it, on her end, by trying to manipulate him." She rolled her eyes, wrinkling her nose. "And listen to me. As if I'm the pinnacle of success in the relationship department."

"You sound pretty smart to me." At least Evie had *tried*.

"Mom, can we go over to the rides *now?*" Alan stopped next to the booth, his siblings in tow. "We've played all the games *twice* and you said we could before fireworks time."

Evie nodded and handed her eldest a few bills. "Keep hold of Trevor's hand," she warned, raising her voice above the sudden blast of music. "Band's warmed up, obviously."

Alan took the money, and the trio raced off again, stopping long enough to tussle with their uncle Stu when they encountered him. But after a few minutes of that, they continued on their way and Stu stopped at their booth. He had a new grass stain on his shoulder.

"Want some chili?" Evie held her ladle aloft. "I'm starting to run low on it here."

He shook his head. "Can I steal Laurel for a few minutes?"

"A *few* minutes," Evie allowed, looking amused. "Actually, I can spring her for the night, I think. I'm almost out of food at this point."

"Did you see the guy Freddie's with?" Stu looked over his shoulder at the pair. "His hands are all over her."

Which was almost exactly what Shane had said about the hug she'd given Stu the day she'd bought the car. "Looks can be deceiving," she said. She hadn't seen any noticeable groping. Just a lot of soulful-looking stares. "Maybe they're just friends."

Stu snorted. "Too friendly if you ask me. Come on. Take off the apron. We gotta dance."

"Go, Stu," Evie murmured, helping Laurel remove the apron.

"Are you sure I shouldn't stay and help you? I was late as it was."

"Sugar, I can handle this with one eye closed. You've helped me as much as I needed. Stu, on the other hand, still needs all the help he can get." Evie waited until Laurel was around the front of the booth, heading off with Stu toward the source of the loud country music. "Have fun dancing," she called loudly.

From the corner of her eye, Laurel saw Freddie craning her head around, watching them go.

Stu's hand was tight on hers. "Come on. Let's make this look good."

She figured it was high time Freddie sat up and took notice of Stu, but she wasn't entirely certain this was the proper means. Nevertheless, when they made their way down the grassy hill to the dance area—in the middle of a natural amphitheater—and Stu swung her into a sturdy two-step, easily moving her among the other couples doing the same, she didn't protest.

"Smile," he said grimly, and pushed his lips into one.

She couldn't help smiling a little. He looked like a man heading off to his execution, not a man having a good time. "This is not going to fool anyone. Why don't you just go ask *her* to dance?"

"No. The only time I ever asked her to dance, she laughed in my face and said her toes would never survive."

"When was *that?*"

"Fifth grade," he said grimly.

She stared. Then she threw back her head and laughed.

She was dancing with his brother.

Shane stood in the shadow of the trees and watched.

Not only was Laurel dancing, but she was grinning and laughing her head off as if she hadn't had so much fun in all of her life.

It was a hell of a note to be jealous of his own brother.

He'd *never* been jealous of Stu. Not even when he'd discovered Denise was seeing him.

"Gonna stand here looking hangdog, or are you going to go cut in?" Beau seemed to materialize out of nowhere. He had a hotdog in one hand and a beer in the other.

Nobody would ever make the mistake of thinking Rev. Beau Golightly didn't know how to celebrate the Fourth of July.

"I'm on duty."

Beau snorted softly. "It's a sin to lie, son."

"Well, believe me, Dad. I've got plenty of sins in mind that are a far sight worse."

"Loving a woman is no sin."

Shane jerked. Stared at his dad. "Who said anything about love?"

Beau just shook his head, taking a pull on his beer, looking amused.

"I'm not in love with anyone," he said flatly. That was a whopper of a lie. "Denise said I was incapable of it."

"Denise wasn't the right woman for you," Beau said equably. "Don't get me wrong. She's a very fine woman. I admire her greatly. But she wasn't the one for you, and I knew it when you said you two were getting married. And it had nothing to do with that boy of hers."

"If you think *Laurel* is the one," Shane kept his voice low, "you're way off base. She doesn't want me."

Beau polished off his hotdog and dusted his fingers down his jeans. "You think Holly and I couldn't see what was going on between you two the summer her mama died? Guess you figured none of us knew about all that sneaking around you were doing."

"That was a long time ago."

"True. So what explains the way things are now? Been a hot topic after choir practices, I can tell you. Everyone buzzing about the special attention the sheriff gives his closest neighbor. The way you hared off to Spokane when she needed you."

His dad would think whatever he wanted, no matter what Shane said. "The choir needed another chaperone. And maybe I just want to help Laurel now 'cause I feel bad about what her father did."

"The charges against Roger were dropped, son. Don't forget that."

"Now you're sounding like her." He jerked his chin at the couple on the crowded dance floor. "She can't bring herself to accept what happened. I pulled the case file to see for myself. Tracked down every person whose name was in it, including Wicks. He shouldn't have dropped the charges. But he did, and it was the end of his career." He shook his head. "Even after all these years he didn't change his story one bit. It doesn't add up."

"Wicks used to date Violet before she married Roger," Beau said, seemingly out of the blue. "Don't suppose he told you that."

He hadn't. "Too bad she chose Runyan," Shane muttered, thinking that fact should have been even more reason for Wicks to want the case against Runyan to stick. "She might still be alive." She might not have become an alcoholic. Might not have done the things Laurel remembered.

"That's a question that won't ever be answered, isn't it, son? Well, what a surprise. Isn't that the prettiest sight you've seen in a while?" Beau's voice went from soberly philosophical to jovial as he noticed a couple approaching. He tossed his beer bottle into a nearby bin and smiled broadly, clearly pleased.

Shane's youngest sister, Hadley, spotted them and let go of her tall husband's arm, breaking into a run. She launched herself at Beau first, her long dark waves bouncing around her shoulders as she laughed and kissed his cheek, then turned to Shane and treated him to the same.

"Hell, turnip. Let a man breathe." He straightened, grinning at his youngest sister. He shook Dane's hand, genuinely pleased. The guy had been born with a silver spoon in his mouth, but Shane had come to like and respect the man regardless of his wealth. "When did you get to town?"

"Just now." Dane's arm slid around Hadley's shoulder. He smiled. "She kept talking about Lucius having the best fireworks display around, so here we are."

Which was a testament to the man's devotion to his wife. They all knew he could have flown Hadley anywhere in the world for any sort of display she wanted to see.

"You're just in time, then," Beau said. "Fireworks go right after dark and it's nearly that now. How are things in Indianapolis?"

"Fair," Dane said.

"Fair," Hadley scoffed, swatting her hand over his arm. "RTM's opening another branch outside of Detroit. Wood Tolliver will be going there. Dane and I are staying in Indy."

"Congratulations." Shane couldn't pretend surprise. There was nothing that Dane Rutherford put his hand on that wasn't successful. But it was the light practically beaming from his sister that made him like the other man. Hadley hadn't ever really come into her own until she'd literally run into Dane. Only half a year ago, yet so much had changed since then.

"That's not our only news." His gaze slanted toward his wife. "Had sold her first novel."

"I did, I did." Her long, brown hair bounced all over her as she did a little jig. "I don't have any of the details yet, but it's official nevertheless. I'm a writer! Where's Evie? She's never going to believe it."

Shane pointed toward the food booths where the lights hanging from a wire strung among the trees were beginning to come on. Hadley set off in a jog, Dane following leisurely behind.

"It's good to see your sister so happy," Beau said. "Worried a little about that. The Rutherford world is a far cry from Lucius, Montana."

"They love each other. They want to make it work, they will."

Beau smiled slowly. "Now that is one of the smarter things I've heard you say lately, son." Looking satisfied, he wandered off, leaving Shane standing there alone among the pine trees.

His dad was too optimistic.

*Two* people needed to love each other, before they could even get into the game.

## *Chapter Sixteen*

Laurel couldn't concentrate. The music was too loud. The dance area too crowded.

She stumbled, her toes knocking over Stu's boots yet again. She mumbled another apology—they were automatic after the first half dozen—but her gaze was caught on the solitary figure standing at the edge of the trees at the top of the amphitheater's sloped grass seating area. "I haven't danced in a while," she told Stu, feeling lame.

Shane looked so alone.

"'S okay," Stu excused a moment later. He was as distracted as she was.

"Mind if I cut in?"

The stranger stopped behind Stu, waiting expectantly. She managed to gather her attention together well enough to realize the man was Freddie's date and immediately let go of Stu's clenched hand. "Don't let her stand there long," she warned him softly and smiled brightly at the man, who quickly swung her into the sway of people. She turned her head, keeping an eye on Freddie and Stu.

"Come on, come on," she murmured under her breath. "Take her hand. Start dancing."

"That's for sure," her new partner agreed, surprising the life out of Laurel.

He spun her around, giving them both a chance to look. "I might be speaking out of turn here, but you two looked about as cheerful as we felt. Something needed to be done."

"Yes," she agreed, a little bemused.

He looked relieved. "Thank God. If I had to gaze adoringly into Freddie's eyes for another minute we were both going to go into a coma. I'm Dan. Freddie's second cousin, up from Dallas. And you're—"

"Laurel Runyan. Freddie's your *cousin?*"

"She was desperate," he said, shrugging. "What's a guy to do when his little cousin calls him up, offering a free trip if he'll come and pretend to be a suitor?"

They'd circled the area. All the dancers were beginning to give the standing couple a wide berth. Freddie had her hands on her hips, her chin thrust out pugnaciously. Stu looked as animated as a rock.

"It's not looking good," Dan murmured.

Laurel looked beyond his shoulder. Shane was no longer standing in the shadows.

No. It wasn't looking good at all.

And she had no more stamina for charades, even when it was presented in a surprisingly charming and wry dance partner. The song ended and she stepped free of him. "Think I'll get back to my post at Tiff's booth," she told him. "Thanks for the dance."

"My pleasure."

Another song had already begun, a slow one that enticed even more people to dance, and she slipped between the people, making her way up the incline to the stand of trees. On the other side of the trees, she could see the food booths.

Evie was there, one arm around Julie and another around a slender brunette.

"We had our first dance on the Fourth of July."

Shivers rippled down her spine. She surreptitiously pressed her palm against the jumping in her stomach. "We had our only dance on the Fourth of July." She didn't turn to look at Shane. It was hard enough not recalling every single detail of that night, without him talking about it, too. "Is that Hadley over there with Evie?"

"Yes. Have you had something to eat?"

"Yes."

"What?"

She pressed her lips together for a moment. "Chili."

"Liar."

Defending the untruth would take too much effort. "I need to be going."

"Before the fireworks?"

Definitely before the fireworks. "I…have things to take care of at the house."

"What things?"

She frowned. "Things. It doesn't matter."

"Then they can hardly be important enough for you to need to leave just now, can they?"

"I don't want to stay!" Her voice sounded loud despite the music and revelry around them.

"Okay."

Wariness pricked at her. That had been too easy. "O-okay, then."

Shane easily fell into step beside her, even when she quickened her step. She finally stopped and faced him, midway through the carnival rides.

Yellow and red lights flashed merrily from the ticket booth where a long line of people—young to old—stood waiting. Carnival workers hawked their games, pennies and nickels pinged as they were tossed into stacks of colorful glass dishes.

It was achingly familiar.

"Don't you have something else to do? Go write some tickets for all the people who are double parked."

"How did you get here?"

"Your father, which you probably already know." His stony expression assured her he did.

"Then you'll need a ride."

"It's a lovely evening and I can walk, thank you."

"It's nearly dark. You're *not* walking."

She pushed at her hair, her hand unsteady, and turned again to walk.

She nearly tripped over a little girl dashing toward the ticket booth, money clutched tightly in her fist.

Shane's hand shot out, grabbing her arm, steadying her as the child sped merrily along her way.

Laurel jerked free and kept going. Past the Ferris wheel. Beyond the Tilt-A-Whirl. The Fun House. When she made it to the street beyond the park, she slipped around and through the parked cars.

She could feel Shane on her heels with every step.

She kept going. Turned up church row. Her breath was hitching in her chest. Her sandals were comfortable if she weren't trying to do a twelve-minute mile. Now, the strappy red things were rubbing a raw spot across her instep. She set her chin and kept walking. Turned onto Main. Strode by the Luscious Lucius. Even it was closed in observance of the holiday. Or—more likely—to pick up the only business in town there was to be had. At the food booths in the park.

"You're limping," Shane commented from behind her when they passed Tiff's, where lights shone from the windows, making the big Victorian look welcoming.

She ignored him. She had a stitch in her side now.

And to think she'd considered herself in fairly decent shape. During the last school year she'd had no problem keeping up with an overfull classroom of third-graders.

Oh, Lord, her feet hurt. She stopped. Ripped off the sandals and continued as the concrete sidewalk gave way to soft ground.

A sudden bone-shuddering *boom* rent the air and she started. The sole of her foot trod on a sharp pebble.

The fireworks had begun.

There was not a single vehicle traveling into or out of town. She began crossing the gritty pavement. Her house was within sight.

"You're not going to have any skin left on the bottoms of your feet by the time you finish proving how damn stubborn you are."

She stopped. Her hands curled. Uncurled. A sharp, whining whistle sounded, and white sparks exploded in the air, a trio of cascading brilliance.

She turned. "*I'm* stubborn. That's ironic, coming from you. You're the epitome of stubbornness."

"I'm not the one making a five-mile walk in my bare feet."

"And I didn't ask you to follow me home as if I needed some sort of watchdog."

"Seeing Eye dog would be more useful," he said grimly. "Maybe then you'd have a clue about where you're heading."

"The only place I'm heading is away from you."

"Because you're afraid of what you might find if you actually stopped and stayed?"

This wasn't about her finding her way to her father's house, and she knew it. "Stayed for what? To live in a town where people still think my father got away with murder? Just because he endured the rumors and speculation doesn't mean *I* want to."

"The only rumors in this town concerning you right now are whether or not *we* are sleeping together. Has anyone made you feel unwelcome? Or have you even let anyone close enough to find out?"

Her throat ached. "I let *you* close." Her voice was thick.

"And you pushed me away the second you found a reason."

"A little *more* than a reason."

"I had that file out—traced Wicks to Orlando—because I was trying to prove you were right. Not me. I'm sick of having a difference of opinion rule my relationships. *You* used it as an excuse to end things between us."

"You would have left, anyway!"

He watched her. "Why? Because I made that mistake a long time ago? If there was one thing I could change in my life, Laurel, it would be that. If I'd stayed with you a little longer, hadn't dumped you off at your house the way I did—"

"You would still have left," she finished.

He didn't deny it. "But you wouldn't have walked in your house when you did. Yeah. I left. I was twenty-three and you scared the hell out of me. But I'm not wet behind the ears anymore, and I am here to stay. *Are you?*"

She couldn't form a response to save her soul.

His face turned grim. "So, you *are* leaving, then. You gonna go back to the *gentleman*?"

Her voice finally broke loose again. "No!"

"Then what are you going to do? Where are you going to go?"

"What does it matter?"

"Because I want you to start living your life instead of running from it!"

Rapid bursts sounded, heralding a shower of green and gold sparks.

"Maybe running is the only thing I'm really good at," she said hoarsely. "I ran out on my father when he needed me most—"

"That's bull."

"—and I couldn't bring myself to go through with my wedding—"

"Thank God," he muttered.

"—and I don't want to do that to you!" Her eyes burned. "What if I were in your life? And I panicked again. They're real, you know. Panic attacks. I…I used to have them at Fernwood. And then not until the wedding, after Mr. Newsome had contacted me about Dad. I couldn't bear it, Shane, if I ran away from you that way."

He took a step closer. "So you'll run away from me *this* way? Laurel, maybe you panicked because you knew you weren't meant to marry him. That you didn't love him the way a wife should love a husband. Damn. For a while after Denise and I split up, I broke out in a cold sweat every time I thought about how close we came to marrying. You think that means anything deeper than that you and I both narrowly avoided making the same huge mistake? Of marrying someone we didn't love enough?"

The fireworks were exploding rapidly, the sky a brilliant display of color after color after color.

He took another step nearer. "I loved you when you

were a girl, Laurel. I shouldn't have, but I can't bring my-self to regret it. And I love you now. I can't change the past, and I can't force you to stay where you don't want to stay." His jaw tightened. "But I will *ask* you to. You want me to trust what you believe. Well, I want you to trust *me*, too."

Tears blinded her. "I'm…afraid."

"Of me?" His voice was gruff.

She shook her head. "Of me! What if I'm like her? Like…my mother."

He swore under his breath, closing the last few steps be-tween them. He swept her off her feet and strode the last yards to her house. Carried her up the plywood ramp and settled her on the old wicker love seat.

He crouched before her. His hands cupped her face, thumbs brushing at the tears. "You're *not* your mother."

"I slapped you that day."

"I said some damned offensive things. A man says crap like that to me, I'd have wanted to take his block off." He pressed his lips to her forehead. Her temples.

His gentleness only made her tears flow faster. "You… should be married. Fill that house of yours with children. I…don't know if I could do that, Shane."

"I've seen you with children," he reminded her softly. "Dozens of times now. And I don't have a doubt in my mind what you can do. Just like I don't have a doubt in my mind about what you would *never* do." He pressed his mouth against hers.

She trembled, her heart aching.

Then he slowly lifted his head. "I love you, Laurel. I want *you* to be my wife. I want *your* children leaving toys on the floor in my house, playing their music too loud, breaking curfew when they're not supposed to. I want Christmas mornings and July Fourth fireworks and Sunday dinners with the rest of the Golightlys. I want it all with you. Only with you." He uncoiled himself, straightening. Stepped a foot away.

She barely kept herself from reaching out for him, begging him to return.

"But I don't want any of it until you can let go of the past and start living *now*. Stop blaming yourself for not remembering a horrific incident that no person should have to witness. Regardless of *why* it happened, it was *not* your responsibility. You have to let it go, Laurel. I'll fight anything for you, but I can't fight ghosts."

She sank her teeth into her lip.

"Only you can do that," he finished quietly. "You've accomplished so much in your life, Laurel, since that night. You finished school. Became a teacher. You made a life for yourself that anyone can be proud of. I don't doubt you. Now you need to stop doubting yourself, too. Have some faith."

The plywood vibrated as he slowly walked down it. He looked back at her once, seeming to wait for some response, some proof that she was capable of it.

She tried to speak, but the words didn't come.

And after a long moment he turned away.

Overhead dozens of fireworks were exploding in the sky in a glorious finale.

Laurel could only sit there and watch Shane walk away, feeling as if every speck of light within her was winking out as surely as the sparks died in the star-spangled sky.

## Chapter Seventeen

"Did you hear the news?" Evie greeted, when Laurel opened the door to her knock the next day. She pulled open the screen door without waiting for an invitation and pushed the large, plastic container she held into Laurel's hand. "Peach cobbler," she said briskly. "Freezer's full up at Tiff's, so I'm farming it out to everyone I see whether they want it or not."

"I, um, don't have room in my freezer, either."

Evie waved her hand. "Supposed to eat it, sugar, not freeze it. So, did you hear?"

Laurel shook her head. She had a splitting headache and was still wearing the same clothes from the previous day. She barely felt like a functioning human. "Hear what?"

"Stu and Freddie eloped last night." Evie nodded and grinned. "He called this morning from Reno. They're well and truly hitched. Finally." She rolled her eyes and flopped dramatically onto the couch. "Oh, geez." She moved rapidly to one side. "Didn't notice before, but I think you have a broken spring in there, my friend."

Laurel's eyes burned. Friend? So far, she hadn't been much of a friend. She stared at the container, blinking hard. "I'm happy for them. Um…thanks for the cobbler. I, I love peach cobbler." She quickly went to the kitchen, slipping the container on the counter next to the percolator.

It hadn't been used since the last night Shane had stayed there.

She swallowed the knot in her throat.

"How long are *you* going to keep this up?" Evie's voice was quiet. "I'm hoping you're not as pigheaded as Stu and Freddie have been all these years. Hate to see my other brother wait even longer before he gets the woman he wants."

Trust Evie not to stand on ceremony. "It's not that easy."

"It's not that complicated, either." Evie stepped into the kitchen. "Did you know that this house is exactly point three seven miles from Tiff's?"

Laurel hesitated, thrown. "Um, no. I didn't."

The other woman was nodding. "Did you also not know that there's a dearth of lodging around Lucius? The Lucius Inn is okay for anyone who doesn't mind rooms with the television bolted down, but there are a whole lot of people who prefer something more homey. There are less than a handful of houses around here that are rented out for vacations—one of them was decked out with a heart-shaped tub in the middle of the living room, if you can believe it. But the owner recently sold it. So we can't even count that one." She propped one elbow on the counter and glanced toward the front of the house, ignoring Laurel's confusion. "Some nice shrubs and trees, maybe a pretty fence and gate, to block off the view of the road. Just one bathroom, right? We wouldn't want to have a heart-shaped tub."

Laurel had never even seen a heart-shaped tub. "Er... yes. One bathroom."

Evie tucked her tongue between her teeth, sliding a glance Laurel's way. "Would take some real money to put things truly to rights, though."

"What's your point, Evie?"

"You and me. A business deal. Between the two of us, we turn this place into a sweet little getaway cottage. I'll manage rental, same as I manage Tiff's. We can either split the profits down the middle and you pay me a management fee, or we come up with some other split. Either way, all three of us stand to gain."

"Three?"

"You. Me. This house."

Laurel's head spun with surprise at the very thought of it. "Did Shane put you up to this?"

"Good heaven's, no. Why would he? He wanted to buy it himself, remember?"

Laurel shook her head a little. "I...no reason."

Evie looked disbelieving, but she let it go. She pulled a piece of paper out of her pocket and laid it flat on the counter. "You know my architect said I couldn't expand Tiff's. So I've been thinking about other properties. And frankly, yours is the most logical choice. These are some numbers I ran on what we might be looking at. Expenses. Income. Take a look. Think about it. Let me know. I've got the financing end lined up, thanks to a certain brother-in-law who gives a great interest rate on a business loan." She headed to the door. "Enjoy the cobbler. Come to church tomorrow. Dad's despairing over what to do about the junior choir. Nancy isn't going to have the job even if she *does* come back to Lucius, which is looking doubtful at this point."

Just that quickly the woman left.

Laurel stared at the paper, not seeing any of the numbers. Turn the house into a vacation cottage? Could she do that?

*Yes, she could.* And she could walk away from it, leaving it all in Evie's more-than-capable hands.

She ought to have felt relief at the idea. Instead her stomach just felt more hollow than ever.

The phone rang beside her, and she grabbed it, answering automatically.

"Laurel? This is Marian Smythe calling again."

She marshaled her thoughts. "Mrs. Smythe. How are you?"

"Fine. Getting anxious, of course. Have you thought any more about the teaching position here?"

Laurel pressed her fingertips to her closed eyes. "I'm sorry, Mrs. Smythe. I know the school board is anxious to fill the position. If you have another candidate, I'd understand."

"I wish we did," Marian admitted, sounding wry. "Wouldn't it be wonderful to have a plethora of willing applicants. Unfortunately, we're more in the position of having to chase down than being chased. Is there anything we can do to help persuade you? I've spoken with your former principal from Clover Elementary. She gave you a glowing recommendation, even though she freely admitted she'd despaired over your departure."

"Mrs. Smythe, I appreciate the school board's confidence. But I'm afraid I'm not ready to commit to a position yet."

Not ready to commit? *Afraid* to commit.

Exactly what Shane accused her of being.

She rubbed her eyes again. "Could I have a few more days?"

Marian agreed, but Laurel could tell the woman was frustrated and unhappy about it as she ended the call.

Laurel picked up the paper Evie had left for her.

She'd come to Lucius thinking she had nothing but her father's rundown house.

Instead she had job offers and options she'd never have thought of on her own when it came to the house.

And none of it meant anything.

She climbed up the staircase and shoved open the door to her father's bedroom. Turned and stood on the landing, her hands clutching the banister. "Why can't I remember, Gram? Why?"

But there were no answers in that empty house.

Only silence.

From where she stood, she could see Evie's page of estimations lying on the counter. The boxes Laurel had packed up for the donation pickup were scattered all over.

Her gaze slowly slipped over it all. What was here that made the house a home, when everything she wanted was in the house on the hill behind her?

She turned and went into her bedroom, where she retrieved the suitcase she'd brought from Colorado. She flipped it open on the bed. She filled it to capacity, then had to sit on it to get the zipper to close all the way.

She found an empty old school backpack on her closet shelf and filled it with her journals. Then she went into her father's room and plucked the graduation picture off the dresser. She added that to the backpack, too.

Then she hefted the backpack and the suitcase down the stairs and out to her car. She took one more look at the house, trying to imagine it the way Evie had described, but failing miserably.

Maybe it was because there were tears blurring her eyes.

Then she got in her car and drove away.

But for the first time in a very long while, Laurel finally knew where she was going.

"You're going to be fine."

Laurel brushed her hands down the front of her pale-yellow dress. She'd bought it new just before the department store had closed the previous day. She needed every bit of confidence she could summon, but the dress wasn't as helpful as she'd hoped.

She was a nervous wreck.

"What if he refuses to come?"

Beau smiled as he unhooked his black robes from the hanger on his office door and shrugged into them. "Evie will get him here."

"Are you sure?"

"Evie has a knack for getting her way. But if for some reason she doesn't get him here this morning, then you'll try again."

She could hear the organist playing the prelude. "I'm going to make a fool of myself. I haven't sung in…well…not since the day my mother died."

"Is that what matters?" Beau stopped in front of her. The Bible he tucked beneath his arm was dog-eared and worn. "Whether or not you make a fool of yourself?"

She shook her head. "He needs to know that I'm here to stay."

"All right, then. You'd better scoot down to the choir room or you'll be making a grand entrance by yourself." He nudged her toward the door.

Her feet hesitated. "Thank you. For everything. For…looking out for me when my mother died. And for opening your door to me when I came to you yesterday."

He smiled gently. "I wish I could have done more for you back then, child. I wish I'd *known* more."

"It's in the past," she said, lifting her chin a little. "What's important is now." She picked up the hymnal that she'd left on the chair inside his office door. "See you in church."

She walked down the narrow corridor from Beau's office to the choir room where the other adult choir members had already assembled and warmed up. She took her place with them, smiling nervously.

Louise Halloran leaned over and squeezed her hand, smiling her encouragement. "Joey's going to be so happy," she whispered.

Well, at least there was that, Laurel thought, her nerves lightening for just a moment.

And then they processed into the church.


The pew felt about as comfortable as the cots in his jail cells.

Shane glowered at his sister's head. She, annoying woman that she was, blithely ignored him.

He shifted again, stretching out his legs. He didn't want to be in church. Couldn't believe he'd let his sister nag him into it. Especially at a time when the sight of Laurel driving away had caused him so much pain.

"Would you sit *still?* You're fidgeting worse than my kids do," she hissed beside him.

Their father was in the pulpit, greeting the churchgoers, many of whom were still filing into the pews. He caught Tom Halloran in the middle of a huge yawn.

Couldn't blame the guy. Shane had a yawn or two built up inside him, too.

He had a whole new appreciation for Laurel's inability

to sleep certain places in that damn house of hers. He was feeling about the same way toward his own bed, because every time he closed his eyes—and even when he didn't—he was remembering her in it.

"Here." Evie opened their hymnal and held it out in front of him. He gave her a look and rose.

And he didn't need a hymnal. It might have been a long time since he'd been a seminary student, but he still remembered most every hymn his father had ever used in a Sunday service.

Just as they'd done all of his life, the choir filed into the church during the first hymn, filling the loft behind the pulpit.

Forty-seven minutes, he thought grimly. It would be just about that amount of time before the service would be finished and he could get out of here. He'd go to the station. Hang out there. Better than going home to an empty house that overlooked an equally empty one.

"Thank you," Beau was saying as the organist finished the hymn on a flourish. "Please be seated. And welcome again. What a beautiful Sunday morning it is, indeed. Ordinarily, I like to save announcements until the end of the service when all of you are awake again after napping through my sermon."

Smatterings of laughter rippled through the congregation as they sat.

Forty-six minutes, Shane thought. He stared at his boots, his father's voice nothing more than a deep murmur in his head.

What could he have done differently? He tried to protect her; she pushed him away. He tried to let her go; she drove away. It was no different than it had been with Denise. Only, instead of a seven-year-old miscreant between them, they had a twelve-year-old memory.

And the end of his engagement to Denise hadn't felt as if he was being gnawed painfully from the inside out.

Evie slowly pinched his arm, and he caught her hand in his. "Grow up. We're not ten anymore."

"Pay attention," she whispered back, yanking her fingers out of his.

His lips thinned. He didn't want to be there. He wanted to be out finding Laurel. God knows where she'd gone. He'd known her state of mind was…fine. Her emotional state, though? That was another matter.

And he hadn't helped it with his ultimatums and demands.

He should be out finding Laurel.

He wasn't twenty-three anymore. He was thirty-five, and he'd be hanged if he'd let another twelve years pass before he had a chance for the kind of love he'd only ever seen between Beau and Holly.

He dropped his hymnal on Evie's lap and pushed to his feet. "I've got something to do." It wasn't the first time he'd left in the middle, beginning or end of his father's service; though before, it had always been his duties calling him away.

This time it was his heart.

He figured God would understand.

He glanced at his father as he moved toward the aisle.

And his boots rooted in place.

She wore a yellow dress. With little buttons that stretched from the scooped neckline all the way down to the hem. Her hair was pulled back in a ponytail, loose curls streaming down her neck.

Her amber gaze was focused directly on him. She had a hymnal open in her hands, but she didn't so much as glance at it when a single organ note sounded, then slowly faded away. And Laurel opened her mouth and began to sing, her voice as pure and beautiful as it had ever been.

When the notes finally faded, the congregation sat there, seeming to be stunned in silence.

Beau returned to Laurel's side. "We all know about the junior choir's wonderful trip to Spokane. And that it wouldn't have been possible at all if this lovely young woman hadn't stepped in for us. So I think you'll all agree, then, with our selection of Laurel Runyan as their new director?"

Someone clapped. The applause built. Laurel's gaze was glued to Shane's. "I'm staying," she said, and even though her voice was too soft to be heard over the enthusiastic response of the members, he still heard.

And he didn't care that there were still a good forty-one minutes left in the service.

He walked up to the chancel, stopping in front of her. Taking her shaking hand in his. "I thought you'd left," he said, his voice gruff. "I saw you from my place. Watched you drive away."

She shook her head. "I only left a house." Her eyes were wet. "Because I want to have a home. With you. If you'll have me."

"Is that a proposal?"

Her lashes drifted down for a moment. The clapping was fading away and the listening had definitely begun.

Her lips trembled. He could see the pulse beating like a butterfly at the base of her lovely neck. Her lashes lifted again and her eyes met his, her lips curving softly. "No," she said. "It's a promise. I love you, Shane. I always have. I always will. I'm sorry if you think I didn't trust you. Didn't believe in you. You were right. It's been me that I was afraid to trust."

"And now?"

Laurel pressed her lips together for a moment, dredging up courage.

But it turned out the words weren't so difficult after all. Not when Shane looked at her with those beautiful gray eyes, so soft and so full of love. She forgot the fact that they were standing in front of a hundred people, interrupting a summer Sunday church service.

There was just her and Shane.

The boy she'd loved when she was just a girl. The man she'd love until they were old and gray, and beyond, if they were lucky.

She settled her hand lightly on his chest. "I'd rather be with you and chance a few fears and mistakes, than be alone and never know what happiness really is. I want the toys on the floor. The broken curfews. I want all that with you. Because I know that *you* are my home. This place. Lucius. These people. Your family. And you, above all else. I love you."

He lowered his head and pressed his mouth against hers, leaving her breathless when he finally pulled away. She could feel the stories forming in the minds of the congregants. "We're in church here," she whispered.

"A good place to kiss my wife."

She inhaled shakily. "We haven't said any vows yet."

He lowered his head toward hers again. "Like you said. We're in church here. And they sounded like vows to me." Then he closed his mouth over hers and slowly kissed her again while cheers and hoots filled the rafters of the church.

It was a moment she knew she would remember all of the days of her life.

## *Epilogue*

"What are you working on over there?" Shane's voice was curious as he came up behind her. She was sitting on the porch, a worn afghan pulled over her legs against the October chill in the air. "Thought you finished grading papers before lunch."

Laurel looked up from the journal lying open in her lap. "I did." She nodded toward the house down the hill where Jack Finn's renovations were newly complete. "Evie's going to be pleased the work is done so early. She says she has a waiting list already for reservations. I went through the house this afternoon. It looks really great. Evie has a real talent."

"My sister. The up-and-coming B&B mogul."

"You know, she and Tony are going to hook up. Mark my words."

"No way."

"That's what you said about Stu and Freddie," Laurel reminded, smiling faintly. "And look how *that* turned out. For a smart lawman, you're sure behind the times when it comes to certain matters."

"The only 'certain matters' that matter to me are you and me." He slid onto the seat beside her, pulling her back against him, nuzzling her neck.

She barely caught the journal from falling off her lap. Shivers danced down her spine and it had nothing whatsoever to do with the dwindling afternoon temperature that boded an early snowfall, and everything to do with *him.* Her husband.

She closed her eyes, tilting her head back against his shoulder.

His hands slowly burrowed beneath the thick sweater she wore. "Come inside with me where we won't be putting on a show for the construction workers cleaning up down there."

She laughed softly. "They can't see what you're doing from there."

"Shameful." He lightly bit her neck. "Who'd have thought third-grade teachers and choir directors were so brazen?"

"All depends on how inspired we are," she said a little breathlessly. She caught his hand before he could start really doing damage to her self-control. "Like I said. I went through the house. The new staircase is a thing of beauty."

"You're a thing of beauty," he murmured, delving his hand again beneath her sweater. "Well, well. You're not wearing a bra."

She smiled faintly. "Write me a ticket, Sheriff."

He chuckled.

She leaned her head back against him again and couldn't

prevent the satisfied sound that rose softly in her throat. "I remembered," she murmured.

His fingers paused on her breasts. "You…remembered."

She closed her hands over his, holding them against her. Maybe she was brazen. But she couldn't get enough of his hands on her. The more days that passed since they'd stood in front of Beau and said their vows—their official vows only two weeks after that memorable Sunday morning—the more she realized that they were only at the tip of the iceberg. The wholeness of their love was simply deeper and wider and stronger with each passing day.

"Hey." He shifted. "Is that all you have to say about it?"

She realized belatedly that he was staring at her, tension stilling him.

"I was going through the house, admiring all the work. The changes are just remarkable. It's as if the old house was barely even there. Just a whisper of it remains. And I was standing there, at the base of the stairs, running my hand over the new wooden banister, and it was all there. The memories. She *did* fall," she said quietly. "When I went inside the house that afternoon after you drove me home, they were arguing. Dad came out of their bedroom and she was right on his heels. When they realized I was standing in the living room, Dad stopped. I suppose it was the suddenness of that, but I'll never know for sure. She just sort of pitched right past him."

"Ah, Laurel." He pressed his head against hers.

"Dad tried to catch her," she finished. "He almost had her, almost went tumbling after her, in fact. It really was *just* an accident."

"Are you okay? Why didn't you tell me earlier?"

She lifted her palm, laying it against his jaw. "I'm glad the doubt can finally rest. But you'd already helped me let it go. Maybe that's why the memory finally came back. Because I knew it couldn't hurt me anymore."

She swung her legs down and swiveled around until she could face him. "*And* I have something much more important to concentrate on." She leaned forward, pressing her mouth to his. "The here and now. With you."

*"Now?"* His lips curved against hers.

"Now," she promised softly. "Today." She tugged aside the collar of his shirt and kissed his throat. "Tomorrow." She kissed the small dent in his chin. "Next year." She slowly rubbed her lips against his. "Twenty years."

His arms tightened around her. "Then let's go inside," he suggested, looking gratifyingly impatient. He pulled her to her feet. The journal slid off the seat with a soft thump.

"Just one more thing." She leaned over and picked it up. "Read."

"Later."

She pushed it into his hands. "Read." Smiling a little, she stepped inside the doors to their bedroom. She knew she wouldn't have to wait long. And she didn't.

He came through the door, hard on her heels. "Seriously?"

"Absolutely." She slowly took the journal from his slack fingers and set it aside, then stepped into his arms. "I love you, Shane Golightly."

He pulled her tightly to him. His touch gentle, his voice rough. "I love you, Laurel Golightly."

Dear Gram,
We're going to have a baby.
Love, Laurel.

\* \* \* \* \*

# A bear ate my ex, and that's okay.

Stacy Kavanaugh is convinced
that her ex's recent disappearance
in the mountains is the worst
thing that can happen to her.
In the next two weeks, she'll
discover how wrong she really is!

# Grin and Bear It
# Leslie LaFoy

HARLEQUIN®
Next™

HN23
Available December 2005
TheNextNovel.com

If you enjoyed what you just read,
then we've got an offer you can't resist!

# Take 2 bestselling
# love stories FREE!
# Plus get a FREE surprise gift!

## Clip this page and mail it to Silhouette Reader Service™

| IN U.S.A. | IN CANADA |
|---|---|
| 3010 Walden Ave. | P.O. Box 609 |
| P.O. Box 1867 | Fort Erie, Ontario |
| Buffalo, N.Y. 14240-1867 | L2A 5X3 |

**YES!** Please send me 2 free Silhouette Special Edition® novels and my free surprise gift. After receiving them, if I don't wish to receive anymore, I can return the shipping statement marked cancel. If I don't cancel, I will receive 6 brand-new novels every month, before they're available in stores! In the U.S.A., bill me at the bargain price of $4.24 plus 25¢ shipping and handling per book and applicable sales tax, if any*. In Canada, bill me at the bargain price of $4.99 plus 25¢ shipping and handling per book and applicable taxes**. That's the complete price and a savings of at least 10% off the cover prices—what a great deal! I understand that accepting the 2 free books and gift places me under no obligation ever to buy any books. I can always return a shipment and cancel at any time. Even if I never buy another book from Silhouette, the 2 free books and gift are mine to keep forever.

235 SDN DZ9D
335 SDN DZ9E

Name _____ (PLEASE PRINT) _____

Address _____ Apt.# _____

City _____ State/Prov. _____ Zip/Postal Code _____

*Not valid to current Silhouette Special Edition® subscribers.*

*Want to try two free books from another series?*
*Call 1-800-873-8635 or visit www.morefreebooks.com.*

\* Terms and prices subject to change without notice. Sales tax applicable in N.Y.
\*\* Canadian residents will be charged applicable provincial taxes and GST.
 All orders subject to approval. Offer limited to one per household.
 ® are registered trademarks owned and used by the trademark owner or its licensee.

SPED04R                                        ©2004 Harlequin Enterprises Limited

# Home For The Holidays!

## Receive a FREE Christmas Collection
## containing 4 books by bestselling authors

**Harlequin American Romance and Silhouette Special Edition invite you to celebrate Home For The Holidays by offering you this exclusive offer valid only in Harlequin American Romance and Silhouette Special Edition books this November.**

To receive your FREE Christmas Collection, send us 3 (three) proofs of purchase of Harlequin American Romance or Silhouette Special Edition books to the addresses below.

<table>
<tr><td><u>In the U.S.:</u><br>Home For The Holidays<br>P.O. Box 9057<br>Buffalo, NY<br>14269-9057</td><td><u>In Canada:</u><br>Home For The Holidays<br>P.O. Box 622<br>Fort Erie, ON<br>L2A 5X3</td></tr>
</table>

- - - - - - - - - - - - - - - - - - - - - - - - - - - - - - - - - - - - ✂

098 KKI DXJM

Name (PLEASE PRINT)

Address                                                                Apt. #

City                    State/Prov.              Zip/Postal Code

To receive your FREE Christmas Collection (retail value is $19.95 U.S./$23.95 CAN.), complete the above form. Mail it to us with 3 (three) proofs of purchase, which can be found in all Harlequin American Romance and Silhouette Special Edition books in November 2005. Requests must be postmarked no later than January 31, 2006. Please enclose $2.00 (check made payable to Harlequin Books) for shipping and handling and allow 4–6 weeks for delivery. New York State residents must add applicable sales tax on shipping and handling charge, and Canadian residents please add 7% GST. Offer valid in Canada and the U.S. only, while quantities last. Offer limited to one per household. **www.eHarlequin.com**

```
FREE
CHRISTMAS
COLLECTION
PROOF OF
PURCHASE
HARPOPNOV05
```

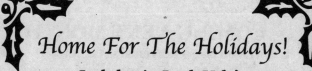

# Home For The Holidays!

## Indulge in Leah Vale's great holiday recipe

### Family Fattigmann
### Traditional Norwegian Christmas Cookies

Have at least one beloved family member or friend within shouting distance. The more the merrier.

6 egg yolks
3 egg whites
6 tbsp sugar
6 tbsp canned milk

1 tbsp whiskey
2 1/2 cups flour
Vegetable oil for frying
Powdered sugar

(and no nipping from the bottle—there's hot oil to follow!)

Beat egg yolks until creamy. Add sugar, milk and whiskey. In a separate bowl, beat egg whites until stiff, then add to egg mixture. Add flour to make soft dough. Chill in refrigerator. No, it's not time for that hot whiskey toddy, yet! When dough is almost ready, heat the vegetable oil in a deep saucepan. It should sizzle, but not smoke. Once dough is stiff, roll out until very thin—about 1/16 inch thick—on a lightly floured surface. Use a floured knife to cut dough into diamond shapes approximately 2 by 1 inch. Cut a slit lengthwise in the center of each diamond and pull one end through the slot to make a sort of knot. In batches, deep-fry the cookies until they are golden brown, then drain on paper towels and cool. Place cookies in a clean paper bag with some powdered sugar, roll the top closed and then dance around the kitchen shaking the bag. Store cookies in airtight containers.

HARRECIPELEAH

# COMING NEXT MONTH

**SPECIAL EDITION**

### #1723 THE SHEIK AND THE VIRGIN SECRETARY— Susan Mallery
*Desert Rogues*
Learning of her fiancé's infidelities the day before her wedding, Kiley Hendrick wanted revenge—and becoming mistress to her rich, powerful boss seemed like the perfect plan. At first, Prince Rafiq was amused by his secretary's overtures. But when he uncovered Kiley's secret innocence, the game was *over*—the sheik had to have this virgin beauty for his very own!

### #1724 PAST IMPERFECT—Crystal Green
*Most Likely To...*
To Saunders U. dropout Rachel James, Professor Gilbert had always been a beacon of hope. So when he called asking for help, she was there. Rachel enlisted reporter Ian Beck to dispel the strange allegations about the professor's past. But falling for Ian—well, Rachel should have known better. Would he betray her for an easy headline?

### #1725 UNDER THE MISTLETOE—Kristin Hardy
*Holiday Hearts*
No-nonsense businesswoman Hadley Stone had a job to do—modernize the Hotel Mount Eisenhower and increase profits. But hotel manager Gabe Trask stood in her way, jealously guarding the Victorian landmark's legacy. Would the beautiful Vermont Christmas—and meetings under the mistletoe—soften the adversaries' hearts a little?

### #1726 HER SPECIAL CHARM—Marie Ferrarella
*The Cameo*
New York detective James Munro knew the cameo he'd found on the street was no ordinary dime-store trinket. Little did he know his find would unleash a legend—for when the cameo's rightful owner, Constance Beaulieu, responded to his newspaper ad and claimed this special charm, it was a meeting that would change their lives forever....

### #1727 DIARY OF A DOMESTIC GODDESS—Elizabeth Harbison
With new editor-in-chief Cal Paganos shaking things up at 125-year-old *Home Life* magazine, managing editor Kit Macy worried her sewing and etiquette columns were too quaint to make the cut. So the soccer mom tried a more sophisticated style to save her job...and soon she and Cal were making more than a magazine together!

### #1728 ACCIDENTAL HERO—Loralee Lillibridge
After cowboy Bo Ramsey left her to join the rodeo, words like *commitment* and *happily-ever-after* were just a lot of hot air to Abby Houston. To overcome her heartbreak, Abby turned to running the therapeutic riding program on her father's ranch. "Forgive and forget" became her new motto—until the day Bo rode back into town....

SSECNM1105